FOR
HONOR

TOM CLANCY'S OP-CENTER NOVELS

ALSO BY JEFF ROVIN

Tom Clancy's
OP-CENTER

FOR
HONOR

CREATED BY
Tom Clancy and Steve Pieczenik

WRITTEN BY
Jeff Rovin

St. Martin's Griffin ✺ New York

TOM CLANCY'S OP-CENTER: FOR HONOR. Copyright © 2018 by Jack Ryan Limited Partnership and S&R Literary, Inc. All rights reserved. Printed in the United States of America. For information, address St. Martin's Press, 175 Fifth Avenue, New York, N.Y. 10010.

www.stmartins.com

Designed by Omar Chapa

The Library of Congress Cataloging-in-Publication Data is available upon request.

ISBN 978-1-250-18301-9 (trade paperback)
ISBN 978-1-250-15690-7 (ebook)

Our books may be purchased in bulk for promotional, educational, or business use. Please contact your local bookseller or the Macmillan Corporate and Premium Sales Department at 1-800-221-7945, extension 5442, or by email at MacmillanSpecialMarkets@macmillan.com.

First Edition: May 2018

10 9 8 7 6 5 4 3 2 1

FOR
HONOR

PROLOGUE

"We are putting one of our hedgehogs down the Americans' trousers."

Rear Admiral Dmitri Merkassov stood on the forward deck of the *Komsomol* class freighter *Mikula*, his winter-bronzed bare hands firmly gripping the iron rail. Like the deck beneath his ankle boots, the bars were slick with sea spray. The fifty-seven-year-old officer had to squeeze tightly to keep from shifting with the sway of the ship. The distant chug of the steam turbine engines was nearly lost in the loud, clapping sound of the ocean water as it met the hull. Each slap tossed a mist of salt spray over the gunmetal jacket of Merkassov's casual service uniform. The dampness evaporated swiftly in the sharp sunlight.

The officer allowed himself a smile. Everything here was different. The spray was warm and the motion of the ship was rolling instead of jerky. The 12,285-ton vessel would shift atilt for a second or two before lolling upright and then dipping in the other direction. This back-and-forth motion required a less firm-legged stance than the choppy, fast-changing waters of the north.

Merkassov had spent most of his career in the Arctic Ocean, serving mostly on Soviet Northern Fleet Novik-class, Type 7 and 7U destroyers. There, under cold blue or even colder slate gray skies, the Beringovsky native experienced nothing like a comforting morning sun and invigorating sea breeze. In just over an hour, shortly after noon, the *Mikula* and the convoy of which it was a part would cross into the southern hemisphere and the winds would blow in the opposite direction. . . .

The rear admiral breathed deeply of the Caribbean-tinged winds. It was the first time in his military career that he had taken this voyage through the Baltic Sea to the Mediterranean to the Atlantic Ocean. To serve in the Soviet navy had always been his dream, it didn't matter where. The son of a father and mother who had fought in the Revolution, that honor was his only goal. But now that he had made this passage, seen a crew that was not dressed in thick winter jackets lined with sheep fur, he began to realize how small his world had been. Full and deep, yes, but in a very narrow field of operation. Perhaps, when this action was complete he would request a transfer to the Fifth Operational Squadron stationed in the Mediterranean. Just for a while, maybe to iron some of the wrinkles from his long, leathery wind-blasted face.

But it was a passing notion. Just to be part of Operation Anadyr was an honor that he did not take lightly. It had been bestowed upon him and his counterpart Rear Admiral Blinnikov personally by Commissar Khrushchev. Blinnikov was the one who would be handling the hedgehog—as Khrushchev had put it in his refreshingly blunt, colorful, peasant's way. That flotilla would be bringing the nuclear weapons to China. But the role of the *Mikula* and the *Vsevelod* was equally important. It would be both spearhead and heart of what the Kremlin quietly referred to as *maskirova*: the art of deception.

A naval infantry intelligence officer in a dark blue work uniform trotted over, saluting and handing the rear admiral an envelope. "Thank you, Lieutenant Bolshakov," Merkassov said, then indicated for him to wait. It was a decoded message from Blinnikov.

Flagship will cross boundary at 12:06.

Merkassov folded the message into his shirt pocket. "Please inform the rear admiral that his message has been received and is acknowledged," he said to the other. "I will be along momentarily to advise the *Vsevelod*."

"Yes, Commander!" the young man said smartly, saluting and turning back toward the bridge.

The rear admiral inhaled. He would not want to be in Blinnikov's position. To mask the immensity of this effort, the small convoys had departed from eight ports: Kronstadt, Liepāja, Baltiysk, and Murmansk in the north, and Sevastopol, Feodosiya, Nikolayev, and Poti on the Black Sea. Western access to these ports was briefly closed off so absolute secrecy could be maintained. The success of his mission depended not just on the proficiency of his own crew—and they were working in a strange land with a different language, unloading equipment that had a low tolerance for any mishandling. It also depended on the reliability of an intermediary, a Cuban woman code-named *Buntovshchik*—rebel—who had no experience with this particular of cargo, only a general knowledge of the science behind it.

The world suddenly seemed to spin around him, around this proud arm of the Soviet fleet. He looked a final time at the serene blue sea and the proud array of freighters, frigates, and corvettes that stretched ahead. To be part of this armada was, yes, an honor. But to be a part of history was greater still. Operation Anadyr would change the world, and his part in it created *maskirova* with a difference.

This deception would have fangs.

CHAPTER ONE

"Will there be vegan hot dogs?"

Meteorologist Gary Gold turned from his laptop to the speaker, Dongling Qui. Gold had been reviewing the morning's low-orbit satellite views of Poland, where NATO maneuvers were scheduled to begin that afternoon. He regarded the young woman with his pleasant blue eyes.

"I don't know," Gold said, folding his arms. "I think we did have turkey burgers last Fourth of July."

"A turkey is meat," Dongling pointed out.

"Yes, I know that," he replied. "But what I'm saying is—there's a diverse menu. I'm sure if you ask, Aaron will make sure he has some."

"I wouldn't want to impose after just a week on the job—"

"Dongling, it's a tradition," Gold assured her. "Everyone shows up, invited or not. And their plus-ones. You can be mine, if you feel like you're forcing yourself."

She made a face that reflected her ongoing hesitancy.

"How about this: I'll ask," Gold offered. "And I promise you: frankless-furters will be served."

The twenty-eight-year-old geologist smiled gratefully and returned to her examination of soil analysis from Syria. She was tracking the movement of soldiers based on samples scraped from the soles of dead ISIS fighters.

Gold lingered for a moment in the silence she left behind. He wasn't sorry he brought up the annual bash thrown by his boss, Aaron Bleich. Dongling was new, just a week on the job, and was coming in early to acclimate herself. Beijing-raised and educated, the daughter of a U.S. diplomat and Chinese embassy worker, she was one of the few women who worked in the Tank, the electronic and scientific brain-center of Op-Center. Along with former U.N. translator, linguist Salim Singh, he and Dongling were also the only people here at this hour.

"All I can tell you is that it's like working as a hedge fund guy," Gold had told his parents when he was hired seven months before. "I've gotta be there when certain European markets open."

The European "markets" were the Royal Meteorological Institute of Belgium, Meteo France, the Irish Meteorological Service, among dozens of other facilities around the globe. It was Gold's job each morning to study the world's microclimates, searching for sudden events that could not be explained by the weather: for example, suboceanic thermal signatures that could be North Korean midget submarines and not whales, or decreased pollution over Beijing or Shanghai that might indicate downtime and thus decreased production for Chinese factories.

There was also a need for actionable global weather reports, since Director Williams never knew when and to where it might be necessary to dispatch the Joint Special Operations Command out of Fort Bragg, North Carolina. JSOC was Op-Center's military wing; military "fist," as their commander, Major Mike Volner preferred to call it. Volner was an observer assigned to the Polish drills. Williams liked to know whether his people were in sun or storm and the most efficient way to reach them in a crisis.

The staff of mostly twenty-somethings trickled in over the next hour, bag-breakfasts in hand and dressed as if they were going to a university protest. Williams and most of his senior staff did not approve of the informality but concessions were the only way to get the sharp, millennial talent Op-Center needed. The sole exceptions to the lazy conformity were three women: Dongling, in her white blouse and black skirt; cartographer Allison Weill, who was said to be descended from one of the noncoms who journeyed west with Lewis and Clark; and thirty-four-year-old Kathleen Hays, a Hollywood computer graphics designer who was discovered, by Aaron, at a comic book convention nearly eight months before. Hays was Op-Center's visual analysis specialist, a shy, private woman who favored black pantsuits that matched her raven hair. Her station formed the third piece of the triptych with Gary Gold in the center. There were no cubicles in the small but open Geek Tank: the stations formed a rectangle with the fourteen "geeks" facing inward. Only Aaron had his own office, though a small one was being carved out for Charlene Squires, the RES—reverse engineering specialist. It was being constructed on the same spot from which her father,

Charlie Squires, had commanded Striker, the military arm of Paul Hood's Op-Center. Charlie was KIA—killed in action—on a mission to Russia with the team.

Gold's row faced the door and he saw Aaron arrive.

"*Six for six*," the meteorologist grumped inside as he saw the network leader smirk in his direction. The first day of Dongling's employment had been orientation, which had been handled by Deputy Director Anne Sullivan. From day two onward, Gold had made it his personal responsibility to help the new hire in any way possible, from walking her to the fast food outlets on the base to understanding the pop culture references and ever-changing slang employed by most of the geeks. Though Dongling was seemingly oblivious to Gold's solicitous attention, Aaron was not. There was no competition for her attention, such as it was. As everyone at Op-Center learned in their post-employment, pre-assignment orientation, proximity to target was nine-tenths of any effective land campaign.

Gold did not look forward to telling his boss why he was asking about the Fourth of July menu. He decided to wait for an opportunity rather than make one. For one thing, Bleich was distracted by all that had to get done in the week before his annual summer vacation. For another, officially, there was a no-dating policy among coworkers at Op-Center. Fraternizing at parties and barbecues was permitted, but pillow talk was not conducive to keeping divisional secrets. These boundaries were strictly enforced even in a confined space like the Tank, when the parties were seated side-by-side. Confidential data was sent to Smart-Ware, eyeglasses that read the irises of the users before divulging and then destroying the information. Unofficially, however—to the disapproval of Anne Sullivan—Chase Williams looked the other way at minor infractions. He had told his deputy he would rather know who was seeing whom rather than have it occur in secret.

To Gold's left, Kathleen Hays nodded good morning to her neighbors and began scrolling through the results of the International Facial Scan program that was automatically run overnight. Until six weeks ago, this kind of research was time-restricted because Op-Center was piggybacking on the NSA's mainframe. Then Aaron and Joe Berkowitz, a technical support associate, cobbled together what they called OpPrime—a nod, she later learned, to Optimus Prime and their affection for the universe of the *Transformers*. Part official, part dark ops, the system was designed to cobble together everything they needed from a variety of sources, without proprietary constraints or permissions. The efficiency of Kathleen's work had increased exponentially.

The IFS was a program that constantly sifted through all social media postings from around the globe, performing facial scans and comparing it to Op-Center's vast database of suspected terrorists. If there were an urgent match, she would have been notified by smartphone and a member of the skeletal evening staff would have accessed the data via SmartWare. Absent that, the morning update fell into three categories: F3, nationals from hostile nations who were posing at monuments or crowded clubs, markets, or sports venues; F2, intelligence service "watch list" individuals who were spotted anywhere; and F1, known terrorists who showed up in an image. The highest level of alert, F0, was for fugitives. That was how Op-Center helped the National Intelligence Agency of the Kingdom of Thailand find the assassin who shot and killed an imam in Sungai Padi: he was spotted on a tourist's Instagram video taken at a halal restaurant. Though he had been masked during the attack, his clothes and bodily proportions matched exactly security camera footage of the killing.

While there was a generally predictable flow of images from around the world, two places had experienced upticks in the last six months as tourism grew. One was Costa Rica, thanks to its emphasis on ecotourism; and the other was Cuba, now that it was directly accessible from the United States.

The world was relatively quiet, though there was an interesting F2 hit from Moscow. She didn't need the glasses to read it. And the classification was F2B, a subset which meant that the identity was "confidently suspected" but with an uncertainty factor.

Kathleen opened the attached dossier.

Konstantin Bolshakov, she read. *Former naval officer who became an arms dealer after the breakup of the Soviet Union.*

There were no warrants or indication of recent activity, just two photographs: a thirty-two-year-old image Interpol had taken when he met with drug dealers in Berlin; and this new image, during the May Day Parade, only just posted on Facebook. The "aging" program applied to the older photograph made for a convincing similarity and a 79 percent certainty that it was Bolshakov.

Kathleen flagged the name and asked for a priority follow-up. That meant that security cameras to which Op-Center had access in and around Moscow, and at many Russian airports, should be searched as well. If the man were still active in gunrunning, he would be a useful bargaining chip if Moscow had anything the White House needed.

Almost at once, the scan returned with an update. Two weeks ago, Bolshakov had flown into an international airport in Russia's frozen northeast. No departure had been noted.

Kathleen dutifully marked the location for further scrutiny: the frozen port city of Anadyr.

CHAPTER TWO

Anadyr, Russia
July 2, 12:40 A.M.

During his twenty-year career as an officer for the Northern Fleet Intelligence Directorate, Konstantin Bolshakov became familiar with the three common designations for cold weather. There was freezing cold, which was the norm when ships were docked in northern bases like Severomorsk and Tiksi. It was the kind of weather when even a clear sun hanging in the sky did not cause the ice to melt. Then there was bitter cold, a classification that described a vessel leaving port and thrusting itself into winds that were restless at best, brutal at worst. And then there was extreme cold, which was the typical at-sea designation for ships facing not just wind but ice, floes that lowered the sea and air temperature by ten degrees or more.

The port city of Anadyr is none of those. Located in the permafrost zone, where the ground was frozen year-round, it is quite literally in a class by itself, nestled in one of the coldest inhabited spots on the planet. With a population of just over fourteen thousand, the port city is a sizeable fishing center, though it is also a significant mining center for coal and gold and is one of the largest reindeer-breeding centers in the hemisphere. Most of the people live in sturdy *khrushevkas*, five-story apartment buildings, and the roads are built of concrete; in the cold, lacking flexibility under heavy traffic, asphalt simply snaps and becomes granular, like little black diamonds.

"When the ground underfoot does not crunch," a fellow traveler on the flight had commented as they deplaned, "*then* I will worry about global warming."

Bolshakov replied with an agreeable smile. The other man—a structural engineer judging by a well-worn leather jacket that announced the name of his firm—had turned and addressed his traveling companion directly, a not-uncommon occurrence. Bolshakov had a wide, open face with relaxed, approachable features. It was one of the reasons that even career criminals and black marketers had trusted him for over thirty years.

The airbus journey had lasted nearly eight and one-half hours, the nonstop Ural Airlines flight describing the shortest path between the two places: an arc over the top of the earth. Now eighty-eight, the former sailor had bookended the trip with sleep, his chin tucked in his shoulder, his ear pressed to the cold, rattling window, his arms tightly crossed to keep his fingers warm. He woke for meals; to stare down at the pole that explorers had clawed across—not in relative comfort, with vodka on a fold-down tray; and to visit the lavatory. At those times, when he moved haltingly down the narrow aisle, Bolshakov found that his once powerful sea legs were woefully inadequate air legs. They embraced inactivity and protested with sharp joint pain and apathetic tendons whenever he rose. The proud part of him wanted to believe he could still make the journey by sea, if required, in one of the old freighters or frigates. But the pragmatic part of him—and the one-time idealist was nothing, now, if not a realist—knew that was not the case.

Still, he thought, now that the trip was behind him and he prepared for bed in his small, utilitarian hotel room, *still, you had that once*. A freedom that most men never knew, the euphoria of serving the Soviet Union and doing it on the great, swelling arena of the sea.

And then came Gorbachev. Damnable, short-sighted, weak-willed Gorbachev. Thanks to him, it was a freedom that men would never know again.

Bolshakov drew the blackout shade over the single, small window. Though it was dark now—not pitch, but a deep dusk-gray—there were just over twenty hours of daylight during the summer months. The sun would rise in less than an hour. He remembered having been excited by those lopsided hours when he was first stationed here. For a kid who grew up in Moscow, a metropolis, everything beyond the city limits was new and fascinating and he had embraced it all. Especially this place, which was God-touched in its unblemished simplicity. He had spent two years here when he was in his twenties. From what the dim light had revealed in the bus ride over, the outpost had grown to a small city. The Anadyr Hotel was a minor showplace: relatively new, the two-story barn-red box did not offer Internet for its guests but did have a private bathroom in each room. This particular room had a pair of twin beds, as requested. But even with a hotel, a supermarket, and a film theater, the town was still dwarfed by the vast skies and the fields beyond. As he lay down, alone, he also remembered—

You fell in love here. You married here, had a son here. Varvara and Yuri, brighter to him than the sun that shined through ice on the eaves of their small military apartment.

Tears formed in the old warrior's tired eyes and fell to the pillow. He had often thought that those years were the best he had ever known; perhaps they were the best that any man could ask for, to know perfect love and purpose and contentment.

"And yet," he murmured.

Perhaps there was still enough of God in this great wilderness to work a miracle. Bolshakov had come to Anadyr a day early not to see old sights, not for nostalgia. He had wanted to be rested for what was to come. Because it was possible that he had one great moment left in his life. The moment when, after three decades, he would finally get to put his arms around the neck of his son.

CHAPTER THREE

Op-Center Headquarters, Fort Belvoir North,
Springfield, Virginia
July 1, 8:55 A.M.

Three levels underground, in the small warren of offices and corridors that comprised Op-Center, Deputy Director Anne Sullivan sat in her office, the door closed—something it rarely was. Virtually all the work done by Op-Center was collaborative and she was the lynchpin among the many offices and their small staffs. Chase Williams called her the gatekeeper; those trying to reach him referred to her less kindly as the bottleneck. Science fiction geek Aaron Bleich had once put it more succinctly: "You're the Mr. Spock to the boss's Captain Kirk."

Anne did not know Aaron well, but the comparison was more apt than even he probably had realized.

Anne was highlighting items in the daily intelligence report from Homeland Security. The flags she placed on the secure tablet were color-coded by day. She took some teasing from Williams and Roger McCord, the intelligence director, about that. Williams called it her own private United Nations while McCord referred to it as her BBC: Big Box of Crayolas.

Sullivan smiled tightly whenever they said that. She didn't get clubhouse humor, the kind of needling coworkers did just for the apparent hell of it. It reminded her of the sorority pranking she experienced as an undergraduate at Smith, dialed back to conform to federal employment guidelines.

The fifty-seven-year-old stared at the tablet as if its size and proximity would obliterate the smart phone sitting to the right of her computer keyboard. Sometime after five minutes from now, she was supposed to get the call. It had been a long night of intermittent sleep and now that it was nearly here she felt a chronic chill, despite the rapid beat of her heart. If she were on her treadmill at home in Georgetown, lost in a novel or short story, a tiny beep would have sounded telling her it was time to slow down.

How? she demanded of the imaginary warning.

Her world had been upended by the biopsy. It wasn't just anxiety that electrified her body. It was a sense that the existence and routine she knew might suddenly have an expiration date . . . if not life itself. For the past few days, work had been a distraction rather than a passion; even *that* was new to her, and she didn't know how to handle it. She didn't *want* to handle it. She had already handled so much, pushing the envelope in a hierarchy where men either filled or controlled the slots.

And there's the self-pity, she warned herself.

She had stopped planting flags on the file and returned to it. Electronic intelligence transcripts from Israel about Western sympathizers in Tehran. Here she was, reflecting on past challenges when there was an entire population of human beings living in mute, terrified obeisance.

But her mind still wandered. The Sullivans were a Protestant family that had emigrated from East Belfast a half century ago. She still had the trace of a brogue in her voice, cherished because it reminded her of her dear father and departed mother, a mother she had lost to the same damn scourge that she was waiting to hear about—

The respectful rap at the door caused her to jump.

"Come in," she said, returning focus to her work.

The door opened slowly; Chase Williams was still answering a text as it swung in. The retired U.S. Navy four-star, former combatant commander for both Pacific Command and Central Command filled the doorway with a quiet authority that betrayed thirty-five years of active duty. He also held a PhD in global history from Tufts University, though Anne deeply respected the fact that he usually deferred to his coworkers who, like him, had field experience.

"Sorry," Williams said, looking up and smiling softly. "Seems my lease was due yesterday."

"Print or electronic?"

"Print," he said.

"We can have someone go over and break *into* the safe," she remarked.

Williams grinned. He lived at the Watergate. "Nice one. I don't think they'll evict me. I know people in higher places."

She smiled back, relieved for the distraction of the banter but aware that it was 9:03 and her phone hadn't chimed.

"Anything?" he asked, his eyes turning from the iPhone to hers.

"Not yet," she said, pursing her lips.

His eyes went back to the phone. "You want to bring it in my office, have coffee?"

"I'll wait here," she said, fighting down the choke in her voice. "I'll come in after—"

"The morning briefing can wait," he assured her. "Let me know if you need anything."

"A call from the oncologist really, really soon," she said.

It was a rare moment of vulnerability and Williams was about to give her a thumbs-up when the seabird chime sounded. Anne looked at the caller ID and took a long breath. Williams gave her an encouraging nod and shut the door.

She picked up the phone knowing that what she had just said was a lie. What she needed was a call that opened with, "Good news, Ms. Sullivan. We've got the biopsy results and the tumor was benign."

CHAPTER FOUR

Op-Center Headquarters, Fort Belvoir North,
Springfield, Virginia
July 1, 9:06 A.M.

Chase Williams was now sixty years old and in good health. But he had never been complacent about that. He had experienced the abrupt and bloody death of men in combat and he had gone to veterans' hospitals where soldiers had lost everything except the will to survive. He recognized that same uncertainty and anxiety in Anne Sullivan's eyes. She was a scrupulously private woman; after the doctor found a large lump in her breast, she had confessed to him that her mother and sister had both died from breast cancer—and that she was frightened.

"I don't think I'm afraid of whatever specific surgery might be necessary," she had admitted. "Worst case, they'll cut with an abundance of caution and I will heal. I'm more afraid of the road I'm starting down."

"I understand," Williams had said, "but you know you've got all kinds of support here if you—"

She had stopped him with a firm shake of her head. "It's not the disease, Chase. It's this." She had tapped a temple with her index finger. "It's like that children's game where you spread out a deck of cards and build a little house on top. You start pulling out the cards one by one and sooner or later—you can't stop *thinking* about it—the house will fall. The 'end' is no longer an abstraction, something that's just 'out there.' I'm waiting to pull my first card."

Williams had had talks like this with soldiers, not office workers. But fear was fear and he had fixed her with his strong, Naval Academy eyes-on-the-prize expression and said, "I don't go in for platitudes, so I won't tell you that the SEALs have a saying: 'The only easy day was yesterday.' But I *will* tell you something I was told by a Marine who took part in the Iwo Jima bloodbath. He said in the midst of a meat grinder like that, when every next instant could mean oblivion, you hold those seconds dear as breath itself."

He had said a lot of things that morning, and there ended up being more chestnuts than he had intended. It was unavoidable; the spiritual bones of the military were all mottos. But all his advice obviously had not taken. The woman he just left was already fighting a physical and mental battle that might not even happen.

Williams took a moment to regard the signed photo of General Douglas MacArthur on the wall—he always communed with the great man at the start of the day—then began going through overnight TAFs, the threat assessment files that were eyes-only and contained summarized analysis from his counterparts at the NSA, CIA, FBI, and other intelligence-gathering services. It was a good morning when the worst news were the dangers you already knew. But he was still thinking of Anne, his selfless and trusted number two. Her office was down the hall and he had left his own door open. The walls were soundproofed, so all he could listen for was the click of her door. He hoped she would come by.

Instead, it was Paul Bankole, the international crisis manager, who stopped on his way to his office. The former member of SEAL Team Six understood pain and recovery. He was an E-8, senior chief, about to make E-9, master chief, when he was severely wounded in a firefight in Iraq. He spent just over a year in recovery at Balboa Naval Hospital in San Diego, California.

"You going to sit in on the video debrief of Brigadier General Ghasemi?" Bankole asked.

"I'll read the transcript," Williams answered flatly. "He was in Iraq helping ISIS kill our people. And frankly, Paul, if you don't want to watch—"

"He says he can help stop that, now," Bankole said. "I want to hear that. Anyway, remember those pictures of Saddam after he was captured? Broken and lost?"

"Vividly and proudly."

"Well, *sic semper tyrannis*," Bankole said. "This Gorgon's lost his snakes."

Williams nodded with understanding as Bankole turned to start back down the hall.

"Paul!" Williams called after him.

The forty-three-year-old African-American leaned back into the doorway.

"Are you sure you don't want Dawson to go?" Williams asked.

Brian Dawson was the operations director, a position which informally made him a jack-of-all-trades backup to the other senior staff members.

"I'll be fine," Bankole said. "I don't want to look at that son of a bitch, either, even in a video feed. But if the guy's a Fizz, that's the only way I'll know."

Fizz was derived from the expression "F is for Fake." Coined in the 1960s, it was briefly used to describe Communist spies who infiltrated the influx of defectors and asylum-seekers coming from Eastern Europe. The term was revived in 2016 by United States Immigration and Customs Enforcement to flag suspicious young, single males who came to the United States with the exodus of Syrian refugees.

Williams gave the crisis manager a short, face-front nod that carried the same show of respect as a salute.

Bankole hesitated, then took a step back into the doorway. "Question?"

"Shoot."

"The Iranians aside, any of this have to do with Trevor Harward?"

Though Williams didn't show it, the frankness of the question surprised him. It also pleased him. Bankole was relatively new at Op-Center, a replacement for the well-liked Hector Rodriquez, who was killed in an assault on an ISIS compound in Mosul. Williams encouraged his team to be frank and open and he was glad to hear Bankole ask something that bordered on the personal.

"Are you asking because the national security advisor is a puppet to the polls or because he's a brownnoser who we just don't like?" Williams frankly replied.

Bankole grinned at the blunt response.

"Both are true, but not a factor," Williams went on. "You're new to this, but not to bureaucratic bullshit. When the administration trots out a defecting Iranian general just when President Wyatt Midkiff happens to need a political boost—I'm wary," Williams said. "It's like when NASA press-releases a story about hints of life on Mars just before their budget review. There isn't an office inside the Beltway whose motives I trust. I just want to read the questions and answers and not be thinking about breaking the guy's jaw because the high command in Tehran is still financing the IEDs that are maiming our troops."

Bankole rubbed his left hip, the one that had been shredded in combat and left him with a noticeable limp.

"I hear you," Bankole said. He glanced down the corridor and smiled, just then. "And I appreciate you looking out for me. I'll get back to you when it's over."

Still smiling, Bankole said good morning to someone and continued to his office. Anne Sullivan replaced him in the doorway. Williams rose as he motioned her in. She was slumping a little, her expression neutral, her energy low. That told Williams nothing: she was probably exhausted. He walked with her to the sofa and perched on the armrest while she sat. She was holding her ever present tablet, which she placed on the large coffee table in front of her. She folded her hands lightly on her lap and stared back at the door.

"I'm all right," she said. "I mean, I'm healthy. The doctor said the growth was benign." It was more of a long exhale than a statement.

Williams looked down at her. Her face turned toward the floor.

"Dear God, thank you," she said.

Anne was breathing heavily. Williams continued to give the woman her space. Finally, she looked up at him. Her breathing was more regular and her eyes were dry.

"When we first talked about this, you said something about being in the arena," she remembered.

"Teddy Roosevelt," Williams said softly. "A speech in Paris. 'The credit belongs to the man who is actually in the arena, whose face is marred by dust and sweat and blood.'"

"That's the one," she said. "I was talking about decay and you were talking about spirit. I was giving up before I had to fight."

"I hope that's not self-reproach," Williams said.

"Maybe a little," she admitted. "You were right. You tried to amp me up while I let myself die inside. Thanks to you—and to Paul, when I think about all that he had to overcome—when this happens again, I'll be better at it."

Williams did not want to patronize her with a speech of gesture; she had said everything that needed to be said.

"Do some work?" he asked, gesturing toward the waiting tablet as he relocated to an armchair at the near end of the table.

Before she could answer, his secure smartphone beeped. He went back to the desk and looked down. He hesitated before punching "accept."

"Mr. Harward," he said thickly. "How are things in the West Wing?"

"Would you come to Quantico for the Ghasemi interrogation?" he asked without preamble and with his characteristic agitation. "We'll arrange a chopper."

Williams glanced at the clock on his phone. The interview was scheduled to begin in about forty-five minutes. "I can be there," he replied. "What's this about, Trevor?"

"I'll tell you when you get here," he said. "I'll need you to bring every hole card you have about black market nukes." He waited, then made a point of adding: "Everything."

Despite the generally successful architecture-for-sharing mandate enacted by the Department of Homeland Security, every top official kept some things to themselves—so-called hole cards. In a town run by power, in a business where intelligence was power, NASA wasn't the only organization that held key information for timely release.

"I'll be there," Williams promised.

Hanging up, he told Anne to pull the EON file—eyes only nuclear—and check the Tank for any late-breaking updates. Williams immediately began organizing his trip, making sure he had the dossier of Brigadier General Amir Ghasemi on his tablet to read on the flight over. In addition to a biography of the sixty-year-old, it included the interview that was conducted when he sought asylum at the U.S. Embassy in Baghdad. The general offered information that was in the process of being verified; in the meantime, to calm the man's extremely high level of agitation, the decision was made to relocate him.

"What's going on?" Anne asked, one hundred percent in this arena.

"From the sound of Harward's voice," he told her, "I'd say the national security advisor may have stumbled into a minefield."

CHAPTER FIVE

Main Intelligence Directorate,
Khodynka Airfield, Russia
July 1, 4:13 P.M.

The *Glavnoye razvedyvatel'noye upravleniye* or simply GRU—
Russia's Main Intelligence Directorate—was also known as the
Aquarium due, in part, to its busy fishbowl configuration of its
most distinctive building. The complex was located on the former
field where Czarist Russia suffered one of its worst domestic trag-
edies: in May 1896, during the coronation of Nicholas II, crowds
eager to see the new ruler crashed through security cordons and
over one thousand onlookers were trampled to death. An airfield
arose on that spot and, fourteen years later, a man named Rossin-
sky became the first Russian to pilot an airplane.

Captain Yuri Gherman Bolshakov was fond of history. He
himself bore the names of two heroes: Yuri Gagarin and Gherman Titov, the first and second Russians to fly in space. Captain
Bolshakov was attached to the Ninth Department, the Division
of Military Technologies. He had previously worked in the Eleventh
Department, Strategic Nuclear Forces, which was one reason he

had been handpicked for this mission. The other reason, of course—perhaps the foremost reason—is that he had the surname of a famous Russian as well, a onetime hero who had found his way into corruption and shame. Yuri's father, Konstantin.

Wearing a modest gray business suit and sitting in the back of the yellow public taxi, Captain Bolshakov looked like any other civilian on his way to the commercial airport, Sheremetyevo International. Anonymity was necessary. Ever since the Russians began expanding the Nagurskoye military airfield in the Arctic, the Americans and Chinese both were paying more attention to flights headed north. The 14,000-square-mile complex could only house 150 troops but it was not a tactical advantage the Kremlin was after. It was oil, over four hundred million barrels of it beneath the ice. Before they attempted to exploit it, the Russians wanted to be able to protect it. Moscow had steadily tested American capabilities and response-times by sending Su-35 fighter jets and Cold War–era bombers to test Alaska's air defense zone. They would not be a threat to Nagurskoye.

But they will be so busy watching that region they will never notice me, he thought.

Still, it was good to take reasonable precautions. In the likelihood that Western eyes and ears were watching and listening either on-site or electronically, nothing about this trip was to appear military. On the surface, it was a fascinating undertaking. But as they lurched through traffic under darkening skies, most of what the captain felt was not on the surface.

The forty-four-year-old career soldier had neither sought this meeting nor was he looking forward to it. He had not even made the overtures. That was done anonymously by the staff of his superior, Lieutenant Colonel Glazkov. The captain was handed the assignment a week before, given a detailed briefing, provided with updates about his father, and that was that. Perhaps Glazkov thought his subordinate would enjoy the reunion. More likely, he didn't care. The elder Bolshakov was needed in a certain place for a specific reason and the GRU was convinced his son could guarantee both.

They drove behind an ambulance headed toward the airport—most likely with a fare rather than a person in need of medical care. Paying customers took priority in Russia's major cities. That was the real spawn of Gorbachev's policy of *perestroika*, of societal "reformation." A breakdown of all controls. The shadow economy that slithered through the Soviet Union was now in the open, muscular and contemptuous of anything decent.

Like my father. A snake.

A slashing rain began to fall. The captain lit a cigarette and watched the smear of lights on the window. His eyes were as resolute as his fixed jaw, as dark as his close-cropped black hair. The driver's side wiper started to beat—the other one didn't work—but Captain Bolshakov saw only the smoke. It was a habit he picked up from his mother, Vavara, who had a moderately successful career as a concert pianist under her maiden name, V. Kochnev. Her specialty was Alexander Scriabin, and her career fell in and out of favor as the nineteenth-century aristocrat did likewise.

Now he looked at the wiper. Only it was a metronome, striking the beat for his own lessons, which he enjoyed. He thought of them, and his mother, often; but not of his father. Never.

Until now.

He looked into the driver's rearview mirror, saw the receding lights of the Aquarium, his real home, his *only* family. He did not want to see the past, his father's face the last time they spoke.

"*Yuri, I have news,*" he had said gravely.

News! As if he were telling the fourteen-year-old about another cosmonaut sent aloft by the proud Soviet people, the way he used to do when the boy would come home from school.

News.

Captain Bolshakov crushed the cigarette in the seatback ashtray. He jabbed the stub so hard the driver started.

"Hey!" the man shouted.

"Sorry," the captain said in a quiet voice.

"My springs are shit. I *felt* that!"

"Again, my apologies," the man replied deferentially.

The driver grumbled his way back to silence. Maybe the captain should have taken an ambulance as well. Or maybe that's who the driver was really angry at. It was difficult to know anything, to see anything clearly, when everything was the tumultuous spawn of *glasnost*—transparency.

If Lieutenant Colonel Glaskov was to be believed, and his own Kremlin sources were accurate, President Putin had it completely right. His goal was to reignite the old ways, rebuild the proud mind-set. Reconnect and expand the old confederacy to create a new entity—not the Soviet Union but the Soviet Empire, a force for equality and progress across the globe.

You're getting ahead of yourself, he cautioned himself.

That was understandable. The officer had been on missions before, but most of that was counterintelligence and disinformation at the nation's long-range nuclear missile sites. The Eleventh Department programs were designed to confuse foreign operatives and to ferret out moles and spies. It was fulfilling and intellectually stimulating work but this project—this was bigger.

The taxi splashed forward and the roar of aircraft came nearer. The captain was actually looking forward to the long flight east. It would be the first time in a week he'd be able to rest. And he had never been to the region of the Bering Sea or the Arctic Ocean. Discovering a new region of his homeland was always exciting to him. He was glad so many of the nuclear silos were in remote places, districts few Russians ever got to visit.

The flight would also give him time to contemplate the reason he was making this trip. The preparations had been intense and exhaustive, from learning geography to studying abandoned mechanical and engineering systems to ice-climbing. He had just enough time to do everything except to fully assimilate the big picture. If Captain Bolshakov lost sight of that, if he dwelled on the man who had caused his mother's murder, whose very name he had almost discarded, he might very well kill the creature on sight.

Potholes outside the entrance to the airport caused his luggage to bounce in the trunk. The rain became a drizzle and the drizzle stopped. He collected his own bags, paid the driver, and stepped to the curb. He paused to smell the clean, warm air of the descending night. Moscow was his city and Russia was his home. However difficult the road ahead, he would do whatever was required to honor them both.

With invigorated purpose, Captain Bolshakov turned and entered the terminal that housed Yakutia Airlines.

CHAPTER SIX

Op-Center Headquarters, Fort Belvoir North,
Springfield, Virginia
July 1, 9:14 A.M.

"He wants you *in* the room?"

"At his side," Williams assured Paul Bankole.

"That's . . . a curious wrinkle," Bankole replied with his penchant for understatement.

Paul Bankole was bouncing beside Chase Williams in the back of an open-top Commando. The sun was warm and the sky was clear and the ride gave Williams a moment to clear his head. The light, mobile vehicle was one of the first Jeeps purchased since the early 1980s; it was returned to the roster as part of the Army's leaner Ground Mobility Vehicle Program in 2017. Williams preferred them to Humvees, which always made him feel as if he were wearing a lead overcoat.

"What do you make of it?" Bankole continued.

Williams shrugged. "He acted as if he were holding a live grenade. Why, I have no idea."

The Op-Center director looked down Belvoir Road toward

the drill field, where a forty-year-old Black Hawk UH-60 was warming up.

"The least they could've done was let you borrow the Black Knight," Bankole sniffed.

Belvoir was the current home to the Advanced Tactics Flying Jeep, which was still undergoing field tests. It had eight piston engines powering two-blade propellers for vertical takeoff and flight, and a Volkswagen engine for ground travel. Williams had seen the ungainly beast around. He was happy not to be riding the ungainly beast.

The retired officer felt a familiar thrill as they neared and the fabric of his blue windbreaker started to respond to the prop wash. It was, he thought unashamedly, like a kiss from the girl who got away: familiar and like no other sensation. It eased through the fluttering breeze caused by the Jeep, caused a familiar "pluck-and-plunge" in the nylon fabric, and reminded him of every command, every hellhole, he had ever been visiting or leaving.

He loved his work at Op-Center, but he missed that. It was the stuff that made him, right to the end. Now, desk-bound, more bureaucrat and diplomat than commander, he missed that deeply.

"Dawson and I will be watching," Bankole said as the Jeep braked. "Anyone else you want in there?"

"Yeah," Williams said as he stepped out. "See if they'll let you patch Bruner into the feed. If not, secure-line her a video. I want a body language analysis."

"Will do."

Meagan Bruner was Op-Center's on-call psychologist at the

Navy's Walter Reed National Military Medical Center. Most of her work involved extreme cases of PTSD; she welcomed every opportunity to work on Op-Center's eclectic challenges.

Williams thanked the Army driver but made it a point not to salute. Like his current position, his past life was supposed to be as anonymous as he could make it. That was why Bankole had not asked more specific questions about the interrogation of the Iranian general, and Williams had not offered any details.

The northeastward flight to Quantico covered the twenty miles in just under ten minutes. Williams landed at the Marine Corps air facility in the southwest sector of the compound. He was met by one of the smaller black sedans in the president's fleet; Trevor Harward was inside, beside a glass partition.

"Thanks for coming out," said the slight, balding man with a set frown.

"Happy to help," Williams said, slipping off his sunglasses and managing to sound believable.

The two men were not friends, were barely even allies. In addition to being the kind of partisan who put politics above nation, Harward had spoken out strongly against the reactivation of Op-Center, describing the last incarnation as reckless and rogue and warning to expect the same from Williams and his people. A flowering of crises caused the president to ignore those objections—concerns which rose from not just Harward but the entrenched fiefdoms of other intelligence chiefs. The irony was, none of the naysayers was entirely wrong. One of the reasons Op-Center had always been so effective is they did very little through channels, and virtually nothing by the book.

"So, my first question, which wasn't in the file: how do you know this is actually Qarazi?"

"We have the fingerprints of the shah's imperial guard on file from a state visit in 1977. It's the same man."

"Then what's got you concerned?" Williams continued. "The man has a pedigree."

"He does indeed," Harward replied. "A long one and a very specific one, the kind you don't often find in Iran. The kind you'd manufacture to sell him to someone as a candidate for defection. Especially the connection to the shah. When the government was overthrown in 1979, most of his loyal officers fled or hid. Some vanished. Many died under questionable circumstances. Few survived the transition to the Islamic Republic. But let's assume he managed to transition—through family connections, a cousin to Ayatollah Khomeini, as he claims," Harward went on. "Ghasemi made his way quickly to a position of high authority and ended up working closely with security personnel covering the *mujtahids* that comprise the Supreme Leader's Assembly of Experts."

"Giving him access to a great deal of privileged information."

"Information we would naturally want," Harward added. "The perfect defector, possibly manufactured for this purpose since the ayatollah came to power."

"Or," Williams countered, "a secret shah loyalist who couldn't wait to betray the theocracy."

"Exactly," Harward said. "But before we take this gift horse to our bosom, we have to know whether this man is the real deal."

He regarded Williams. "Matt Berry says you've got a special talent for what he calls 'the real deal military.' The president needs that kind of perspective. So do I."

Matt Berry was Midkiff's deputy chief of staff and a close friend of Williams's operation head Bob Dawson. The secretive Berry was Op-Center's unofficial inside man at the White House.

"I'm flattered and more than a little curious myself," Williams said.

Harward shook his head heavily. "We cannot afford to embrace a Red Rose, Chase. Not with a high profile get like this one."

A Red Rose was an intelligence "catch" who smelled right and looked good on the lapel, then poked you in the heart with thorns.

"Who else will be there?" Williams asked.

"January Dow and Allen Kim," he said. "We had a bit of a turf war with the INR so January will handle the initial questioning."

Williams nodded approvingly. Kim was a good man, a longtime colleague of Op-Center's intelligence director Roger McCord. He was the executive director in charge of the FBI facility at Quantico and had personally driven the Iranian to this facility. Williams knew of Dow, the young deputy director of the State Department's Bureau of Intelligence and Research, the INR. She studied political science at Harvard and had spent two years apiece at the embassies in South Africa and Turkey. He had read some of the papers she published on the Shia-Sunni struggle in the *American Intelligence Journal*; a little too much academia, too little boots-on-the-ground for his taste. She was ivory-tower formality to the point of never using the nicknames for the FBI, the CIA, and Op-Center—the Bureau, the Company, the Ranch. But her presence made sense. The INR had a liaison at the embassy in Iraq, who took charge of the general. Qarazi had obviously remained in joint custody of the INR and the FBI; Williams could imagine both the pique and relief at CIA that this great catch—or great burden—was not their responsibility.

Williams hoped that Dow didn't mind *him* being there. Even well-meaning bureaucrats could get prickly about their dominions.

Harward thanked Williams again as they reached their destination. The first "thank you" had been for showing up; the second, warmer and more sincere, was apparently a blanket self-pardon for past infractions. Williams knew it had a shelf life of about an hour.

The sedan had stopped at the FBI's Technology Services Unit, a nondescript building that Dawson once described as being the color of macaroni and cheese; it was severe and featureless and would not have been out of place in an industrial park. Because the entire base was secure, they didn't need much of a holding area and this complex would provide the electronics they'd need to record and securely transmit the interview.

Williams did not often get away from the office—except to go to someone else's office—and this was more than a welcome change. Routine was necessary in government, and his was strictly regimented. He was widower, his son and daughter were adults with lives and careers and homes in other cities, and by the end of the week he was too tired for get-to-know-you dating. Especially after the love he had with Genie, as gracious and lovely an angel as ever walked the earth—and whom he felt, more times than not, was still beside him at night. For social interaction and downtime recreation, he had his regular Saturday game with the lacrosse team from the Department of Defense and occasional squash matches with his domestic crisis manager, James Wright.

Before they could walk through the glass doors, a tall, handsome African-American woman emerged and strode briskly toward them. She held a large tablet with a secure-wireless receiver plugged in the USB port. Williams recognized her as January Dow; Allen Kim followed close behind. Their pace caused Harward to stop where he was.

"Something wrong?" the national security advisor demanded.

The woman looked around to make sure there was no one else nearby. They stood away from the twin security cameras positioned above the door.

"Before you go inside, there's a video you have to see," she answered without answering.

"What kind of video?" Harward unhappily demanded.

She replied bluntly, "The kind that turns humanists into cynics."

CHAPTER SEVEN

Op-Center Headquarters, Fort Belvoir North,
Springfield, Virginia
July 1, 9:41 A.M.

He was the man who came back from the dead.

Because each keystroke was recorded and, if questioned, had to be justified, Kathleen Hays created a small dossier on Konstantin Bolshakov. It wasn't just a matter of recording personnel efficiency or safeguarding national security; it was a form of "negative deduction," as Aaron had described it, a way of determining how much time employees spent out of the office or on private cell phones during business hours.

The more Kathleen wrote, the more automatic algorithms kicked in, connecting the subject to events that might not occur to individuals with highly specialized knowledge. In this case, only an historian of the Cold War would have linked the minor intelligence officer to the Cuban Missile Crisis—though, as even the computer acknowledged, the "threatcon" level of that information was an insignificant 0.7 percent. The connection came through a Lieutenant Ilya Myshkova, deceased, who belonged to the same intelligence unit and who was placed in Havana the same day Bolshakov disappeared from official Soviet military records. When he reappeared, a quarter-century later, Bolshakov was a private citizen.

"Where were you all that time?" she wondered aloud. "And were you or weren't you a soldier?"

Gary Gold did not look up from his own computer. "The Question Whisperer," he whispered, imitating her breathy speech. It was like kicking a snorer, a knee-jerk reaction doomed to fail.

"Sorry," she said. Her cheeks reddened a little.

Thinking aloud was a habit that dated back to finger painting and continued through graduate school. It inevitably surfaced when she was faced with a puzzle. She returned to her monitor.

Gold grinned and reached for the earbuds plugged into his phone. "I will vanquish you with talk radio, that I may also know what's really going on in the world."

They both went back to work, Kathleen receiving an instant message from Bankole that she would be needed for a VIE—a video internee evaluation—in five minutes. He told her he would send the code when he had it.

Kathleen acknowledged and returned to the mysterious Konstantin Bolshakov. Despite the May Day image, there was no record of that name, even then. No bank statements that she could find in Russia or the United States and other preferred investment locations for wealthy Russians.

"Did you survive on cash?" she wondered.

That was more likely in Russia than anywhere else, where

thriving black marketers left as few financial electronic fingerprints as possible. But there was no evidence that Bolshakov went
from being an intelligence officer to a criminal. Playing the per-
centages, those individuals were usually given new identities and
sent abroad as spies.

Kathleen began to feel that she was wasting her time. Like
the collapse of the Third Reich, the breakup of the Soviet Union
was accompanied by the mass destruction of records. If material
weren't stored in the files of foreign intelligence services, it was
most likely lost.

"Still . . ."

The Cuban connection was interesting. Among the first influx of American tourists to those newly opened shores had been
undercover CIA operatives looking for Russian, Chinese, South
American, and even Middle Eastern agents looking to make connections and establish influence for whatever the post–Raúl Castro
regime looked like. It was a game of political chess, a throwback to
wartime Casablanca where Allied and Axis agents moved clandes-
tinely in public but knew each other by sight and often by name
in the underground. It was like being on vacation where the occasional sport was murder. The one area where these agents did
not have to go was the Lourdes SIGINT facility just a few miles
southwest of Havana. Run by the SVR—the *Sluzhba vneshney
razvedki*, the Russian Foreign Intelligence Service—it earned the
Cuban government 200-million-dollar "rental" fee annually. Lourdes
had been a primary target of electronic counterintelligence after
the Russians successfully blocked radio transmissions overseen by
the private Broadcasting Board of Governors. The bulk of these

were newscasts being sent from the United States to Iran. Lourdes was finally hacked by the Department of Defense listening station at MacDill Air Force Base, Tampa, in 2015, using a signal that was undetectably routed through SVR headquarters in the Yasenevo District of Moscow. The communications between Havana and Moscow gave U.S. intelligence a chance to break their code and keep track of whatever the Russians had picked up from our own intercepted electronic signals. Most of what the SVR captured was either trivial or disinformational. But they continued to listen.

Sadly, one thing Lourdes did not provide was insight into anything that occurred before 2014. The station had been closed in 2002, after fifty years of operation, and most of those files were either destroyed or relocated to Yasenevo. But a few of them made their way into American hands via nighttime couriers to the Guantanamo Bay Naval Base, some six hundred miles from Havana on the other side of the island. Those had been scanned and she searched them for Lieutenant Ilya Myshkova.

His name returned with a single ping: hospitalization for a pernicious case of diarrhea.

"This is getting me nowhere," she muttered.

Closing the file on Cuba, she was about to do the same with Bolshakov when the surname returned a hit. She read the alert.

July 1 2019—9:48 A.M.
INTERPOLlink/datafeed/Sheremetyevo-security
Bolshakov, Yuri Gherman, passenger.
Yakutia Airlines/Flight464/DME-DYR

Kathleen looked up the codes. From the Sheremetyevo reference she knew that DME was Moscow. The other—

Well, that's a little present, she thought.

Yuri Bolshakov was flying to Anadyr. She ran a check of the man, found his home address in Moscow, birthplace—Anadyr—and his parents, Konstantin and Varvara, status unknown. There were no photographs, but that wasn't unusual; Russia was far behind the United States about digitizing school, passport, and motor vehicle records. That was where most photographs turned up.

So this whole thing might be nothing more than a family reunion. That was the double-edged sword of having access to virtually unlimited information: sometimes the trail lead nowhere.

"But at least you get there quickly," she thought aloud.

Kathleen left the file open for auto-updates, expecting she would at least get an image of the man when he reached Anadyr. She had no idea what she would do with it, what relevance it had to anything. She noticed her own dark, blurry reflection on the monitor. This was—*she* was—the Big Brother that George Orwell had warned about, the all-seeing government of *1984*. And nearly without justification: she was eavesdropping on a man's private affairs without his permission or knowledge in a statistically nonexistent pursuit of possible ties to a potential gunrunner who might be retired; and even if he weren't, Op-Center had practically no skin in that game. There were so many qualifiers that she felt like a voyeur.

She made a point of not saying that word aloud, certain that Gary would have heard it through whatever he was listening to.

A red flag instant message appeared on her screen. It was from Paul Bankole.

```
Access   Ghasemi   feed,   code   Qu/i/
[71] . . . pB10/Red!
```

She acknowledged and went to her routing file, typed the code, save-name Ghasemi. The analyst knew who the Iranian was, but that was all . . . until now. The code told her he was at Quantico, that he was being interviewed—as opposed to inter-rogated, which tended to involve a prison setting—and after the date, authorizing officer, and time, that Bankole was asking for a body language and voice analysis. As soon as Ghasemi had de-fected, Homeland Security had assembled and distributed a com-plete video and photographic file on the man. Kathleen's computer would compare the general's body language, thermal readings, and speech to his own baseline movements and expressions. It would then form a flowchart assessing the truth of his statements. The woman noticed that in addition to the international crisis manager, Meagan Bruner was also on the feed at Bethesda. The psychologist would be offering her own take.

Strangely, this activity did not make Kathleen feel as if she were eavesdropping. Possibly because Ghasemi was complicit in the process. Still, as she waited for the interview she considered the surveillance cameras spread through the nation, the world; the satellites able to read dog collars or keyboard strokes in exurbia; and the law enforcement software being applied to much of it. And she wondered if members of any security team would ever again—*could* ever again—feel personally secure or socially un-wired.

The computer showed ten o'clock. The feed opened on a seat at what looked like the end of a conference table. A small, serene man was seated there. He had a closely cropped beard and slightly thicker moustache. His eyes were dark and sunken, his mouth relaxed but shut. He wore a bulletproof vest and a black baseball cap without any markings that might indicate who had him, or where.

She watched for two minutes as the man stared at the table. All the indicators in her FRISC program—Full Range Interrogation Scan Composite—read normal. Facial heat reading, restlessness in hands and shoulder, eye movement, breathing . . . everything suggested what Kathleen once described to Chase as "someone in the middle of a long train ride through rain." He seemed to prefer that to the official classification of Guard Down Alpha.

Then, at 10:03:22, the man suddenly looked up. And exactly three seconds later, the feed ended.

CHAPTER EIGHT

FBI Academy, Marine Corps Base, Quantico, Virginia
July 1, 10:14 A.M.

As far as Chase Williams was concerned, the skirmish had settled nothing.

Fifteen minutes before, he was still standing in the sunlight as January angled the tablet so he and Harward could see. It was nauseating, but that was not why Williams had felt a chill run riot through his torso.

Combat produced adrenaline and caused the body to exceed perceived limitations. Command created intense focus and, in times of war, deep anxiety for the well-being of others—not just his troops but the civilian population.

What he had just seen was different. It showed a middle-aged woman wearing a black *hijab* that covered her head and breast. Beneath it was a floor-length black *abaya* with gold trim. She was on the concrete floor of a bare room. The walls were cinderblock. A man was with her and he was lashing out repeatedly with a whip. Each time it landed on the woman she shrieked piteously and scudded away—only to be found, again, by the snapping leather tongue. Her clothing was shredded in spots, the torn hem stained with blood.

In the lower left corner of the video was a photograph. It was a photo of General Ghasemi in uniform, stamped with the seal gun-and-laurel seal of the Army of the Guardians of the Republic of Iran. It was probably used for the general's military ID.

The sixty-second video had seemed much longer. When it was over, Harward had asked, "Who is it?"

"We don't know," January admitted.

"More importantly, how did you get it?" Williams asked.

"It was delivered to the embassy in Baghdad on a flash drive."

"When?" Williams asked.

"About four hours ago," January told him. She knew why he had asked. "And no, I don't think it was timed to this interview per se. Need-to-know was highly restricted. I agree with my colleague in Baghdad that it was meant to be seen at *some* point early in the debrief process."

"Forensics on the drive?" Williams asked.

"No prints, U.S. Army issue."

"How do you know it was ours?" Harward asked.

"When IT dug in they discovered the clip had overwritten a training video for Excalibur GPS–guided artillery rounds."

"From Iraq," Williams said. "That's not good."

"Meaning what?" Harward asked.

"Tehran either had people with Ghasemi or shadowing him," January said.

"So—he's a plant?" Harward asked.

"Not necessarily," January said. "Officers are routinely surveilled, though that's something I intend to find out."

"If they were watching him, why didn't they stop him before he defected?" Williams asked.

"I have some thoughts on that," she told him, but said no more. Williams let it sit.

"Is there an interpreter?" Williams went on.

"The general speaks English," January said.

"Which strikes me as a little too convenient," Harward offered.

"Not really," Williams said. "It was expected of those who worked close to the shah."

January looked at him admiringly. Apparently, she hadn't read up on *his* curriculum vitae.

The chill had faded and Williams glanced at his watch. "We're late. Do we show him the video or not?"

"*Before* we interrogate him?" Harward demanded. "If this is a relative, he may shut down. That is the intent of it, isn't it?"

"We can't assume anything right now," January countered, "other than that the general had to anticipate something like this."

Williams glanced over at Kim, who hadn't watched the video. "Allen? Thoughts?"

"Show him," the FBI officer replied. "His reaction will probably tell us as much as anything he has to say."

"How?" Trevor asked. "He could be acting."

"If he's faking, we'll know," Williams told the national security advisor. "A reaction of horror is more than just a scream. It's made up of markers like wariness when he first sees the tablet, then anger, grief, self-reproach when he watches the video. You look for those in the eyes, the hands." He added, "Let's show him."

"I like your analysis, very much," January said to Williams. "But I want to wait. There are a few things I want to ask him first."

This was her interrogation and Williams had no strong feelings one way or the other. She went inside and the others followed her into the lobby. There was no further discussion, since there were pockets of young men and women here. Ghasemi had been brought in shortly before dawn, by January and a guard who remained with the general at all times. Despite the facility's high-profile guest, the INR intended that business should go on as usual to avoid calling attention to this location. Often, enemy agents who could not access secure sites watched people coming from those places for meals, eavesdropped on their conversations, intercepted their smartphone Google searches.

January turned the three men down a corridor to the right. They took an elevator to the second floor and walked to a room at the end of another corridor. The group was silent the entire time; Williams was chewing on what they knew.

The team leader knocked on the door and waited for it to be unlocked form the inside.

"I assume your guest was fed?" Williams asked her.

"Fruit and coffee, per his request," January replied.

"Did he also request a prayer rug?" Williams wondered.

"At the embassy," January said, once again regarding Williams with admiration. "He brought it with him."

The door opened and the group entered. Ghasemi was seated at the far end of a short conference table. A camera on a tripod was positioned on the near side. January stood beside it and the men lined up inside the door.

January did not introduce them. She lay the tablet on the table, smiled at the general, and made a point of shutting off the camera.

"Ms. Dow?" Harward asked, questioning her action.

Ghasemi seemed as surprised as the national security advisor.

"My first two questions will be off-the-record," she said, still looking at the general. "I believe there is a cover story that must be preserved."

"What are you talking about?" Harward asked. "I have intelligence experts watching."

"Not this part," she said.

Williams and Kim exchanged looks. Neither man knew where she was going with this.

January regarded Ghasemi. "Sir, I shut the recorder because I want to reiterate what I told you earlier: you are perfectly safe here. But we need a truthful answer, one that will not leave this room unless you are comfortable. Do you understand?"

"I do, and thank you," he said in a quiet voice—a voice accustomed to deferring to very powerful men, Williams noted.

"My first question, General Ghasemi: are you a Christian?"

Ghasemi's reaction was instantaneous. He said nothing, seemed to be unable to speak, but he began to tremble.

Harward was no less startled.

"No one will find out, I promise," the woman moved quickly to assure him.

"I ask you again: are you a Christian?"

The general nodded. He seemed to want to say more but was unable to find the words. January helped him.

"Where did you worship before the Revolution?"

"My family, my parents, we all worshipped at the Central Assemblies of God in Tehran," he said with a tremulous voice. "It is gone, now," he added sadly.

"Protestant?" January asked.

Ghasemi nodded once.

"Why is that relevant?" Kim asked.

"It speaks to plausibility," January said. "Many Christians fled the country, certainly the big cities, but the Protestants were the first and the largest group to go underground in 1979. They hoped to ride the storm, which they prayed would be brief."

Harward was shaking his head with open disgust. "General, you're saying that you and your family have been posing as Shia since the Revolution and the government *never* suspected your true background?"

"Many records were lost, destroyed," he said. "Then as now, no one can be sure of anything in Tehran. The more time that passed, I felt we were safe, that I was accepted. Then—this happened."

January held up her hand to Harward in order to continue the interview.

"Thank you for your honesty, General," she said. There was compassion, not triumph in her voice for having exposed him. "My second question, sir: who is the woman they're holding?"

If Ghasemi had been rattled by the first question, reference to the woman broke him. He pushed back in the seat, exhaled, and remained deflated.

"General?" she coaxed softly.

Ghasemi's eyes found the woman and stayed on her as though

seeking support, comfort, anything kind. "It is my daughter," he answered, then inhaled slowly. "They have my only daughter. She . . . in a cell where they . . ."

He couldn't finish and the room fell utterly silent, but only for a moment.

"You've seen the video," Kim said with sudden understanding.

"All right," Harward said with disgust. He stepped forward and stopped beside January. "What is this? What's this *about*?"

"It's about Islam and Christianity in the twentieth century with Professor Bani-Etemad at Yale University," she replied.

"That doesn't help," he said impatiently.

"It was a paper initially discredited because the professor believed that leading members of the Revolution were both theocrats and pragmatists," she said. "He was later proven to be correct. The shah had recruited a large number of Christians in his personal guard, men who were not likely to be swayed by Islamic revolutionaries. After the Revolution, as much as the clerics wanted purity of faith, they also needed tactical advantages. The general had a young family and made the choice not to try and flee. Am I correct?"

The general nodded once, stiffly.

"For decades, the Revolutionaries watched men like him, men who stayed," she went on. "The men didn't know it, of course. The soldiers were allowed to rise in the ranks, and in the case of General Ghasemi to get close to the top clerics. Knowledge of potential moderates, of the schedules and personal habits of each cleric hostile to our interests, would naturally make him a very desirable candidate for a staged defection. They saved him until such time as they wanted to sell us some story. Saddam Hussein used to infiltrate Iran with the same tactic. He would let Shi'ites rise in his Sunni inner circle, then hold their families hostage and send them to Iran with a mission. Iran's SAVAMA and its successor VAJA did the same thing to Baghdad."

"Is all of this true, about you being a plant?" Harward demanded of the general.

"This woman understands," he replied, looking at January.

"Dammit, I need this on the record," Harward said, turning the video recorder back on.

"Mr. Harward," she said, "the general was turned over to the INR—"

"And a phone call to the president can change that before you're a minute older," he said.

Flashing displeasure at Harward, January stepped in front of the camera, facing Ghasemi. "Is it all right?" she asked.

"Yes," he said. "I-I have made my choice and now that you know the truth . . . I will stand by it."

"Thank you," January said. She stepped away.

"I'll take it from here, Ms. Dow," Harward said. "General, you just informed Deputy Director Dow and the others present that contrary to your initial claim, this is *not* a defection but that you have been sent by the Iranian Ministry of Intelligence."

"Yes."

"Who is in charge of this operation?"

It wasn't so much a question as a challenge. Harward had come here in search of actionable information; thwarted by a defection that was suddenly a failed infiltration, he refused to leave empty-handed. Williams understood the man's frustration, if not his bullying tactics.

"I was sent here by Prosecutor Ali Younesi of the Special Court, *Sazman-E Ettela'at Va Amniat-E Melli-E Iran*."

"That's the SAVAMA, the Ministry of Intelligence," Harward said.

"Yes."

"What was your mission?"

"To be accepted as a defector and become an advisor to your government," Ghasemi replied. "That video of my daughter, Parand—it was given to you, I suspect, to reinforce my trustworthiness."

"Let me see if I understand," Harward said. "They captured her to force you to stage a defection—"

"Christian women can be treated most . . . unkindly," he offered.

"We understand," January said.

Harward was frowning. "Yes, we understand but we have a problem here. Your superiors imprisoned your daughter. They made this video, showed it to you, to force you to come here. You're saying that they let us see it so we would *believe* you're sincere? We're supposed to trust you because of all that you're sacrificing?"

"I cannot say what was in the mind of the prosecutor, Younesi," Ghasemi replied. "I am telling you how it came that I am sitting in this seat."

"Can you tell us how you are supposed to get information to him?" Harward asked.

"They are to send me time-stamped images of my daughter,"

he replied. "Those stamps are meeting times with someone from my embassy."

"Where?" Harward asked.

"I don't know," he replied. "That was going to be embedded in a message they would allow my daughter to send." He anticipated the next question. "Syllables in words that would be rearranged to form a location."

The code was a throwback to a World War II–era German system, something that sophisticated decryption systems were likely to overlook in their search for hidden audio or data streams.

"What do you want us to do?" Williams asked.

The general held up helpless hands, looked at them with eyes forlorn of hope. "I cannot help these monsters," Ghasemi said. "But if I am sent back, I will most likely be executed and my daughter will die in prison. For myself, I have no concern—"

The general did not finish. He did not have to.

"When were you approached by the prosecutor?" Williams asked.

"Five days ago," the general replied.

"That's not a lot of time to mount an operation," Harward said.

"Or to consider it carefully," January noted for Harward's benefit. "That's part of the psychology of putting a reluctant player in the field."

"Yes, thank you," he replied insincerely.

"What Miss Dow says is true," the general said. "I had no time to think about it."

"Where were you at the time this proposition was made?" Williams continued.

"An Iraqi village, Badana Pichwk," the general said.

"What business did the Assembly of Experts have there?" Williams asked.

The general smiled crookedly. "I, of all people, was sent to assess the faith of a small force of Houthi who had come up from Aden to fight Kurds."

"That would be an extension of the tactical and financial support your government has been providing the Houthi throughout Yemen," Williams said.

"That is correct," Ghasemi said. "The council did not want to support Muslims who were not strongly committed Shia."

"Lunacy," Harward muttered.

January shot the national security advisor a look. "How is that different from our own internecine struggles?" she asked. "Between the groups we represent, for instance."

"That's not murder," he said.

"I'm not sure this is an appropriate conversation," Kim interrupted, nodding in the direction of their guest.

Williams was not surprised by January's show of teeth. Many younger generation upper-echelon bureaucrats were bringing their own struggles into the workplace and using their new positions as platforms for payback. Unfortunately, she was right: the strife between generations, genders, races, had caused exactly the kinds of conflict Ghasemi had described, albeit with the bloodshed. It was one of the reasons Williams had agreed to take an intelligence post in the first place: he had no interest in identity politics. He was results-driven and that was all the president had required of him.

January and Harward fell into a tense silence. Williams had taken advantage of the exchange to study Ghasemi.

"Have you been to Iraq before?" Williams asked.

"Several times," Ghasemi acknowledged. The unhappy smile returned. "When there is danger, Tehran does not mind sending its Christian officers."

"Same with black soldiers in our Civil War," January noted.

"And Jews under the czar," Williams pointed out. "We call it slow-burn genocide. General, who delivered this message about your new assignment?"

"An adjutant to Corps General Heydar Najafabadi summoned me to a forward encampment in Kermanshah," the general told him. "From there, I was flown to Tehran."

"What about the cover story you provided at the embassy?" Harward asked. "Is anything in that true?"

According to the dossier Williams had read, when the general turned himself in he told the intelligence attaché that he was in Iraq to interview Iranian advisors working with ISIS in Iraq. He had provided the names, places, descriptions, which were as yet unverified.

"Several of the names and places I gave them are accurate," Ghasemi said.

"They had to be," Kim pointed out. "Sacrificial lambs."

"But lambs nonetheless, not wolves," Harward said. "They wouldn't have given us anyone of importance."

"That has nothing to do with our guest," January said.

Harward's normal frown deepened. He looked at January, clearly unhappy with this dead end—and with her.

"I think we've exhausted this line of questioning," January decided. She faced the others. "Why don't we take a recess?"

"Fine," Harward said unhappily.

January turned back and smiled at the general. "You will remain here, please. I'll be back to let you know what happens next."

The officer nodded but otherwise made no reply. The others filed out, leaving the guard. The door closed firmly behind them and the four stood clustered at the end of the corridor.

"Well, shit," Harward said, broadly addressing the entire situation. He turned on January. "When did you first suspect any of this? Not that professor and his paper—"

"No," she said. "General Ghasemi took the prayer rug from the embassy, pretending to be Shia for our sake. Right before you arrived, I saw that it was still right where the general placed it hours before."

"He was in there for seven hours but missed the morning *salaat*," Williams said.

"Exactly," January said.

"So we have a Typhoid Mary," Harward said, using an old euphemism. "If we give him nothing, his daughter dies. If we return him, he dies. If we give him real intelligence to send to Tehran, our people may die."

"I'm not ready to call this," Williams said.

"Oh?"

"For one thing," Williams said, "everything he told us hinges on something we cannot prove."

"Which is?"

"His story about being a Christian." Williams's eyes sought January. "The prayer mat is interesting but circumstantial."

"I think we have stronger evidence than that," she replied. "His daughter. That lashing was real, and severe. Did you watch the man with the whip? He wasn't just whipping her for effect. He was every Sharia-obedient man prowling—and I mean that word—*prowling* after someone he considered a lesser being. The man I saw in that room knew that. To me, he was struggling with something millennia-old: whether another Christian should die for his faith."

No one spoke for several seconds. It was Harward who broke the silence.

"This still gives us nothing," he said.

"I don't agree," Williams replied.

Once again, Harward turned to him eagerly. "All right. What do I tell the president we have?"

"The question of Christianity aside," Williams said, "this defection did not occur in a vacuum. One way or another it was crafted in Tehran, possibly by this Ali Younesi the general mentioned. And at the moment, I am disinclined to believe most of what he told us."

"Why?" January asked.

Williams replied, "Because I don't think the general has been where he said he was."

CHAPTER NINE

Anadyr, Chukotka Autonomous Okrug, Russia
July 2, 6:00 A.M.

It was frustrating and counterintuitive: the older Konstantin Bolshakov got, the less sleep he required.

Well, anyway, he thought tiredly, *the less sleep I get.*

He certainly felt he needed it, especially after the previous day's odyssey. But the sun was up and so was his body; the rest of him eased from the narrow bed and joined the new day.

Pulling his heavy fleece bathrobe and slippers from his suitcase and shuffling into the tiny bathroom, Bolshakov washed his face and cupped a handful of water to his lips. He smiled at the familiar taste and smell of the water. It had a mineral quality that the tap water in Moscow and other major Russian cities lacked. If not the water, then the memory of it made him feel lighter, younger. He might even have been giddy with it if Vavara had been here to share it—

"No."

If he started to poke among the what-ifs of his life, he would lapse back into the depression that had caused so much damage. But he did permit himself to relive the what-was.

The old man finished his morning routine and returned to the bedroom to unpack. The electric heat was only heat in name; the room was marginally above freezing. Businesses and residences here counted on the sun to do the necessary warming . . . and it would, in another hour or two. Warming his hands with his breath—how often he used to do that—he placed his clothes carefully in the drawers of the single dresser.

He stopped without realizing it and stared into the small compartment. Once, that was where he would have kept at least one of his handguns. Loaded at all times. There would have been another in his nightstand and one in the bathroom, among the folded bath towels.

"Once . . ." he said.

The word hung in his memory and then Bolshakov smiled as a lyric came into his head, one his father used to sing as he reached out with strong fingers, gnarled as gingerroot, and collected eggs on their small farm in Magnitogorsk. He hadn't thought of it since he was a boy, and he only remembered the first verse: "Once there was a man with chicks, who traded eggs for candlesticks, which left him hungry every night, but not in darkness, praise the light!"

It was years before Bolshakov understood the meaning of the classic verse: everything is a compromise.

He remembered what he was supposed to be doing and, with a sudden sense of purpose, shut the drawer. He also shut out the reverie that was taking him where he did not wish to go. The past was littered with lumpy roots that too-often caught his toe and sent him sprawling into depression.

"You are in Anadyr," he reminded himself. "Only good happened here. Only good *will* happen here."

He went to the closet and ran his fingers down the quilt lining of his overcoat. It was still damp with sweat that had cooled while he slept. No matter. Bolshakov went back to the drawer, pulled a black sweater over his head, and put the coat on over it. Then the warm shoes, the heavy ushanka hat, the scarf around his mouth, the sunglasses—as much to protect him from wind as from glare—and finally the gloves. He tucked his key inside the gloves, an old habit from when he had an important key that must never be lost. He had worn it attached to a leather band tied to his left wrist, the silver key thrust into the military-issue tactical leather gloves.

Bolshakov crossed the quiet lobby and pushed through the revolving door, the rubber flaps stiff and scraping in the extreme cold. He stopped just outside the hotel on Otke Street.

The flaps of the hat deafened him to most outside sounds, but enhanced the drumming of his own heart. Warm breath slipped from under the scarf and caused his sunglasses to fog. He hadn't realized that; it never happened with the goggles he used to wear. He removed them, slid them into a pocket.

The years and the exhaustion seemed to leave his body as the nearly white northeastern sun struck his partly exposed face. He felt joy but reminded himself not to weep or his skin would freeze.

It couldn't *be sixty years*, he thought. It all felt so familiar.

He hooked a leather-clad finger behind the scarf so it rested under his nose. He could smell the water from here, cold and fresh with just a hint of salt air. There was water on three sides of the town, none of it more than a few minutes' walk from where he was standing. Except for the great, wooden Holy Trinity Cathedral, few structures were more than two or three stories high; the sun, as it rose higher, glanced sharply from the multitude of red and blue rooftops, from buildings with green or yellow brick sides—the only real color in the otherwise bleak landscape. He had first come here in October, just after the seaport had been modernized. That ambitious construction was fresh, then, but the rest of the settlement had seemed shopworn. There were a few low, white structures, a few bare trees, a few badly rusted war-era trucks. The only thing ripe was the smell of fish. That odor was mostly gone now, suppressed by modern processing techniques.

Not that he had spent a lot of time here in those early days, except on leave. Most of Lieutenant Bolshakov's stay was to the southeast, on a crag overlooking the Bering Sea. After he met Vavara it was different, but by then the mission had changed . . . life had changed.

Though they were squinting down the empty street, the old eyes saw the sea from the precipice that was home for a dozen years.

Pissing distance from America, as the rear admiral used to say.

Bolshakov missed that place and he missed Dmitri Merkassov, a man of ferocious conviction, patriotism, honor. He missed that time, when adventure was high and responsibility limited. Other men made the heavy decisions; Bolshakov simply carried them out.

Shivering in a way that was familiar and strangely comforting, he pulled his scarf back up over his cold nose and began walking slowly along the two-lane street toward the center of town. As he walked, he kept his mind from going back by looking ahead.

People change, he thought. *They* do *forgive.*

Two days before, when Yuri called and asked to see him in the town of his birth, Bolshakov could not believe what he was hearing. The two had been estranged since Yuri had joined the army. Bolshakov, the elder, had bought a safe retirement from his trade, paying most of his fortune to former rivals and current enemies not to seek retribution. That was the code. In the unlikely event that any gunrunner survived to old age, he was permitted to retreat for a price. Given that Bolshakov had not become involved with the South and Central American drug dealers, there was no fear that he would ever be abducted or persuaded by a foreign government to turn evidence in exchange for sanctuary. He wasn't like the notorious "Tarzan" Fainberg, who negotiated the sale of a ninety-foot Foxtrot class attack submarine to the Colombians in the 1990s. All Bolshakov did was serve as middleman for the privatization of vast amount of Soviet weapons.

And what did it get you? he asked himself. Not what he had planned. A very tiny *dacha* just outside of Moscow, a one-room log cabin on a small square of land where he gardened in the summer, read and studied chess in the winter, and lived the lonely life of a widower. *Your work*, he thought, *deprived you of the only thing you really wanted. A family as close and loving as the one he had on the farm.* He smiled a little, thinking of how sad they had been when he went into the navy, but also how proud—

He sighed tremulously and stopped walking. Why did thinking about the future invariably circle him to the past?

Bolshakov was at the corner of Dezhneva, outside a small, new Bank of Russia building. His eyes turned to the north. At the end of that long straight road was Lenina. That was where his old apartment was, where his wife and son lived when he was at the bunker. The drafty wooden structure was almost certainly gone now; he couldn't see from here.

It was too cold to continue on; he would wait until later to go there, when his son was with him, when they could walk together.

The sun had crept a little higher. The cold shadows were less expansive, the areas of sun on the ground making it marginally warmer walking back to the hotel. That was relative, of course; it was still at least fifteen degrees below freezing. Bolshakov's cheeks were still the most reliable thermometer he knew.

He would have breakfast, nap, maybe read one of the newspapers he had seen in the lobby. There would be time for all three. And then his boy would be here for the reunion, although Yuri hadn't actually said so.

Bolshakov was an old hand at sensing when something—a deal, an individual, a situation—wasn't right. It was instinctive, a talent that had been nurtured at sea, refined in Anadyr, and polished to a shine when he ran his operation. The chill the man felt as he reentered the lobby was a sudden feeling that came from having avoided a question, let alone an answer:

What else could *it be?*

CHAPTER TEN

Op-Center Headquarters, Fort Belvoir North,
Springfield, Virginia
July 1, 12:10 P.M.

Takeout food had the odor and taste of crisis.

There was an unspoken rule in the nation's capital that any time the government was managing a hot global situation, meals were not to be ordered in bulk: no dozen pizzas, no wagon-load of cartons from a Chinese restaurant, no hamburgers in quantities to feed a team. Enemy operatives frequently watched the popular eateries, and from the size and destination of deliveries ascertained who was working hard and late. From that information, a delivery to Homeland Security or the Department of Defense, or a command facility abroad, could indicate an attack was imminent at home or against targets abroad. That would give domestic terrorists a time to move up their timetable or disburse.

Since returning to Op-Center, Chase Williams felt as though he'd been on a crisis footing. There was nothing that pointed to an imminent operation, as far as he knew; no one had made an actionable threat; but he could not shake the gnawing sense that something had been seriously off in the meeting at Quantico.

Pulling Anne, Paul Bankole, Kathleen Hays, and intelligence director Roger McCord into his office, he ordered lunch from the fort's taco hut. Williams was at his desk, the others arrayed on one side of the coffee table. While everyone ate, he played the video of the Ghasemi interview on the 4K large-format screen on the wall of his office. Anne hadn't seen it and Williams quietly observed her reactions. When it was done, Williams put the prison video on the screen. Anne and Bankole both looked away. Afterward, Williams filled the group in on what they had missed.

"So," Williams said, "at present, we have several possible but very sketchy scenarios. First: Ghasemi is everything he says he is, a defector who came here with a mission and wants to continue that kabuki. We make him an advisor in some capacity, he sends scraps to Tehran, and maybe he leverages that into his daughter's release. Certainly verified information keeps her alive. Second: he's a Christian who is wrestling with what is more important, his strong faith or his daughter's life. If we allow him to stay, perhaps he becomes a spokesperson for oppressed Christians in Iran . . . I don't know and that's not our concern. Or third, and this *is* my concern: he's a liar who is on the surface a good actor, one with a mission whose purpose is unknown." Williams waited for that to sink in before continuing. "Before we can answer any of that, my question is, what do we make of the man and his story?"

Williams proceeded to call on each member of the team to give their reactions, beginning with the video analyst.

"The profiling checklist isn't much help," Kathleen said. "General Ghasemi has had very little sleep the last few days so his responses, across the board, were bound to be verbally laconic and physically torpid. We don't have a record of what was apparently the most reactive response—to Deputy Director Dow's opening questions—but even there, had thermal readings perked, it would have told us nothing definitive. Increased blood flow is to be expected under those circumstances and is no indicator of guilt. It is more likely a fear of being exposed. The rest of the readings were consistent with a tired and also very cautious, guarded man who is being questioned. He was free of tics or gestures, he didn't cross his arms defensively, his nostrils didn't flare as if he were panicked and oxygenating. That could all be the result of exhaustion or simply the lack of any artifice, or both."

"Shouldn't the repeated mentions of his daughter have produced some kind of active response, at least a blip?" Williams asked.

"He already knew she was a prisoner—"

"Hostage," McCord interrupted sharply.

Kathleen—who was not accustomed to being in these senior meetings—closed her mouth. Williams frowned with displeasure at his intelligence director.

"Ms. Hays will use her own words," the director cautioned.

The forty-two-year-old former Marine nodded deferentially toward the woman. His reaction hadn't come as a surprise to Williams. McCord had been a company commander in Iraq and had witnessed the kinds of brutality that caused severe PTSD in many soldiers; suggesting a stronger, more honest word was a mild reaction. But Kathleen was a civilian. Williams had crafted a careful blend of backgrounds at Op-Center and wanted observations and choices from that perspective.

Williams pointed toward Kathleen, who continued.

"So, yes," the woman recovered and went on. "Our algorithms found nothing out of the ordinary."

"Nothing inconsistent with what he said and how he behaved . . . looked?" Williams asked.

The way he'd asked suggested Kathleen had missed something. She reviewed the findings. "There's nothing here," she said. "Absent the opening panic which you've described, we have no evidence of inconsistency."

Williams thanked her and moved on to Bankole.

"I'm not going to be much help here, either," the international crisis manager told him. "I've never witnessed a preliminary interrogation where the subject wasn't severely sleep deprived or afraid for his life, and this fit that template. Lethargy, monotone, distraction. Without being in the room, I can't say more. *Was* it different there, Chase?"

"Somewhat, but I'll get to that in a minute." Williams turned his eyes to McCord. "Roger?"

As always, McCord was sitting in a leather armchair that was too soft to support his athletic, six-foot-two-inch frame. It diminished him slightly, which may have been his intent; a man who was often a target for enemy fire, who had been wounded in combat, had his own ways of coping.

"You know what I'm gonna say," McCord told him.

"Say it anyway," Williams coaxed.

McCord slapped his hands on his knees and looked at the director. "He's a serving Iranian officer. I don't trust him."

Williams saw Anne's expression shift from neutral to disapproving. Unlike Kathleen, Anne was an aggressive voice for the civilian point of view; maintaining equilibrium between the factions was tougher for him than actually crafting any of Op-Center's fieldwork. That was the main reason he tried to keep these meetings equally balanced. Williams spoke before she could.

"Taken at face value," the director said, "Ghasemi has asked for asylum. That would make him a former officer."

"I thought we had a big question mark on that request," McCord said.

"That's why Chase said, 'Taken at face value,'" Anne pointed out.

"Yeah, well, as we used to say at Special Operations Command, 'Once a Marine, always a Marine,'" McCord recited the unofficial motto of his branch of service. "When it comes to these guys, you're safer assuming, 'Once an Irguck, always an Irguck.'"

Anne was professional enough not to expand on her irritation, but she was clearly displeased by McCord using the derogatory name for an Iranian soldier. Derived from Islamic Revolutionary Guard Corps, he pronounced it "irgook" to evoke the disparaging name for Communist soldiers during the Vietnam conflict.

A tense atmosphere had settled on the group. Williams took a sip of the orange juice he'd ordered with lunch. "Anything else, Roger?"

"I'm sorry if I offended anyone," he said sincerely. "But this is too important for niceties."

Anne waited before saying anything else.

"If Roger's done—Anne, would you like to talk about the video?" Williams asked.

She leaned forward in her seat on the couch. "My reaction is pretty much in line with the others, though I feel strongly that we have a potential asset here who should not be dismissed without a complete and objective vetting. I understand there's a shelf life, that the general will be expected to communicate something to Tehran, but he can delay a while—take a meeting or two and give progress reports, not hard data. That will give everyone time to get behind an approach."

Williams considered this. He threw his taco wrapper in the trash, then sat back. "I hate to be the perfect diplomat," he smiled, "but I agree with Roger and I agree with Anne."

He noticed Bankole smile crookedly, like a man who would have won a bet if he'd bothered to place one. To a degree, that outcome was predictable. While the director encouraged his people to talk freely, to disagree respectfully with one another and him, he did not have that luxury. A group leader, any group leader, was obligated to listen to advice from all sides. Otherwise, there was no reason to have a team—"other than to delegate blame," as operations director Brian Dawson had once put it.

"I'm not willing to dismiss Ghasemi as insincere," Williams continued, "but Roger—you were in Badana Pichwk."

"I passed through," the crisis manager said, perking.

"It's open terrain with big winds and a hot sun this time of year, yes?"

"It's a goddamn desert, mostly," McCord agreed.

Williams pointed the remote at the TV, pressed play and mute. The video began to run again. "That man's skin hasn't seen harsh conditions for quite a while, if ever."

Everyone looked. Anne sat very still while McCord seemed to rise a few inches in his chair. Kathleen dove back into her tablet, wondering why her analysis hadn't picked up skin tone.

"There are some things algorithms haven't been trained to do," Williams told the young woman. "Iranian and Iraqi officers don't pull scarves over their mouths in the field. They're too busy talking to subordinates, who usually need very specific directions because many of them are mercs. Ghasemi *should* be red from neckline to hairline. He isn't."

"I will write that into the program, sir," Kathleen replied. It came out as an apology.

McCord stifled a snort though Williams caught it. The intelligence director had an "algorithm," too. One which Williams would be eager to hear when he'd had time to work it out.

"How do you know Ghasemi wasn't there at night?" Anne asked.

"Unlikely," Williams answered for Kathleen. "The general's stated purpose for being in Iraq was to talk to the Houthi fighters. Since 2015, when those fighters joined the larger war to establish a caliphate, they have waged their sorties in darkness. They are guerrilla fighters who are accustomed to ambush, not combat."

"Like they did in Yemen," McCord said. "Pick a target, destroy it, get the hell out under cover of darkness."

"Exactly," Williams said. "So they would have met Ghasemi during the day. Now, avoiding sun or windblasting is possible if the general went from an armored vehicle to a tent or building, but those guys don't like to be inside because of our drones. Seconds matter where incoming is concerned, and they like to be able to hear the engine and dive for cover."

"The IRGC," Anne said, speaking the letters individually, "is rarely across-the-board careless. How could they not have foreseen all of what you just said?"

"Anne is right," Bankole said. "The military would have evaluated all of this before sending Ghasemi over. An hour under a sun lamp would have passed muster."

"This Prosecutor Younesi may be running a rogue operation," McCord suggested.

"Again, all of that is possible," Williams said. "Which brings us to this pinch point: that someone in Tehran is using Ghasemi to buy time."

"We piddle while something burns," McCord said. He looked at Williams. "Sound familiar?"

The director nodded. Anne shot him a quizzical look.

"There was a Russian who we believe was a defector in the fall of 1962, name of Dr. Shukur Kuzmina," Williams said. "He was a rocket scientist who helped develop the R-14 intermediate-range ballistic missiles Moscow sent to Cuba. We can only assume he was here to seek asylum because he was found floating in the Potomac with his throat cut."

"Why didn't the Russians just grab him and take him back?" Anne asked.

"An autopsy showed he had colon cancer," Williams said.

"A powerful stimulant to one's conscience," McCord added.

"The CIA concluded that he had been sacrificed to confuse us," Williams continued. "Gave rise to an expression, 'Being

Shukur-punched.' What was he going to tell us? We tied up dozens of agents and man-hours pursuing leads, had over one hundred analysts drawing concentric circles on maps of Germany, Turkey, NATO bases looking for potential targets. No one seriously explored the possibility of the U.S. as a target from Cuba. The consensus was: 'The Russians wouldn't dare.'"

"But they dared," Anne said thoughtfully.

"Boldly and with a damn big head start," McCord said.

"Which brings us to Ghasemi," Williams said. "My concern is that while we vet him, his job is to take our eye off the ball." He looked out at the team. "I'm not quite willing to go Roger's route—not yet—but I want you to find me the ball."

CHAPTER ELEVEN

Ministry of Intelligence, Tehran, Iran
July 1, 8:50 P.M.

Prosecutor Ali Younesi was not a patient man. Yet he had waited, not for years but for scores of years.

He had been a young student of the Haghani seminary when Ayatollah Khomeini returned from France to replace the shah, a day that he and his fellow seminarians had prayed they would see. They immediately drove the seventy-eight miles from the holy city of Qom to Tehran to join in the mass prayer and celebration to welcome the establishment of the new Iranian republic, the great theocracy that would one day spread its light around the globe. The students were certain of that. With the same kind of patience that devout Shia had shown during the centuries of rule by the Qajar and Pahlavi dynasties, they worked underground . . . and they waited. Cracks formed between laic and secular Iran as they provoked Shah Pahlavi's secret police into excessive brutality and then, in September of 1978, on Black Friday, when 10 percent of the nation marched against the shah, the military was provoked into firing upon protesters.

The long wait for power had come to an end. With power, the new wait had begun . . . with the same kind of careful planning. It had never been about achieving goals within any individual's lifetime. It was about serving the faith, day by day. So doing, undistracted by personal needs, goals would once more be achieved as surely as one day followed the next.

The fifty-seven-year-old sat in his ministry office on Damavand Street, District 13, Tehran. As usual, it had been a challenging day, full of incident and decisions. The filter of Allah made the process simple; managing the impact of his decisions on national and international affairs was not. As a member of the Special Clerical Court, Younesi oversaw and investigated Iran's clergy, making sure that transgressions were uncovered and punished. He also made certain that influential persons who were not Shia or adherents to the orthodoxy were watched and persuaded to serve the one true faith. Most complied, since incarceration or execution were the only alternatives. But each was a thumbprint on the intricacies of politics. That was exhausting, especially when there were still a few moderate voices in government, in the press, in banking, on the Internet, and in other necessary institutions.

He enjoyed being here after sunset, when the sounds of traffic had diminished and the activity within these walls had quieted and ancient Persia seemed so close. Prayer at the assigned hours was the means to worship Allah; reflection at any time was the way a devout man understood his place in Allah's plan. Where the two met, there was the path of Younesi and his people:

"God's curse be upon the infidels."

"Give us victory over the unbelievers."

Allah did not set a timetable, only that whatever the objective, it be done. And so the ministers and the council and the clerics likewise did not give themselves deadlines. Just the one holy objective.

The smartphone on the polished, uncluttered surface of Younesi's ornate mahogany desk beeped. He drew it closer with a long finger and looked down. His associate was coming. He texted permission to enter the building, the floor, and his office; then he pressed his index finger to the screen. A scan of the print sent the message to each of the three checkpoints that must be passed.

Younesi sat back. He overlooked his natural and understandable revulsion of this creature for the greater good. Possessing a knowledgeable and creative mind, few people impressed him the way this physicist did. And in forty years of professional service to the Revolution, few plans had been as ambitious and yet as obvious, once stated, as this one. Most of the prosecutor's work was small and managerial, supporting existing operations at home and abroad. This was the first he had taken to the Supreme Leader, the first in his career to be assigned a Highest Priority classification.

The first that put elements of the Islamic Revolutionary Guard Corps—of which his ministry was a division—under his direct authority. It was not a heady feeling but a humbling one, the opportunity to serve in a way that could accelerate the incremental advances of the ultimate world order.

He heard the shuffle of simple shoes approaching on the

other side of the door. There was a soft knock and he pressed a button on his phone. There was click. The door cracked slightly; it was pushed inward by a small figure garbed entirely in black, from the *roosari* on top to the floor-length *chādor* that covered all but the face. The prosecutor rose not to honor his guest, but the extent to which the visitor respected his own beliefs. And it was not in just the attire.

Younesi gestured toward a chair facing the desk and looked out with a mildly cross expression. "You disobeyed your surgeon," he said. "He wanted you to stay."

"The ointments and bandages would have worked no faster in a hospital bed," the newcomer replied. "I had to know how the project is proceeding."

The prosecutor felt a small sting of disappointment. There was a fine demarcation between eagerness and impatience. It was good to be hopeful. Anything more had a feral, subhuman quality. The question belied the confidence in ultimate victory that a truly devout individual would possess.

"All we know from the license tags recorded by our gardener is that several intelligence services were present for the interrogation," Younesi replied. "They departed after only twenty-five minutes. We are confident from this that not a great deal was gained from the questioning."

"That is very good," she said. There was no hint of emotion in her voice, no acknowledgment that it was her father who was in the hands of a hated enemy. "Do you have any idea what is next?"

"They will talk, consult, consider," he replied. "That is what they do best instead of acting. Then they will questioning him further and analyze further."

Dr. Parand Ghasemi's delicate mouth pinched slightly. She had not bothered to tell the prosecutor of the painful sutures that were required to close several of the wounds.

"Doctor?" he asked solicitously. "Is everything all right?"

"I'm fine," she assured him. "What of the field team?"

"They are ready to move when we know that the materials have been acquired."

"The agent—?"

"Also en route," Younesi assured her. He looked at her covered shoulder. "Now I suggest you return to the doctor. My driver will take you."

She seemed puzzled.

"There is blood," he informed her.

The scientist glanced to the side the government official had indicated. Her dark eyebrows rose slightly against her fair, smooth skin. That was one of the early blows, the whip having struck her back with such force that the tip wrapped around to the front.

"All right," she said, more like a petulant child than a woman. "May I come back in the morning?"

"Let us say the afternoon," he replied. "You really must be more fully recovered before I can send you on such a journey."

"I will be healed, Prosecutor Younesi, I assure you," she replied.

"Then—bed rest, as you were advised."

"As you wish," she answered. "There is no way I will not be ready for this task."

Rising with the help of the armrests, she bowed to the official and he rose as she left the room. Once again, the woman was more impressive than admirable. Like the beating to which she had willingly subjected herself, she had reasons that transcended personal safety. Ever since she had uncovered this secret in her research, Dr. Ghasemi had been driven by her desire for the ultimate professional challenge rather than by patriotism. But—*no matter*, he told himself. As long as the two ideals converged, Younesi was content.

And, apparently, as long as Dr. Ghasemi was able to work with a pair of nuclear weapons, no sacrifice was too great—not just her own health, but the safety of her father.

CHAPTER TWELVE

Op-Center Headquarters, Fort Belvoir North,
Springfield, Virginia
July 1, 12:55 P.M.

The meeting in Chase Williams's office ended with a simple mandate from the director: find out everything there is to know about Amir Ghasemi and his family.

"Solitaire?" Anne had asked before everyone left.

"Solitaire," Williams had replied.

The order meant that despite the Quadrennial Homeland Security Review defining homeland security missions as "enterprise-wide," across all assets available to the government of the United States, Williams wanted this search conducted in-house, for in-house use only. For Williams, this wasn't a turf war. He simply wanted to be sure that the information he received was solid. Too many appointees in too many offices watched clocks instead of data streams. The Geek Tank drew the daughter, Parand Ghasemi.

Informed of the assignment by Anne, Aaron Bleich decided to work on that himself, with Kathleen, from their respective workstations. Bleich had three monitors arrayed on his desk, plus a tablet for emails; the leftmost monitor was networked with Kathleen's screen so he could see what she was doing. She briefed Bleich on the presentation in Williams's office through the audio link built into their SmartWare glasses.

The thirty-two-year-old was a math and computer science prodigy who won a full ride to Stanford University where he dazzled Nobel Prize–winning professors with his computer and network skills. He was recruited by a video game company at the San Diego Comic-Con; that company was actually MARSOC——Marine Corps Forces Special Operations Command—where he came to the attention of Roger McCord. When McCord came to Op-Center, Bleich went with him. Not for the salary bump or added responsibilities, though those were appealing; it was the fact that he would himself be able to recruit at the Comic-Con each mid-July, at the government's expense; and that he'd be permitted to wear branded T-shirts that sold him. Bleich's favorite designer labels were *Star Trek* and *Stargate SG-1*; a sign above his office door read CAPTAIN KIRK. Short and slender from the metabolism-boosting energy drinks he lived on, Bleich ran what was without dispute the freest-wheeling intelligence department in Washington.

Which was one reason the results were invariably so extraordinary. Information flowed in unobstructed, where some of the sharpest young technical minds on the planet processed it with uninhibited free-association.

"A student lounge for eccentric geniuses," was how Williams once described it.

Gary Gold and Dongling Qui were at lunch, so Kathleen's

side of the Tank was as quiet as Bleich's office. It did not take a genius to find Parand Ghasemi. She held a PhD in nuclear physics from the University of Oxford. Bleich had found that even before Kathleen had settled in.

"Okay," Bleich said, openly perplexed. "For what mortal, foggy reason would the government of Iran, which desperately needs nuclear physicists, incarcerate and whip someone with her credentials? To threaten her father to come home? Is that what the story is?"

"That's what the story is," Kathleen told him.

"Then it doesn't make sense," Bleich said. "And what's more, they knew we'd spot that first thing."

"They didn't *kill* her," Kathleen pointed out. "And maybe there's a kind of perverse logic to it: 'As much as we need her, we're going to make an example so no one else will try this.'"

"Maybe," Bleich said. "It's strange, though. It doesn't look like she's been working on their supposedly nonexistent nuclear weapons program. Employment records have her teaching undergraduate physics at the Iran University of Science and Technology."

"The future needs scientists, too."

"Yeah, here's a YouTube video from one of her lectures," Bleich said. "But this still seems to fall under the cut-nose, spite-face category."

"That's because you're not thinking like a radical cleric," Kathleen suggested.

"Maybe," he said, scrolling through other data streams. With a slight delay, the automated Language Intelligence, Government Operations system—LINGO—provided split-screen translations of Persian, Azerbaijani, and Kurdish, which comprised the majority languages in Iran. "Our girl is unmarried, has no siblings, mother deceased—"

"Also no religious activism," Kathleen said, searching police records, "which seems to fit with the idea that she's a closet Christian."

"Who doesn't want to be hanged from a crane," Bleich said.

Kathleen moved as quickly as she could through the official documents, which included images that graphically demonstrated Tehran's preferred method of public execution. Once reserved primarily for gays, it was increasingly used to deter what the Supreme Leader described as "all forms of anti-social conduct." Treason was still punishable by automatic weapon fire to the front of the head. The woman had grown up on a ranch in New Mexico. She had witnessed horses being put down, gelded, and even being mauled by coyotes. She had seen riders suffer grievous injuries in falls. To design panicked quadrupeds for animated films, she had to study often graphic footage of prey animals.

Kathleen was familiar with bloodshed. What was unfamiliar before she came to Op-Center was the open cruelty that attached itself to these images. Gladiatorial-style sacrifices made in the name of religion was as obscene a concept as any she had ever encountered.

During her search, there had been several pings alerting her that an open file had been updated: a pop-up reported that Konstantin Bolshakov had been identified by a security camera outside a bank in Anadyr. She closed the box, finished the search on Parand Ghasemi, and looked at what they had.

A nuclear physicist who taught physics in Tehran, no known

relatives other than her father, possibly a Christian. It was as bare-bones as any online biography she had ever assembled.

"Either our lady's had a very quiet life, or the details have been scrubbed," Bleich remarked.

"No social media," Kathleen said, continuing her search.

"Iran," Bleich said flatly. "Not surprising. If she is a Christian, God help her if she were contacted by another Christian other than her father."

"Which is strange," she said.

"What?"

"There isn't even a birth record to connect them," Kathleen said.

"Pre-Revolution records were not routinely digitized," Bleich said, "and these may have been pulled by Ghasemi himself."

"Here are her British visas," Kathleen said. "Nothing special there, and nothing else in the usual databanks." She began a second search, saw that Bleich had already run it. "Nothing in her university-era activities either, I see."

"No, and Iran couldn't have obliterated all of that," Bleich said. "The woman was as off-the-radar as a person could be. No clubs, no travel, no traffic tickets, no anything."

"Here's something, though," Kathleen said. She had gone to the Bank of England. "A bank account."

"Again, not surprising," Bleich said.

"No, but the sum is. Amir Ghasemi was a colonel then. Checking his pay grade—uh-uh. There was too much money here."

"Maybe he had savings," Bleich suggested.

"A junior commissioned officer? No. Checking her address on the bank application—"

"She lived in an apartment, not a dormitory," Bleich said, following along.

"And it doesn't look like anyone else shared that address while she was there."

"So she could have had a sponsor," Bleich said.

"Tehran?"

"Cannot be dismissed," Bleich agreed.

Kathleen was only vaguely aware of Gary Gold and Dongling returning. They took their seats quietly, having noticed Kathleen's uncommon focus.

"This is as small a footprint I've seen on anyone," Bleich said. "Even someone keeping a low profile leaves something behind."

"Hold on—"

"I see it," Bleich said with moderate interest.

There were photographs from a symposium of nuclear physicists, which Parand attended in Moscow in 2015. She had not submitted a paper, given a lecture, and was not listed on any panels. Kathleen immediately engaged the FRA—facial-recognition analysis—to try and ascertain who the Iranian woman was speaking with in the photographs.

Five names came up:

Professor Vladimir Tyagushev—Moscow State University, Russia

Dr. Pak Yong-nam—Hamhŭng University of Mathematical and Physical Sciences, North Korea

Dr. Sadeq Farhadi—Tehran University of Medical Sciences, nuclear medicine and radiotracers

Dr. Gustav Rasp—Max Planck Institute for Nuclear Physics, Heidelberg, Germany

Dr. Adoncia Bermejo—University of Havana, Cuba (emeritus)

Kathleen ran background checks on each.

"Dr. Farhadi is a former revolutionary, has lectured at the university where Parand teaches—" Bleich commented.

"Almost everyone in a position of influence has the same bio," Kathleen said. "Hold on, this is interesting: Farhadi has done work for Iran's TAG program, trace and geosynchronize."

"Obviously our acronym."

"Correct. Injections of very small doses of radioactive iodine, absorbed by the thyroid, could be overlooked as the result of medical treatment. Clever."

"If you don't mind cancer."

"Not at these levels, according to the report," Kathleen said. "Aaron, I want to take a few minutes to check on something else."

"What?"

"Something else that popped up today," she told him. "Probably hasn't got a thing to do with this, but I want to be sure."

"Make it so," Bleich said. "Damn cash-only country. I'm going to dig into smartphone and landline accounts, see if there's anything."

Kathleen left the connection open as she returned to the

four nuclear physicists. Each of them had a very full biography with the exception of Dr. Bermejo. Her file was nearly as thin as that of Parand Ghasemi. That wasn't surprising, given the limited access the United States had to information from Cuba. As much as possible, the Cuban government conducted its business analog or face-to-face, not online.

But the lack of information was telling. There was no obituary, and Cuba always acknowledged their key Revolutionaries. There was a bank account in Havana with a steady income: higher than that of a government-supported retiree or even a former university professor. She was still working, at least on a stipend. Cuba did not have a nuclear program but other nations did. If she were consulting with a rogue state like North Korea or Iran, there should be travel records from those countries—

"Iran has interests in Cuba," she said to herself as she read a top secret budget from then-president Ahmadinejad to a "Caribbean field officer," who was otherwise unidentified. It was an authorization to increase funding. It coincided with a slight uptick in Dr. Bermejo's deposits.

Iran was thought to have placed observers at the SIGINT station at Lourdes at the invitation of Moscow. Lourdes had a "retirement village" for individuals who formerly had high security clearance; it was thought to be less an accommodation as it was a place to keep an eye on them and monitor visitors. The idea—not unique to Cuba—was if a government provided uncommon comfort and safety for former spies and high-level workers, they would be unlikely to consort with enemy agents.

"Lourdes is the place," she decided, flagging it in case they were going to look for a retired nuclear physicist. And there was one notation in the Bermejo file, part of an old CIA report, that grabbed her attention sharply. It was just two words: Operation Anadyr.

CHAPTER THIRTEEN

SIGINT Base, Lourdes, Cuba
July 1, 1:11 P.M.

For Dr. Adoncia Bermejo, it was a job, not even full-time and not necessarily every day. She was able to spend most of the time writing her memoirs. All her employees wanted were her memories, a little of her knowledge—and a large slice of her soul. A soul that had somehow managed to survive nearly seventy years relatively intact.

Until recently, the old base at Lourdes had been nothing more than a comfortable apartment where cigars were free and there was a large green field to go walking. After the morning haze had burned away, that is what the eighty-three-year-old woman did every day. She left her room at the fenced-in facility and walked barefoot on the soft, green grass. On these daily treks, the woman was especially grateful for the gentle winds that rolled into the northwestern coast of Cuba from the Straits of Florida and the Gulf of Mexico, a steady breath that kept the humidity and the biting insects at bay.

Adoncia did not need more than those modest comforts.

She certainly did not need academia anymore, which she had happily given up five years earlier. She disliked the Halls of Bile and Jealousy, as she called them; she disliked them even more than the eleven months of deprivation she spent in the Sierra Maestra Mountains with Fidel and Raúl Castro and her lover Che Guevara. That was on the southeastern side of the island, the tropical Caribbean Sea.

Not that the white-haired woman had a right to complain about any of it, she knew. She aggressively blew smoke from the thickly rolled Sancho Panza, a habit that had earned Adoncia the nickname *el dragón* at university. Unlike so many people she met at home and abroad, she had not only lived, she had lived the way she wanted. First, as a twenty-four-year-old rebel against the corrupt regime of the dictator Fulgencio Batista. She had met Fidel when they were both students at the University of Havana—he studying law, she physics. He was president of the University Committee for Democracy in the Dominican Republic, opposed to right-wing ideology to the east and wherever else it oppressed the masses. She was president of the University Committee for Nuclear Parity, dedicated to battling American imperialism. The two groups had one great ideal in common: unleashing the strength and passion of the peoples of the Caribbean who had been oppressed for five centuries.

It was inevitable that they fight together to liberate Cuba. They both learned English, to battle the Americans in their own press, show them their own corruption. What a time; what a triumph. Even as it was happening, after a few hundred guerrillas managed to defeat a seasoned force of ten thousand regulars, Adoncia knew that nothing would ever be as pure or sublime as that victory. And it wasn't.

She squinted out through dark slits of eyes that had seen so much, squeezed warm soil with her toes as she walked. The legs of her orange jungle jeans stirred the occasional butterfly from its perch. She liked the black and tan ones the most—she didn't know what they were called, only that their wings looked like fingerprints. They were like felons, trying to get away. They made her smile.

She had been that, with the others. Wanted, hunted, always on the run, living in trees or in caves. Then they were suddenly the liberators, the new leaders. The United States and the Mafia, which owned Batista, were gone with the deposed despot. And then—

She pulled hard on the stub of the cigar, then crushed it under her left foot. It burned a little, just behind the toes, but that spot was calloused from years of running—first at university, from police, then in the mountains—and from walking barefoot because she hated shoes, loathed any kind of restraint on her person. She actually enjoyed that little bit of a furnace; that was what it felt to be alive.

She turned those narrow eyes out toward the quiltlike cover of green that rolled before her, peered beyond that to the coastline and the distant seas. The dying smoke of the cigar wafted upward and she inhaled it, and the grass, and the sea air. It was a mix that made her weep with contentment.

Batista and the Americans and the crime lords gone. And then the Soviets came. First with agricultural advisors, then with loans to replace the lost criminal revenue, and then with nuclear missiles to point at the shores of America. Adoncia had gone back to school—at the insistence and expense of the Castros—and as the only trusted lieutenant with a knowledge of physics, she was appointed to be an intermediary between Havana and Moscow.

How to go from a guerrilla band to a global power with a single embrace, she thought.

That hug between Castro and the Soviet Union's First Deputy Premier Anastas Mikoyan was an end to a dream.

Adoncia turned back toward the sprawling complex of satellite dishes and low-lying buildings. That deal had allowed forty-two ships to sail to Cuba with "agricultural equipment" and Russian officers. It opened the door to a burst of power and paranoia that caused Fidel Castro to mistrust and execute some of those who had been closest to him. She remembered fondly, still, Camilo Cienfuegos Gorriarán—Castro's chief of staff and fellow revolutionary, an anti-Communist who was killed in a mysterious plane crash. Adoncia had accepted, if not embraced, the idea of dying for Cuba . . . but not for the Castros. The killings, the imprisonments, the substitution of one bearish ally for another—all of it had turned the physicist's own dreams to ash. She had envisioned Cuba as a haven for nuclear energy, not nuclear destruction. That was what the Revolution had been about, after all. Free education, free health care, free energy—freedom.

Adoncia had never complained to the Castro brothers. She had simply withdrawn. Part of that was growing revulsion over their ruthless tactics to preserve personal power; part of that was simply a desire to survive and serve Cuba in any way she still might. More and more she would say to those around her, "*¡Tu maletín!*"—"That's your problem"—until she no longer had to say it, only look at someone a certain way. After completing her doctorate, long after the Soviet missiles were removed, she was able to pursue ways to bring nuclear technology to the island-nation. When the SIGINT station was closed in 2001, the living quarters remained open for government retirees. Adoncia was given a charitable retirement by Fidel in a place where she could nonetheless be watched.

Too valuable to lose, too dangerous to release.

That was how they used to describe government officials when they cleaned house after Batista. Fortunately for her, Fidel was sentimental about women in general and her in particular. She always seemed exempt from the worst of his purges.

And then in 2014 the Russians returned—along with a quarter-billion dollars in annual payments, replacing the Colombian drug trafficking in which the government had been complicit. The physicist was allowed to remain, though to the many Cuban workers she was an almost mythical fixture, like Medusa, gliding from her cave and slithering through the countryside, snorting puffs of smoke. She actually approved of that image. Who wouldn't enjoy the ability to turn meddlers like these arrogant, arrogant *apparatchiks* into stone? If she had that power, Cuba would be free and a chief exporter of glorious statuary.

The rumors? she thought.

There were mutterings against the Russians in the cafeterias and in the local market. Violence in the otherwise peaceful little city of narrow streets and a poor but contented citizenry. It began months after the Russians arrived with an unsolved sexual assault in town: the victim was the young daughter of a mail carrier, who sometimes helped her father with deliveries to the base. Some said the crime was never solved. Others said it was Russian soldiers and it had been covered up. Fights were increasingly common in taverns frequented by the Russians, and damage was never paid for. Cubans justified their tolerance as a net gain since the Russians brought commerce. But young Cuban men, who were frequently the targets, did not have patience or reason. And it was they who ended up in prison. Then there was prostitution. It had never been a problem, now it was an underground pandemic. And it wasn't only the local women but girls from neighboring Havana. The occasional child, however—that remained a problem for Lourdes.

The young Russians, the scientists as well as the soldiers, thought this was a playground. To the Cubans it was home. The two were not a good match.

As much as the old rebel in her enjoyed that dynamic, she was too old for war. Fidel was gone. His eldest son had committed suicide. The legacy was dying.

Adoncia stood there loving the sun and the sky and every wonder and sensation beneath them, not feeling the least bit guilty about the indulgence of it all. She did miss Che, though, every day. If there were a human counterpart to fissionable material, that being of light and energy was it. She missed the physical man as well as his intelligence, his commitment, and his passion for everything he did. It was that fire, coupled with boundless courage, that drove him to join the revolution in Bolivia in 1966 where he was captured and executed.

Adoncia was born to a family of sugarcane cutters in Cienfuegos. Cuba and Cubans were her only concern. The ideals that had interested Che globally held no appeal to her, which was why she had been able to find some measure of peace just working and living among them.

She looked down at the once-proud cigar pressed raggedly, brokenly into the soil.

"You and me both, *compadre*," she smiled humorlessly.

Adoncia turned back to the compound without joy in her step or eagerness in her pace. It wasn't just that she was reluctant to leave the field, she was not looking forward to going back. A new generation of madmen was out and about in Lourdes. They did not have the grounded maturity of those old Soviet generals, who had lived through a terrible war and did not, at heart, want another. They did not possess the dignity and judgment of Che. In the three weeks since she had been called into the meeting at Central Headquarters B, all she could think about were the lunatics Raúl had let into the country.

You may well get what you wish, she thought unhappily. *A parting act on the world stage that will eclipse anything your older brother ever did.*

CHAPTER FOURTEEN

Ugolny Airport, Anadyr, Russia
July 2, 6:33 A.M.

Konstantin Bolshakov had not only taken some breakfast and read a newspaper in the lobby of the Anadyr Hotel; fully dressed, with his overcoat draped over him like a blanket, he had napped there as well. It wasn't difficult. As a sailor, he had learned to grab a nap wherever he was, whatever the time, since he never knew when he might get another opportunity.

"Maybe that's why you don't sleep so long at night," he said to himself when a blast of cold air from the front door jolted him awake. "You nap all through the day."

He looked at his watch. Now he was more fully awake. His son's plane should be landing at Ugolny Airport within the next few minutes. If he hurried—

Shedding years and infirmity, Bolshakov asked the desk clerk to phone for a taxi. The stand was only a few blocks away, and the driver was there in three minutes.

Located nearly seven miles east of Anadyr, the airfield was built in the 1950s as a base for the Arctic Control Group of the Russian Air Force. As the Chukotka region expanded, the aerodrome was multi-purposed to serve as a terminal for civilian flights to and from the province. Supply flights from Nome, Alaska, were also permitted, the best-kept secret route for black market goods in the region. Ugolny remained a commercial hub during and after the Cold War, and the 171st Fighter Aviation Regiment retained a strong presence there until 1992, just after the dissolution of the Soviet Union. The only military visits since then had been during air exercises, typically long-distance training missions to and from Engels Air Base in Saratov, just over four thousand miles to the southwest.

The heat was uncomfortably high in the white minivan and the driver was a man in his fifties. He was one of those Russians who Bolshakov knew well from his years here: a fisherman who had been injured—in this case a hand injury suffered when he fell from a ladder and landed on it.

"Lucky for Boris he could still drive," he boasted in the third person, showing how he held the wheel with his left hand and right palm. The right fingers were stiff and bent outward, like broken lady's fan. "My sons fish now. We still eat well," he added, in case his passenger was worried.

The man's red eyes peered into the rearview mirror.

"You walk like a sailor," the driver said. "Were you? Here, I would guess?"

Bolshakov was in a good mood so he smiled. "Yes to both," he said proudly. He hadn't had a reason to brag about anything in decades.

"A surface ship in the navy!" the man exclaimed. He rolled his shoulders. "I watched you—side to side for balance, I knew it."

The conversation turned back to fishing, to the old days,

held there for the twenty-minute ride by the enthusiasm of a driver who felt he had found a true comrade. When he pulled to the curb, Boris thanked his passenger for a generous tip and then said, "You are here to meet someone from—then?"

"In a sense," Bolshakov had replied.

Boris nodded his bare head. "As Tolstoy said, 'The two most powerful warriors are patience and time.'" The man shrugged. "I have always had a lot of time to read."

Bolshakov thanked the man in earnest. That advice was worth hearing.

Boris said something else but his passenger didn't hear him through the flaps of his hat. The cold was a shock after the cab and Bolshakov hurried into the terminal. Ugoly consisted of two structures: the glass terminal, which was sun-warmed and resembled an isosceles trapezoid. At right angles was a three-story office building that had also served as the field's military headquarters.

The large, sunny interior was quiet. Solar warmth was definitely preferable to the dry heat blown through the taxi by a fan. Yuri's plane was due in eleven minutes. Bolshakov settled into a plastic seat and stretched his "sea legs," smiling again at the pleasure they had given to Boris. It was good to reflect on that part of his life, especially when the second half of it had been increasingly corrupt and degrading.

You even sit like a gangster now, not a naval officer, he chastised himself when he realized how he had sprawled outward from the seat. He straightened his back, pulled in his legs, then rose because he was too anxious to sit. He walked around the terminal, glanced at the fronts of magazines at the single newsstand, let his eyes roam over the candy and beverage selection—and saw none of it. He was listening for the sound of airplane engines. He was also thinking, wondering. Not just about the concerns any father would have—is my boy happy, is he married, am I a grandfather, a great-grandfather?—but even more basic questions: what does Yuri look like? What does he *do* now? Is he a soldier, a doctor, a train engineer? After the incident that drove them apart, after buying his own safety, Bolshakov had neither the funds nor the contacts to keep tabs on the young man. And the Internet provided no assistance. It was as if he had vanished.

Intentionally? Did he work for the government or did he not want his father to find him?

And then Bolshakov heard the low buzz of the engines. His heart slapped upward to the top of his throat and remained there. He went to a window that was part of the wall of windows overlooking the field. There were two commercial jets and three private planes just sitting there. He looked out and then to his left and saw the jet easing its way in. His heart was still slamming hard and his breath came in tiny gasps as he fought down sobs. The gleaming white Ilyushin Il-62M had the appearance of something celestial, magically bridging generations and injury.

For several minutes, Bolshakov was barely aware of what was going on around him. The plane landed, taxied quickly, the jetway rotated outward, staff gathered, and then passengers emerged.

Bolshakov could barely breathe. Would they even know each other?

A man of moderate height but confident stride entered the terminal alone. He was about forty-five and was smartly dressed, like a moderately successful businessman. He carried an accordion-style black shoulder bag—the kind favored by attorneys and government officials, Bolshakov noted—and he slowed long enough so that he could look around.

The man's eyes found and stayed on Bolshakov. He immediately turned toward the older man and strode ahead with that same purposeful stride. The younger man did not smile; perhaps he still was not sure. . . .

Bolshakov smiled. He could not help it. As the man came closer he recognized Vavara's fine mouth, and then her alert eyes. Tears rolled openly down the older man's face. The man neared, stopped, and Bolshakov threw his arms around his shoulders.

"Yuri," the older man sputtered, kissing his cheek before sobbing into the collar of the new arrival's overcoat.

Bolshakov felt his son move away. With confusion, he released the man, took a step back. Yuri did the same. He met the searching eyes of his father with stern disinterest.

"The bags will be a few minutes," Yuri said flatly. "I'm going outside for a smoke."

Without waiting for his father, he pulled on his gloves as he walked toward the front door. Shouldering his way past a small group of skycaps and a police officer, he stepped into the icy light.

Bolshakov looked after his son with a puzzled expression, but he did not follow. Maybe Yuri was overwhelmed by this reunion and did not want to show it; perhaps he needed time to adjust to seeing his father again. Or maybe he really needed that smoke. It had been a long flight, through nighttime hours; perhaps he had not slept.

In somewhat of a daze, still somewhat oblivious to whatever

was going on around him, Bolshakov made his way to the baggage claim area where the passengers stood silently around the equally silent carousel. Only a few had met family here; the rest were most likely in either the fishing business, construction engineers, or naval contractors. Most had their faces turned to cell phones and tablets.

His mother was reserved, too, Bolshakov remembered. When she played the piano, you could never see what she was feeling. But you could hear it.

A red light came on at the head of the carousel and an alarm blared locally. The ring began to turn and luggage began to roll down the conveyor belt. Bolshakov glanced behind him, saw Yuri terminate a cell phone call and reenter the terminal. He was wearing sunglasses now, and a stylish Cossack hat—mink, it looked like.

The older man smiled hopefully. *Now*, he thought. *Now things will be as they should be.*

But they were not what the older man wanted. Yuri shouldered his way into the small crowd several spots from where his father was standing. He waited with his back to the older man, and when his small, black bags appeared he snatched them both with clean, practiced moves. This was a man accustomed to traveling, but that was all his father knew.

Give him time, Bolshakov thought, forcing himself to heed the admonition. It had been many long years and an unhappy parting.

"Do you have a car?" Yuri asked when he had his bags and approached his father.

"No, Yuri. I-I wasn't sure we would need one."

"Yes," the young man said. "I want to go to the hotel and shower. Then we can see to it."

Yuri turned toward the exit and Bolshakov grabbed his arm. The younger man turned back, his eyes hidden behind the impenetrable sunglasses.

"Son, what *is* this?" Bolshakov asked unhappily. "Why did you ask me to come—you clearly didn't want to see me, to talk to me."

"That is correct, Father," Yuri said; he practically spat the word. "I wanted to do neither. But as much as I would prefer to be back in Moscow, it is necessary that we *do* talk. At the hotel, if you don't mind."

"No, I don't—*mind*," Bolshakov replied, puzzled why something so trivial should matter. "Whatever you like."

His shoulders sagging dejectedly, drooping almost as low as his spirits, Bolshakov gestured weakly toward the exit. He offered to take one of the bags from his son but Yuri said that he was fine.

The men stepped out and a cab pulled over; it had been waiting away from the stand. A familiar face jumped out.

"I told you I would wait," Boris smiled, rushing over to grab the new arrival's grip. "I didn't think you heard, but I took a chance."

The men entered the cab and heat blasted over them and the driver asked if they wanted to go back to the hotel. Bolshakov answered quietly that they did; it was all he could do to find his voice. He wanted to do more than cry now, he wanted to scream in helpless despair. This was not what he had been expecting, and it hurt far worse than estrangement—to be so close and so obviously detested.

He tried to understand, to put himself in the boy's position, but it took all his concentration and resolve to keep the scream in his throat.

"So you are related," Boris said joyously, glancing in the mirror. "I see it in the jaw, the cheekbones. The stoic demeanor," he added, dropping his voice to give it gravitas. "Well, father and son, or uncle and nephew, I welcome you to Anadyr and am at your service for whatever you would like to see or do." He pointed to the glove compartment. "There is my number . . . I will give you a card."

The men did not answer. They barely moved. Yuri looked out the window and Bolshakov stared ahead.

At a long, straight road with very little on it, the older man thought. And suddenly that was his life again.

He reached into his pocket and withdrew his own sunglasses, not to shield his eyes from the sunlight but to keep his tears to himself.

CHAPTER FIFTEEN

One trip had been enough.

Chase Williams was grateful to this president for having given him the chance to rebuild Op-Center and, ordinarily, he'd have gone running to the White House when Midkiff called a meeting. But Williams was just finishing with the briefing from the individual members team about General Ghasemi's background, and it was not the best use of his time to drive to D.C., return to Op-Center, and then drive home again to D.C. At three months shy of sixty years old, logistics—and conserved energy—were more of a concern than they had been in previous years. Williams would not have his focus broken or vigor depleted just to honor outdated protocol. He could participate with January Dow, Allen Kim, Trevor Harward, and the president just as effectively—and more efficiently—via secure videoconference.

Williams saw each participant in a separate box on his own

big monitor. The others watched on tablets, the president on his desktop monitor. Harward was no more relaxed than before. If anything, sitting in an armchair facing the president's desk, he seemed even more agitated. The president also seemed somewhat out of sorts.

Harward chaired the meeting.

"Mr. President, from what the team has just been telling me, we have nothing more solid than we did at Quantico," the national security advisor said. "Chase, what have you got?"

"Very little that isn't circumstantial," he admitted.

"Like goddamn election night when a state's too early to call," Midkiff said. "Glad I'll never have to face that again."

Williams understood the president's frustration. His popularity was at a personal low. Though he was nearing the end of his second term, he did not want to go out with crushing disapprovals . . . or, hopefully worse, something brewing that remained off his administration's radar.

"The thing about that, Mr. President," Williams said, "is that while election numbers are not ready to be tallied, you know there's always a gut feel how something is going."

There was a disapproving turn of the mouth from both Harward and Dow.

"True enough," the president agreed.

"All right, so we go with instincts," Harward said. "What's your 'feeling,' Chase?"

"He's lying," Williams said.

"We have to assume that," Harward agreed. "What does he gain?"

"We're supposed to believe that General Ghasemi was sent to spy on us but had a change of heart," Williams said. "We grill him, he doesn't seem to know very much, we learn nothing. But we'll keep questioning him, refining and retooling what we ask. Doing that, we tell him—and Iran—where our intelligence has gaps, what we suspect, what we're *concerned* about."

"Those are not state secrets," Dow said. "There are bloggers telling Iran everything we don't know."

"Except that he's made it clear some action is being readied," Williams said. "When something does get underway, our questions will no longer be general. How better to keep tabs on us than by having a 'defector' on the inside?"

The Oval Office was silent. Then the president spoke.

"Chase, we're all suspicious because a father does not normally do what this man has done," Midkiff said. "Abandon his daughter, watch her take a beating. What makes *you* think he's lying?"

"I love the military," Williams said, "but no secret operation, large or small, is put into motion without soldiers and especially officers having *some* opinion about it, some sense of what's going down. This man claims to know nothing."

"Is it the same in Iran as it is here?" Dow challenged.

Kim was the one who answered. "It's in the nature of any government hierarchy," he said. "My father experienced that in South Korea when he was deputy speaker of the National Assembly."

"But Iran," Dow repeated. "We're talking about a very strict theocracy."

"Some of my people fought in Iraq," Williams said with a hint of impatience. "I'll conference them in to talk about that, if you like."

Williams was normally not confrontational, but Dow's academic and embassy experiences did not include the military. That didn't prevent her from expressing an opinion when she should be listening.

"You were going somewhere with this, Chase?" Harward asked.

"I'm sure you saw that Parand Ghasemi is Dr. Parand Ghasemi, a nuclear physicist—" Williams said.

"A man's profession in Iran," Dow interrupted. "They had her teaching, not building weapons—"

"Not where I was going," Williams said, cutting her off. "We found her at a symposium a couple of years back."

"In Moscow," Harward said. "That one?"

"Correct. She met there with Dr. Adoncia Bermejo, University of Havana."

"We caught that, too," Harward said.

"Did you catch a reference to Anadyr in Bermejo's résumé?" Another silence.

"What's the significance?" the president asked.

"I know that name," Harward said, suddenly interested. "Russian—"

"Northeast port city."

"Name of the operation used to send nuclear missiles to Cuba," Harward said. "What could that possibly have to do with General Ghasemi?"

"Maybe nothing," Williams admitted. "Only it showed up twice today in intelligence scans."

Now the president was interested, too. "Connection?"

"We're digging into it," Williams told him. He explained about the two Bolshakov flights and reported what Kathleen Mays had found out about the revolutionary and post-revolutionary career of Dr. Bermejo.

"So let me understand this," Dow said. "You have an imprisoned nuclear scientist who once met Dr. Bermejo, who appears to have worked with the Soviets on their Cuban missile emplacements. Is that right?"

Williams nodded.

"And you have two Russians who went to a city whose name that operation bore—though there's no known connection between these men and Dr. Bermejo, whose whereabouts are not known, or more importantly to Parand Ghasemi."

"All true, which is why we're investigating," Williams said.

Dow looked skeptical; he tracked her eyes as they moved from Harward to the president. It was a practiced response from a politically savvy woman. Dow knew that if a rival intelligence officer had access to the president, that would be less time she had to further her own interests. That was the part of Washington Williams disliked more than any other: putting agency or party or special interest ahead of nation.

Harward seemed less interested than before; Kim was neutral. The president seemed to be weighing everything he'd just heard.

"Trevor?" Midkiff finally asked.

TOM CLANCY'S OP-CENTER: FOR HONOR

"Worth checking, though I agree with January about not seeing how the dots'll connect."

Williams looked at the bingo card of faces on his monitor as the conversation moved ahead . . . but not forward. He understood, and generally ignored, those kinds of fence-straddling cover-your-ass comments as well. But it was difficult working with people whose basic tenet was to withhold rather than offer support. Throughout his military career, if an officer showed initiative in the field—even contrary to orders or stultifying rules of engagement—Williams and practically every officer he'd ever known did not hesitate to throw the full resources of his command behind the action. There was no room for functionaries and playbooks when situations arose suddenly putting lives and national security at risk.

Kim had an interesting piece to add to the puzzle, and Williams wondered if the others even heard it.

"We've had this on the agenda before, and have been watching it," Kim said. "General Ghasemi mentioned Corps General Heydar Najafabadi as his contact in Iraq. In the very early 1990s Najafabadi was a new recruit to *Nešān*, which—according to records from the time—means 'a distinguishing ensign.' The graphic that went with it was a warhead. They were an elite, highly secretive military unit charged with purchasing nuclear arms or weapons-grade uranium or plutonium from former Soviet republics . . . in this case, Ukraine, Belarus, and Kazakhstan."

"But they didn't succeed," Harward said hopefully.

"Apparently not," Kim said, "but we only assume that because Iran would most likely have used them against Iraq during their struggles, or given them to a third party after the fall of Saddam Hussein."

"Is Najafabadi still part of that group?" the president asked.

"We don't know," Kim admitted. "We were watching them through one of our Ukrainian contract agents in the Crimea. He was captured by the Russians when they rolled in."

And there was the link the others may not have heard. Williams wondered if the Russians even knew about *Nešān* before that. Learning of it, he could see an opportunistic officer in a vast and corrupt Russian military looking to make tens of millions of dollars helping them fulfill their mission.

Williams did not want to play the my-turf, your-turf game the others played, but he also did not want contrarians tripping his people up. Kim might already be following up on this, but while he was still on the videoconference Williams sent Bankole and McCord a text:

```
Look for any Najafabadi-Russian con-
nections.
```

CHAPTER SIXTEEN

Cargo Ship Nardis, *The North Pacific*
July 2, 5:31 A.M.

It did not matter how many layers of paint had been thrown on the ship. On deck as well as below, from the bridge to the engine room, the Iranian general cargo vessel *Nardis* smelled of melted plastic, charred enamel, and soot.

On January 27, at 6:30 A.M. Moscow time, the ship had been en route from Astrakhan, Russia, to Enzeli, Iran, when it caught fire in the Caspian Sea channel. The ship's crew, with an assist from water cannons onboard the Russian service ship *Kapitan Checkin*, was able to save the vessel though it was carrying cotton and other highly flammable goods, which fueled the blaze for several hours. Though the *Nardis* was able to reach its destination under its own power, it was in dry dock for well over six months. While it was there, in addition to repairs, the 1980s-era ship was fitted with an S-type long-stroke main engine with electronic fuel injection for greater efficiency. It would need that: the 150,936-ton, 1,209-foot vessel was being withdrawn from commercial service and put at the disposal of the Iranian military.

Though it continued to make commercial runs as its cover, the vessel—under the command of "retired" Revolutionary Guards' navy officer Captain Ahmad Salehi—sailed the Middle Eastern, Asian, and South American seas delivering and acquiring black market weapons. Proficient in both blue-water open sea and green-water coastal operations, the sixty-one-year-old officer prowled the oceans like some mythical sea captain of folklore, in search of the ultimate prize: nuclear weapons he could bring to Tehran.

For Salehi, it was not a particular affinity for the ruling ayatollah or his lieutenants. He loved his homeland, whoever governed its people, and he would do whatever it took to recover and shine its ancient glory. That was important, for he was a keen student of history. And there was a time, during the reign of Cyrus the Great in 550 B.C., before the era of the Greeks under Alexander, before the Rome of Julius Caesar, when Iran *was* the world.

None of which changed the fact that the *Nardis*, though back at sea for over two years, still reeked of its former misfortune. Like human beings, mechanisms retained trauma—if not in their workings, then in their frames. Nothing solid came through its life unscathed.

Only ideas and beliefs did that, he told himself

Salehi had wakened with the sun and, after making his morning tea, dressed in gray sweat clothes and came directly to the bridge. He did not pray in his cabin; he allowed the crew and his commanders to assume he was secretly devout. He did not drink and he refrained from smoking . . . though before the Revolution he had been quite fond of his pipes. He also grew a beard of the proper length, and now he absently played with strands of that beard as he sat on the bridge looking out the panoramic windows.

Prayer wouldn't have helped now anyway, he thought, watching as the sun continued to illuminate the calm waters of the North Pacific. He was eager bordering on anxious to be about this mission. They were proceeding at a slow four knots off the coast of the Kuril Islands, Russia's pearl-strand of possessions that ran northeast from Japan to the Kamchatka Peninsula. Despite his current impatience, it was a sight that never failed to stir him, to make him happy for his career. And the view had never looked better: the windows were the latest style, treated with a coating that cut down on UV glare without diminishing brightness.

The rest of the bridge had gotten an overhaul, too, though not as extensive as it needed. A company in Hamburg, Germany—the same firm who had designed the electronics for Iran's centrifuge program—had installed new navigation and communications equipment, but while the panels were new the walls and floors and chairs were all original, and they all bore the telltale odors of the fire. Every time he sat on the reupholstered swivel chair, he seemed to jar some bolt or fitting that had been witness to the conflagration.

Lieutenant Commander Chitchian arrived and saluted the captain; military formality was only observed on the bridge, where enemy satellites might not observe it. He took his seat to the left of the commander. Though dressed in seaman's clothing, the entire ship's company was Revolutionary Guards' Navy or Navy of Islamic Republic of Iran Army—NEDAJA—the latter of which served almost exclusively in the vital Gulf of Oman, and the five-man bridge crew went about their work quietly and efficiently. In fact, there wasn't much to do other than monitor the ship's course up and down the island chain and keep a watch for military vessels of any nation. In international waters, no nation had any right to approach or question the ship's activities. The narrative, if it ever came to that—most likely from the Japanese, who were concerned about Russia's new militarization of the islands—was that Salehi was testing the new systems. In fact, he was just waiting for the next stage of the operation, one that wouldn't have them "pacing," as he put it to the admiral in Tehran.

The radio operator turned from his console off to the left. He pointed to his ears and removed his headset. Salehi switched his tea to his left hand and reached under his right armrest to grab his own headset. Though the bridge was quiet, this mission was ears-only.

"Salehi here," he said, without acknowledging the identity of the caller. The involvement of the prosecutor's office in this matter was need-to-know only.

"The Russian parties are in place," said the communications liaison. "Your passenger will be en route shortly. Your orders are to continue standing by."

Salehi acknowledged the message. Government and the sea had a great deal in common. Both were vast and deep, both were subject to dangerous eddies, and both could upend everyone who depended on them with sudden storms. He would stand by, the crew at ease, as they had been for two days. Salehi tried to console himself with the reason he was here—what was the phrase Prosecutor Younesi had used in their brief meeting? "*This glorious result.*"

Words that were both florid and celestial, as only a cleric could be, Salehi thought.

Finishing the tea, Salehi informed Chitchian that he was going down to the ship's exercise room.

"Restless, sir?" he asked.

"How can I be?" he asked. "I've only been awake for forty-five minutes."

Chitchian grinned knowingly. "Don't hurt yourself, sir. Or Amiri," he added.

The captain threw him a little two-finger salute in acknowledgment. He still wore a bandage on his left wrist from where he was cut by a four-and-one-half-inch fixed blade the day before.

The officer took the circular staircase that snaked to the deck. The bridge access adjoined the vessel's main forward stairwell, which he took to the next level.

He was already beginning to feel the blood flow. The morning drill was not for limbering up; the sailors got enough of that throughout the day. It was hand-to-hand combat, three classes for groups of ten to twelve morning, afternoon, and evening. Salehi liked the morning activities best since he was freshest. And since the knives were real, alertness was a key.

He entered the small, brightly lit room. The men were already on the matts, doing push-ups. There were no salutes, not even from the trainer, Lieutenant Amiri. He was on the ground with his team shouting out the count. Salehi immediately fell in and joined the three sets of fifty, which were just getting underway. His chest seemed to expand twofold as he took deep breaths with every push from the mat. It was exhilarating. When they were finished they rose, formed a circle, and ran with the powerfully built Amiri at the head of the circle. The lieutenant changed the pace from fast to faster; if he stepped on the heels of the man in front, the entire group was punished with another set of fifty push-ups.

That didn't happen today. When they were finished, half the men grabbed blades from a rack along the wall and lined up in two rows of six. Salehi had Amiri, as usual. The lieutenant was not convivial on his best days, but he seemed more intense than usual as he returned with his own knife.

For this first round, the moves were all regimented. The irony was lost on no one that the style they used was Krav Maga, the Israeli form of hand-to-hand combat: in-close, hard-hitting, forward-moving, violent. The drills were bruising but not especially dangerous. The attacking knife sweeps down; the defender meets it with an upraised forearm. The attacking knife sweeps in from the side; the defender meets it with a windshield-wiper sweep of the arm. The attacking knife sweeps upward; the defender meets it with a downward motion of the forearm. Both sides, over and over, faster and faster. The skin takes a beating, there are occasional nicks and tears, but the reflexes are honed. Then the roles are reversed, attacker becoming the attacked.

A half hour of regimented back-and-forth and then it was time for free-form. The objective here was different, designed to employ all facets of Krav Maga: blocks as well as body-throws over the shoulder and hip; kicks with the foot, leg, and knee; and strikes with open hands, fists, and elbows. During this half hour, the knife assault not only had to be prevented, the weapon was to be taken and turned on the attacker, who was then expected to defend himself in a similar fashion. Ideally, the exercise was uninterrupted for the duration.

Unless someone was hurt.

Lieutenant Amiri was nearly half the age of Salehi and had three inches on him. His reach was greater, both with hands and feet. That was how the captain had been cut the day before. He was determined not to let that happen today.

Everyone donned protective headgear and padded vests to protect vital organs and then spread out so that flashing steel or tumbling bodies would not strike a neighbor. Except for the hum of air from vents high on the wall, and the occasional creak of structural metal, the room was silent. As the two officers faced off, with Amiri as the attacker, the rest of the room seemed to vanish for both men. There was no rank here, just two objectives: to win and to be better than the day before.

Amiri opened with a straight-ahead lunge, leaning forward as if he were a swordsman. Typically, Salehi would have turned to one side, so he was perpendicular to Amiri, to let it go by. Instead—partly from his growing impatience—Salehi took a different tack. He stood his ground and met the attack with a block: crouching slightly and thrusting both arms forward, one over the other in the shape of an X. He caught Amiri's forearm, stopping the hand with the knife so the tip of the blade was just two inches from his vest. Unfazed, Amiri took a step ahead and pushed forward to ride over crossed arms; Salehi allowed him to do so. This second lunge brought Amiri much closer to the captain—within kicking range. Salehi drove the flat of his right foot hard into the other man's left knee. The shock caused a brief convulsion throughout the lieutenant's body. The captain seized on the distraction to plant that right foot directly in front of Amiri and swing his bent elbow from the outside, driving it solidly against the side of opponent's head.

Even with the vinyl-covered foam padding, the blow staggered the lieutenant. As he wobbled slightly to his right, Salehi grabbed the man's extended wrist, twisted it round so the knife was pointing up, and then bent the wrist back, in a direction it was not designed to move.

Amiri yelped and dropped the knife. His cry surprised the room, and the fighting stopped as the combatants looked over. They saw Salehi scoop up the blade and turn on the lieutenant.

A veteran at hand-to-hand combat, the younger man recovered so quickly that Salehi was caught off-guard. Amiri charged like a bull the instant Salehi was upright, burying his head in the older man's gut and wrapping his arms around the captain's waist. His momentum carried Salehi backward with such force that he landed on the mat, on his back. With the speed of youth and training, Amiri pinned the captain's wrists to the ground, hard. The knife jumped free and Amiri scrambled off to get it.

Rather than get to his feet as instinct dictated—a maneuver that would have left them back where the fight had started— Salehi remained on the ground and scrambled after him. Amiri recovered the blade but Salehi rolled hard against him and they ended up tangled together against the wall. The knife hand was buried under Amiri's side, pinned there by his own weight. Elbows and knees struck back and forth but Salehi just dug himself in deeper, refusing to let the knife out.

It was a war of attrition now, jabs in close proximity doing only minor damage.

And then something struck the mat behind the captain.

"Sir!" a voice yelled.

Salehi knew what it was. He pushed off his adversary, spun around, and grabbed the knife a crewman had tossed him. He got to his feet and Amiri did likewise. They had not drilled for this, but that didn't matter: in combat, nothing was guaranteed. Neither man had protection on his arms. That, too, would be the case in a combat situation.

It was difficult now to remember that this was a drill. Aggression was like a missile, rising until the fuel was spent, ungovernable by any other force including reason. The men faced one another, breathing rapidly, eyes missing nothing, the knives no less a part of them than the hands that held them. There were feints, short lunges, small *tings* when the blades struck in passing.

And then, suddenly, Salehi relaxed. Amiri waited a moment longer, then did the same.

"We—*I*—seem to have disrupted the class," the captain said, breathing heavily. "I'll withdraw and allow you to continue."

"Not on my account, please," the lieutenant said.

Salehi smiled. "No, Lieutenant. On mine. One must recognize when simulation becomes too much stimulation."

"I understand. Perhaps when you have free time—?"

"I will be back," Salehi assured his subordinate. He looked out at the others. "We must all be our best for what is to come."

The crew did not yet know the mission, but from the way they had been marking time here they sensed it was something out of the ordinary. His words underscored that.

Amiri acknowledged the captain's departure with a bow, followed by a salute. Salehi gave him the knife, then thanked the others before removing his gear and departing.

As he made his way back to the bridge, the officer was both disturbed and intrigued by how quickly he had been roused from drill to fight. Perhaps he, too, was only now just beginning to realize how vital this mission truly was.

CHAPTER SEVENTEEN

Anadyr Hotel, Anadyr, Russia
July 2, 8:11 A.M.

Bolshakov was perspiring, but it was much more than the forced hot air in the taxicab. He saw nothing outside the cab, was not listening to Boris describe the variety of fish in the region. All he knew, all he felt, was the presence of unchecked hate. It was seated to his left—his son, his boy.

Yuri's head was turned. Seeing the upturned collar of his overcoat, the scarf draped around it, he remembered a spindly child with a brown-and-white checked scarf his grandmother had knit . . . a boy's size cold-water coat Rear Admiral Merkassov had requisitioned for him . . . big boots lined with wax paper for easy removal when he came in from skating-without-skates on the ice pond that used to sit not far from where the hotel now stood. He saw a small, pure Yuri who always seemed to be so happy, as a boy should be in a playground that was all ice and snow and ocean and the distinctive, charcoal-winged Fulmars— dive-bomber seabirds that stole food and deposited droppings and battled for primacy along the coast.

Bolshakov had not expected to see that Yuri step from the plane. But he had not anticipated seeing no trace of him, anywhere. Just the same contemptuous eyes he had last experienced, now hardened by time.

It had been about access to the stores of Kalashnikov rifles, Stechkin automatic pistols, and PMN-1 and 2 anti-personnel mines left behind in Georgia. They were wanted by his clients in the Middle East; the Colombian drug cartels also wanted them, and they were the clients of Sergei Bilguun—the Marauder, they called him. The half-Mongolian arms dealer had so many weapons on hand, and enough cash for mercenaries, there was genuine concern that he would be able to stage his own coup in any former Soviet republic he chose. That was what kept the authorities from closing in on his base in Kyzyl in south-central Russia.

Bolshakov's operation had been small compared to Bilguun's, less than one-tenth the size. And it was domestic, not global. But the Russian had territories the Marauder wanted. Rather than negotiate, Bilguun abducted Vavara from their home in Severnoye Chertanovo. She was taken to the basement of one of the industrialized housing complexes in the Moscow suburb where she was murdered. Written in her blood on the concrete floor beside her stabbed, naked body: "Your son is next."

It was a time for deep grief but not for capitulation. Failing to strike back would have left Bolshakov vulnerable to every small arms dealer in Russia. But it was not the kind of assault to which any black market was accustomed.

Bolshakov flew to Kyzyl on a private jet and, through a combination of bribes and intimidation, found the private school where Bilguun's eight-year-old daughter was a student. From that point, these many years later, the Russian could vividly recall everything that had happened. It was a warm day, misted with drizzle, and he had on a black raincoat. He stood across the street from the modern, two-story school and looked for the car that did not belong. There were a number of parents in expensive cars picking up their precious sons and daughters but only one of those vehicles rode low on its tires, weighted down by heavy armor plating. It had smoky windows, and as he walked toward it he smelled the diesel fuel—ideal for maximum torque to move heavy loads, reinforcing the assessment that the chassis had added protection. He waited not far from where other parents stood under umbrellas, outside the closed gates. He pulled his fedora low, shielding his eyes from the rain, and stood with them. When the school doors opened and children came out, he waved and smiled—as if he had a child in the group.

Bolshakov had raised no obvious suspicion as he quickly scanned the figures under the umbrellas and saw the one who was not a parent: a giant of a man with a big, black umbrella. The Russian maneuvered easily, unobtrusively, shouldering his way through the group so that he was closer to the man. A pretty young girl in a yellow rain slicker and with traditional Mongolian braids falling straight from under her pink wool cap stepped to the side of the big man. Dwarfing her, enveloping her as he extended a protective arm behind her, they turned and walked toward the car. Bolshakov was just a few paces away. The bodyguard would open the door and stand behind it so the girl could enter—

The Russian pulled off his right-hand glove, unbuttoned his raincoat. He could still feel the chill of the brass on his fingers—*snap, snap.* The wind had picked up a little then and he recalled the busy motion of the vented storm flap over his upper legs. He actually felt his heart with his palm as his hand snuck into the interior pocket for the snub-nosed .38, his personal weapon since he began his career as a private citizen—

He approached the vehicle from the front. The girl was just getting inside, the bodyguard was behind the door. With a single, clean move Bolshakov drew the gun and put a bullet cleanly through the forehead of the big man. A big, black, red-rimmed hole appeared in front even before anyone had turned in response to the loud, sharp report of the firearm. The girl—

The girl, Bolshakov thought now. She was the most vivid of all. Not the bodyguard's frozen, neutral expression as he dropped behind the open door. Not the shrieks and shuffling feet that penetrated the fading *crack.* Just the pretty yet perplexed mouth, the innocent cheeks, the big brown eyes that stared at Bolshakov as he approached. He was much smaller than the bodyguard but so much more dangerous, he remembered thinking as he pulled a stiletto from his outside pocket. The blade in his gloved left hand, he used his right to grab the back of the head of the suddenly terrified little girl and pushed the sharp point through her large, staring left eye. He left the knife—in his trade, a sign of contempt, leaving "the goods" behind because it had surely been paid for.

Turning back to his car, he left her shrieking in the street and flew back to Moscow.

Bolshakov breathed as his thoughts returned to the present.

Even today, he felt no remorse. To the contrary. It was the last act that had left him feeling fulfilled. The message was clear. Bolshakov could have retaliated in kind, killing the girl. He did not. If there were another incident, he would.

The poor little thing, he finally thought when he was back in Moscow and the rush of the planning and execution had worn off. The girl was just a pawn, as his wife had been. This was between him and the Marauder, and if there were ledgers to keep such grotesque records, the Russian would have come out on top. Bilguun had ended a life but Bolshakov had ruined one, not just with physical scarring but emotional and psychological trauma.

Bilguun did not bother him again, and to protect his son and himself, Bolshakov phased himself out of the arms business. He did this by selling his contacts and his territories. Much of that money went to concealing his whereabouts, buying new identity papers and passports under multiple names, and placing his young, teenage son in the care of his mother's sister, Natalya. She ran an accounting firm in the large city of Novosibirsk, to the south. To protect the boy, Bolshakov did not visit him—though his sister-in-law occasionally sent him photographs. The pain was almost unbearable, but Bolshakov dared not go to him. By the time Bilguun died in a plane crash of suspicious origin, Yuri was grown. He had finally left Natalya's care with one request: that she never reveal his whereabouts to the man whose corrupt life had directly caused his mother's death.

That was over three decades ago. *Thirty years.*

The older man could not sit here like this. He wanted to reach over and take his son's hand, squeeze it, do *something* to show Yuri that he loved him. He wanted to tell him, *Do you think I don't miss her, too? Do you imagine I would not have left my trade, the country, done* anything *to save her?*

He turned toward the back of his son's head and yelled inside, *"Yuri, that loss should have brought us closer, not torn us apart!"*

But that was not what crept from his mouth as a rough, dry whisper.

"Son—do you still like *kvas*?" he asked, referring to the drink made from fermented bread. "The man with the cart used to come and you would run—"

"Don't, Father," Yuri said, half turning. "It is all I can do to sit here. Do not make it worse."

"Then why *have* you come? To hate me . . . to my face?"

"We have business," was all he told the older man. He said it without emotion or interest, as if it were dictation.

Bolshakov slumped back. Boris had been talking on the phone to his dispatcher; he hung up and did not resume his monologue about Anadyr.

A minute later the taxi arrived at the hotel. Bolshakov paid while Yuri gathered his luggage from the trunk.

"All will be well with you," Boris said quietly as he made change. He jerked his eyes toward Yuri, then back. "Trust a fellow sailor: he will see what I see, that you are a good man."

Bolshakov had not been thinking about the driver and, in most other circumstances, he would have ignored the unsolicited opinion of an outsider. But right now, those words were something human.

"Thank you," Bolshakov said. "I will hold you to that."

Boris offered his hand across the back of the seat and Bolshakov left the cab. Yuri had not gone inside but was standing there with his bags. He looked at his father as he approached.

"Do you know why I retained my name," the younger man asked. "Why I did not adopt one of the new identities you offered me?"

"Tell me," Bolshakov said encouragingly. "I wish to understand."

"Because one day I hoped to be able to wear it again proudly," he said. "That day is now."

Grabbing his bags and turning, Yuri entered the hotel. Bolshakov stood a moment longer in the cold sunlight, letting his own upset dissipate by reminding himself of everything Yuri had lost—mother, father, adolescence—before following him inside.

CHAPTER EIGHTEEN

Op-Center Headquarters, Fort Belvoir North,
Springfield, Virginia
July 1, 2:10 P.M.

When former Marine Roger McCord commanded the Intelligence Battalion at MARSOC, he had a simple approach to counterintelligence enigmas: reverse-engineer them. It could be expressed as an equation, he discovered:

$$\text{Goal} = \text{Desire} + \text{Plan (Intelligence} + \text{Experience)} + \text{Tools} + \text{Will}$$

Fill in the elements and one would know how to find and stop the enemy—or, indeed, to solve any conundrum. The so-called McCord Method was one of the frequent discussions he had with his wife over dinner. He was convinced that it must work with the raising of their three daughters, since human nature was inevitably human nature. But it had failed every time, leading him to finally conclude—fairly recently—that teenagers were less predictable than terrorists.

Mary McCord was the only one who could not only hold her own with McCord but get him to cry uncle—however many months it took. The two had met when they were both at Princeton, where she got her doctorate in banking and finance and he earned a PhD in international affairs. Drs. McCord and Williams were frequently at cross-purposes, something the director handled with greater deftness than McCord. *But then*—McCord thought but never said—*Williams was never wounded in combat.* McCord had been injured in Ramadi, his right leg so torn up by an RPG that he walked with a noticeable limp. It hadn't made him inactive: he was still passionate about the single-scull rowing he'd pursued at Princeton, and he loved his Harley; but it had made him self-conscious and occasionally combative. The months he was forced to stay in bed had also turned him into a reader of classic works, which taught him to see life through the eyes of others. He usually apologized when he was wrong—but he wasn't this time. Not about Ghasemi. The man might be everything he said he was, but McCord refused to give him the benefit of the doubt.

After the videoconference with the Oval Office, when Williams had texted Kim's bit of information—to look for any Najafabadi-Russian connections—McCord went to work on his equation. Alone in his office, the door shut, he needed quiet and privacy to access everything he knew—or once knew. There was over twenty years of military and intelligence minutiae in his brain. Silence and concentration were the only way to let it out.

In the equation, the Desire was simple: Iran wanted nuclear weapons or the high-grade material to make them. The Iranians also had the Will: nothing else was as important to Tehran. And they also had the essential Tools by way of a globe-spanning navy and a great deal of cash. The only one that was partially complete

was Plan. That required intelligence, experience, and relation-
ships. They had a great deal of HUMINT—human intelligence—
eyes and ears on the ground around the world. There were also
rumors—

And there's a piece, he thought suddenly.

Iran was suspected to be buying information from Russia via
Lourdes in Cuba. And if Ghasemi had been sent here to spy—and
still might be, while telling January Dow he wasn't—intelligence
was a certainty in the equation. Experience? They were known
to be purchasing nuclear know-how from Germany and North
Korea.

So the Iranians were known to have a few of all the pieces
needed to execute a method. The trick, now, was to find out
which way the elements in the equation pointed to achieve G—
the Goal.

The key to solving that puzzle was "evidentiary weight," as
McCord called it. He looked to see which elements showed up the
most, directly or even obliquely, throughout the equation. When
he laid out the random pieces of intelligence they had acquired, the
ones that stood out—Operation Anadyr, Bermejo, Lourdes, and
even the Shukur-punch. And they all fell under the same heading,
one that completed the equation.

He did a word-search on a CIA white paper from 1962,
then called Williams.

"What have you got, Roger?"

"A bunch of roads if not leading to Cuba, bringing us close,"
McCord said.

"As a staging area or for more intel?" Williams asked.

"The latter. We've got four associations with the Cuban Missile Crisis. That's too high for coincidence. I just skimmed a CIA postmortem on Operation Anadyr and it's amazing what we did not know, and what we still do not know."

"We weren't doing flyovers by then," Williams said.

"Uh-uh."

Williams was referring to the capture of U-2 pilot Francis Gary Powers when the Russians shot the spy plane down over Sverdlovsk during a May 1960, mission. Powers's release, in 1962, came with a tactically timed caveat that the U.S. effectively stop overflights of Russian interests.

"The CIA concluded that one of two things happened in the fall of '62," McCord went on. "One, that Khrushchev didn't clear out all the nukes and that they are still somewhere in Cuba. Or two, that Cuba was only one of the destinations. Syria was aligned with the Soviet Bloc back then, and Moscow was not happy about our missiles in Turkey."

"Christ, if there are nukes in Syria—"

"Could be," McCord said. "Off the radar and buried for over a half century. Or Khrushchev might have deployed them somewhere else in Russia. Our eyes were on Cuba, then. Our HUMINT eyes were on the silos we knew about. He may have wanted a secret stash, possibly within striking distance of an allied target."

"Kathleen reported a Russian arms dealer showing up in the northeast."

"She also said that could be nothing more than a family reunion," McCord said. "She should watch that, but we really need to follow the nuclear trail from where it began. There are only three places where records like that might be found. Russia, Syria, or Cuba."

"Cuba," Williams said thoughtfully. "Bermejo and Operation Anadyr. Your equation."

"Kathleen also zeroed in there," McCord said. "She places the SIGINT station at Lourdes as a likely place for Dr. Bermejo to be."

"Pretty tightly bottled up," Williams said. "Even if you had forged papers, you don't look Cuban and you don't look Russian."

"Cubans are a mix of everything from African to Chi—"

"You only speak high school Spanish—"

"*Cuatro años.*"

"*And* they'd follow the hell out of you. Or if you could sneak inside, how will you find her and what makes you think she'll talk to you? Or that she's fully compos mentis?"

McCord sat thoughtfully. "She emerges from time to time," McCord said. "She has an account at the National Bank of Cuba. Kathleen is looking to see if she makes withdrawals."

"There's probably an ATM *and* a commissary at Lourdes, for the Russians. To keep them happy when they're not on leave."

"Russians," McCord said. "All the more reason for a Cuban to want to get the hell out of there. Look—we have to look into a possible connection. I've got a sculling background. The sport's been big in Cárdenas for over a hundred years and that's near both Havana and Lourdes. Might get me in."

Despite the establishment of diplomatic relations, travel to Cuba for tourist activities was still prohibited by statute. The

United States Department of Treasury's Office of Foreign Assets Control still issued general licenses for a dozen categories of travel of which athletic activities and competitions were one.

"I'll go with your gut on this," Williams said, glancing at his computer. "It may not have anything to do with this matter, but I'm looking at our file on Cuba and it's full of SIGINT and ELINT, not eyeballs. Also, ask Aaron to have his team watch for anything that has to do with Dr. Bermejo—travel, bank withdrawals, photos . . . anything. She may have routines that'll make it easier for you to get to her."

"Good. I'll brief Paul and the Tank," McCord said, "and I'll stay in touch via the usual channels."

McCord hung up feeling as though a weight had been lifted, one he hadn't even realized was there: being office-bound. Injured, in his middle forties, a family man, he had simply accepted this evolution into the routine of middle-age. After his own recent adventure with Mike Volner in New York, operations director Brian Dawson had suggested to McCord that he do the same thing, get himself a field assignment. McCord hadn't been sure that he was up for it physically or psychologically. At least as far as the latter was concerned, McCord had been wrong.

Getting up and going down the hall, he had a chat with Dan Carbonero who was Op-Center's one-person travel office. If documents were needed, legal or not, the sixty-five-year-old former Washington, D.C., travel agent was the man to see. His sister Jodi was a retired engraver at the U.S. Mint. It was a useful partnership.

After telling Carbonero what he needed, McCord got in

touch with Mike Fogel, secretary general of the United States Rowing Association. McCord told him he had some vacation time coming and wanted to spend it in Cuba, where he had never visited. Fogel said he'd call his counterpart in Havana to make it happen—provided McCord could get his papers in time.

"Already taken care of," McCord assured his old friend.

"I forgot," Fogel chuckled. "You *are* plugged in down there."

"Rowing is the only thing I do solo," he replied.

McCord returned to his formula to see what other data he could apply. He was interrupted after a few minutes by a call from Aaron Bleich.

"Need you in the Tank, if you're free," he said.

"What've you got?"

"Chase asked me for surveillance of where you're headed," the tech wiz replied. "I think you're going to want to see this."

CHAPTER NINETEEN

SIGINT Base, Lourdes, Cuba
July 1, 3:09 P.M.

Adoncia was in her tiny living room, listening to a recording by singer Xiomara Alfaro and working on her autobiography, when she smelled smoke. Moments later, a fire alarm sounded. A few seconds after that, a second alarm sounded—from the opposite direction. Then came a peppering of shouts.

The smells and sounds were not in her three-story building; they were coming through the open window, from the direction of Listening Post A about a half mile away. She rose from the desk, no real urgency to her movements as she walked out her back door onto the small patio. Leaving the door open behind her, she walked closer to the burning buildings. By the time she arrived she heard the siren of the fire truck that was stationed permanently at the base. In the distance, to the north, was the sound of sirens coming from the city.

The blaze was churning black smoke from two ends of the long, two-story wood-and-brick structure. The wind was carrying it inland, to the southeast, away from where she was standing.

Either the first-story windows had been open or the heat had blown out the glass. Fingers of flame were beginning to reach up along the façade as both Cuban workers and Russian officers ran onto the paved streets of the compound. The old red fire engine arrived from behind the far end of the building and plugged into the nearly sixty-year-old hydrant; she couldn't quite make it out, but it looked as if the firefighters were having trouble unscrewing the cap.

Adoncia decided to go inside, save her work, and power down her laptop in case it were necessary to evacuate. She remembered, from the days of campfires and Batista's jungle defoliation-by-flamethrower, how fast and unpredictable fire could be. It was survival instinct honed around those same campfires, at night, that told her at once she was not alone.

"Forgive me, Dr. Bermejo," a voice said from around a corner. It was followed by a cough.

The physicist walked through the living room. There was a small kitchen and dining area to the far left. To the right was a short corridor that lead to the bedroom, bathroom, and closet. The sound had come from there.

"Who is there?" she asked. There was no fear in her voice. If someone had meant her harm, he would not have announced himself. Whoever it was must have slipped through the open door when she went to look at the fire.

"I-I am Enrich Sanjulian. I work here as a janitor."

"Why are you hiding?" she asked, though she already suspected the reason. "Did you have something to do with the fire?"

"Yes." He coughed again, apologizing.

"It was not an accident?" she asked.

There was no answer. Adoncia stopped just short of the hall.

"Come out and talk to me, Enrich," she said.

A man of medium height, middle age, and modest build came into the afternoon light. He was dressed in coveralls and wore a black baseball cap with a Cuban flag and the slogan *¡VIVA CUBA!* beneath it.

"Hello," she said with an encouraging smile. "Do you know me?"

"I know of you," the man said. It occurred to him to doff his cap and he snapped it off, revealing a damp tangle of graying hair. Adoncia just now noticed that his dark skin was speckled with perspiration and he was slightly out of breath. "My parents used to speak of you, along with Che and Señores Fidel and Raúl. They were very proud of what you had done."

"Thank you," she said graciously. "Now, Enrich—tell me what *you* have done, and why—but before you do, I'm just going to save some work I was doing. In case we have to leave."

He nodded, was squeezing his hat as she sat. She turned the screen partly toward him so he could see she was doing nothing more than saving the material and shutting the laptop down. He exhaled audibly.

"Would you like to sit?" she asked, gesturing to a cushioned wood chair opposite a small flat-screen TV.

"Thank you, no," he said. "I stared those fires because—what you fought against is happening again. A new era, but an old taskmaster."

"Russia, you mean," she said.

"Yes. Each week, there are more and more of them. My friends are harassed in town, my nieces—we no longer feel safe here."

"And you thought that setting fire to their primary intelligence station would send them home," she said. "It will only bring more of them, for security."

Sanjulian held out his hands. "We considered that, my cousins and I. But we wanted to get the attention of our leaders. Show them our displeasure."

"Our leaders are paid a great deal by the Russians, by the Iranians, by the Colombians," Adoncia said. "A fire won't change that."

They heard shouting outside as security forces—Russian, from the voices—spread out through the complex.

"Not one fire, but many fires," Sanjulian said. "We will do this the way *you* did, rousing a people who are ready to fight back."

The scientist considered this, then rose.

"We can talk of this later, Enrich. First—go into the bedroom and stay there. They are sure to come here. I will send them away."

The man nodded, his lips pressed tightly together to keep from sobbing. She shooed him off, tucked the computer under her arm, and walked toward the door.

Two men were running along her side of the building. Dressed in khaki trousers and matching short-sleeve shirts, they were trying doors, looking in windows. Each man carried a Taser. Noticing her, they hurried forward.

"Have you seen a running man?" a man asked in fractured Spanish.

"Only you," she responded in perfect Russian.

The men stopped. It wasn't her knowledge of the language but her slightly mocking tone that caused them to look at her more closely.

"Who are you?" the second man asked in Russian.

"Dr. Adoncia Bermejo," she replied. "I frequently advise your superiors." She nodded toward the radio he wore on his belt. "You can call them, if you'd like."

The men moved forward in unison as cold spray from the fire hoses misted in their direction. They were standing in front of the small window at the front of the apartment. The one nearer glanced over a window box that was rich with mariposa. The interior of the apartment was dark, still.

"We're only interested in the man who set the fire," the Russian said. "He was seen running from the building, under cover of the smoke."

"I have been working here on the patio," she said, indicating the laptop. "I saw no one."

Two other Russian guards came running around the apartment block from behind Adoncia. They were dressed, and armed, like the others.

"Is this anything?" one of the newcomers asked in Russian.

"No," one of the others replied. "Was everything secure?"

"No doors or windows forced. Here?"

"Everything secure," the men said.

"How do you know he is not a resident?" Adoncia asked.

The first man who had addressed her replied. "The fire started near two custodial stations. Manual laborers do not live here."

A radio crackled on the hip of one of the newcomers. It was a sentry at the gate: no one had gone through and none of the perimeter alarms had been tripped.

"We are gathering the workers," the caller said. "Proceed to Listening Post C to assist."

The man acknowledged and indicated for the others to go with him. The fire was already abating, two engines from the village having attacked it from other sides, the smoke now mixing more and more with steam. The spray had begun to abate as the breeze calmed. Mostly what lingered was the odor of the smoke and whatever oily accelerant had been used.

"We're sorry to have disturbed you, Dr. Bermejo," the first speaker said.

"You didn't," she replied. "It's been an education."

The man was perplexed but moved on with his companion. Adoncia waited until they looked back. Then she waited some more in case they had talked among themselves and came back. After several minutes, when neither of those had happened, she went back inside.

She closed the door and quietly locked it. She did not draw the shades; Russians might still come by and look in. Adoncia could still hear the man breathing, only now it was not from having run, but from anxiety.

"Enrich, I'm going to sit in here . . . I want them to see me alone if they come by. You stay where you are."

"All right," he replied.

"They're still bullies," she complained mildly. "The Russians. They were crude and thuggish in 1962, they are crude and thuggish still. They're gathering the employees. They're going to find out who's missing. They'll go to your home."

"I live alone," Sanjulian replied. "If I can get away, I will go to allies in Manzanillo. I can go from there to Jamaica if necessary."

"How many of 'you' are there?"

"Only a dozen or so now," he told her. "We needed something to embolden others—the way you did with your strikes at the Moncada Barracks."

"We lost those," she pointed out.

"But started a movement," Sanjulian replied.

"Sixty years ago. It was a different world, with weapons and communication that were less efficient at crushing a small insurgency."

"We can use those means, too," he replied. "The social media. Our phones."

The man had a point. Here, she experienced globe-girdling, space-based equipment. On the ground, technology was an equalizer. It had created a terrorist- and anarchist-friendly universe. Like ants, scouts and lone wolves could communicate with the hive in a way she and the other revolutionaries had never been able to.

"Will you stay here, at least until nightfall?" Adoncia asked.

"If you will have me, I would be grateful."

"Tell me, Enrich. How had you planned to escape?"

"My shift was over. I would have been able to walk out before the fire spread, but the bins of shredded paper were quite full. They just went *whoosh*. I ran, and running—well, I was seen and pursued."

The scientist smiled inside; she understood. It would never have occurred to him to wait. When someone was mentally and psychologically prepared to fight, when the spirit and muscles were as primed as they would ever be, adrenaline coopted judgment and survival. The energies had to be expressed.

"Would you answer another question?" she asked.

"Gladly. I appear to have the time."

She laughed. There was the Cuban worker she knew and loved and had once fought for, a soul of humble, realistic, unvarnished candor. "What would you have done had my door not been open?"

He replied as she half expected: "I would have been captured. I was prepared for that. Señor Fidel was."

Adoncia smiled. Enrich Sanjulian was correct about that. It was only by the greatest luck and family influence that the Castros were released in a general amnesty. Their number two man, Abel Santamaría, was captured, tortured, and executed the same day as the raid.

"I'm not sure how we'll get you out," she replied thoughtfully.

"Doctor, that is not your worry—"

"How is it not?" she asked pointedly. "When I was fighting, farmers who did not know us, fed us. Peasants who could spare machetes turned them over. Peasants who could not spare machetes turned them over. We were given buckets to collect rainwater, blankets, old shirts to make bandages." Her eyes drifted to the coffee table. "We were given cigars, which not only relaxed us but allowed us to light fuses without striking a match to give away our location. Cuba is the concern of us all, Enrich. All Cubans are our concern."

The man was silent—though Adoncia thought she could hear him weeping.

"If you leave now you are sure to be caught," she thought aloud.

"Do you have a car?"

"I do not," she replied. "No, whatever we do must be done at night. Or . . ." Her voice trailed off.

"Yes?"

The woman settled back into her chair. "Just make yourself comfortable. Would you like something to eat or drink?"

"Not at present," he replied. "May I ask what you're thinking?"

"Fission," she replied. "A way to get you to safety."

CHAPTER TWENTY

Anadyr Hotel, Anadyr, Russia
July 2, 8:30 A.M.

Yuri took his time.

Perhaps this was his way, his father thought: purposeful, silent, meticulous. Bolshakov had no way of knowing and he did not intrude.

They went to the hotel where the beds had already been made and clean morning light came through the open blinds. The young man showered. He told his father he'd be gone a few minutes and grabbed his coat on the way out the door. He had taken his phone with him; no doubt he had sent emails or texts or whatever he did in his line of work—of which Bolshakov still had no idea. He could be a banker, he could design computers, he could own a liquor shop, he could be an actor or a teacher . . . there was nothing about his walk or the smooth skin of his hands to suggest anything other than that he did not do manual labor. He was not a rancher or paleontologist. That was about all Bolshakov knew.

The older man sat on the edge of one of the beds the entire

time Yuri was gone. Bolshakov had been brought to trial just once in his criminal career and had been acquitted at great expense—most of that a payoff to the judge. This was like waiting for a judge to return a verdict. Then and now he sat, reviewing the deed that brought him here and reviewing his entire life as an adjunct to that. Before the collapse of the Soviet Union, the black market had been a thriving underground. After the collapse, it became the primary economy in Russia. Whether one trafficked Western goods or guns or drugs, there was no legally enforceable right or wrong. Trials were theater, staged to show the rest of the world that Russia was not what it, in fact, was: a criminal enterprise with a military and nuclear weapons.

It was true: Bolshakov could have remained in the military and collected his pitiful wages and retired to a tiny apartment in a box of a tower among other boxes of towers and lived without anything but the basic necessities. But he wanted more for his family so he chose a path that made him wealthy. He wished he could convince Yuri of this fact: it was his innate morality that doomed him. Had he been as corrupt as Sergei Bilguun, the Marauder, as unscrupulous as the vultures who descended to feed on the savaged carcass of Konstantin Bolshakov after the death of his wife—he could have owned the illegal arms trade in Russia.

No, he thought. *You were content with* enough. A comfortable *dacha*, a cottage plus apartments in Moscow, St. Petersburg, Novosibirsk, and Yekaterinburg. Money to travel, to buy things for Vavara and Yuri. The lesson was hard-learned: there is no middle ground in crime. Either you are a petty thief or a gang lord. He had taken Yuri to the Paleontological Museum and a diorama made his world seem so clear: there were the giant carnivores tearing the flesh from giant herbivores while, underfoot, tiny mammals went unnoticed as they sought berries and leaves.

He had tried to be a middle-sized omnivore. He was killed from both sides of natural selection.

Yuri finally returned, dragging with him cold air from outside and the reek of his cigarettes. Bolshakov looked up at him—not hopefully but expectantly, believing the silence would finally be broken, something, anything said or discussed.

The younger man shut the door, removed his coat, hung it in the closet over his unpacked bags, and put his phone on the room's one dresser. He did not sit on the bed but remained standing. He fished his cigarettes from under the heavy, red wool sweater he wore. He shook one from the pack, lit it with a match, and sought the ashtray on the desk. He drew heavily, then shut the blinds. Bolshakov sat with his hands on his knees. Suddenly, he was half-waiting to be executed. A silenced bullet to the back of the head. The thought made him angry and afraid—not because he might die, he had been there before. But because he would die without a trial.

But Yuri did not produce a gun or a knotted cord to strangle him and crush his windpipe with, and his hands seemed relaxed enough, the cigarette tucked between two fingers. The son looked down at his father.

"I have rented a four-wheel-drive vehicle so we can take a trip along the coast," he said thoughtfully, quietly, like someone accustomed to carefully divulging secrets. His voice became even softer. "We are going to *Gornyy Khrebet*."

Bolshakov showed the surprise he felt. Mountain Ridge was the name for the old Operation Anadyr base. Questions piled up in his brain, a disorderly queue, but emerged as a single question: "Why?"

"I work for the government, the Russian government," he added quickly, not sure whether his father even recognized what came after the fall of the Soviet Union. "They believe the nuclear missiles brought there by the *Mikula* and the *Vsevelod* are still in the facility."

Bolshakov frowned. "Those were going to be dismantled. Surely there are records."

"After Gorbachev, records of many nuclear facilities vanished," Yuri replied. "People like you were interested in making a profit from them."

"I never traded in weapons of mass destruction. *Never.*"

"I'm sure that was a mark of great honor to you," Yuri said, with his first show of contempt since they'd started talking. "Others had no such scruples. Surviving records show that the missiles and the launchers in the bunker were made inoperational in 1974. You left shortly before the official closing, before the materiels were disposed of."

"Half of us were transferred to other posts," Bolshakov replied. "Command personnel were no longer needed. They used the engineer corps that had been brought in."

"There is no evidence that they did anything at all, not even to take things apart," Yuri said.

"Why?"

"Budget cuts would have been the internal explanation,"

Yuri said. "But the real reason would have been selling them or simply reactivating them with an easy soil-to-soil reach to the United States of less than five miles."

"They put out false stories in case the Americans intercepted," Bolshakov said.

"That, and Gorbachev wasn't a fool," Yuri replied. "The nation was in turmoil. You don't leave a turnkey nuclear operation where a rogue general can get to it. Such a man could have held two nations at bay. But as far as we know, the nuclear material itself is still there, which is why I have to go. Without blueprints, even the roadmaps, or even American aerial surveillance, that could take months."

"'We,'" Bolshakov said, still taking all of this in. "Who do you work for, Yuri?"

He stiffened slightly, proudly, as if presenting himself for inspection. "I am a captain with the GRU."

Bolshakov was openly surprised. "The operation was military. Why is the Intelligence Directorate interested in nuclear materials?"

"That is classified and it is not your concern," Yuri replied. "I only need you to take me there."

The older man considered everything he'd been told. "For you to see me—to *ask* to see me after all these years—this must be important to you or to Russia. Possibly both."

Yuri remained implacable. Bolshakov shook his head without taking his eyes off the young man.

"You won't give me anything, will you?" the older man said. "You ask for help but will give me nothing. Not love, I didn't expect that. No warmth, fine. But not even courtesy. Is that too much to ask?"

Yuri pulled thoughtfully on his cigarette. "My mother taught me many things while you were off building your new life," he said. "Chief among them was decency toward others. I'm not naïve. Survival demands compromise. You raised your little empire knowing who the players were, what they were capable of. Did you ever ask yourself, 'What would my wife and son prefer?' Having a father, a family, a *life*, and even life itself—or a BMW, the cottage, the apartments, the nice clothes?" He came closer, blowing smoke from the side of his mouth. "And even—*even*—if you thought that was worth the risk, did you ever consider how many families the work you did might be tearing apart? We have a file on you at the GRU. The weapons you sold—which were not yours to sell, I might add—ended up in the hands of killers in Vietnam, in Colombia, in Japan, in Germany—"

"I sold only to Russians," Bolshakov said defiantly.

"Yes, boast of your integrity! But you had to know you were selling to men who were themselves intermediaries. The Marauder knew! He got to them and they led him to you . . . to my mother." He turned, crushed his cigarette, and spun back angrily. "And when he killed her, your retribution was legendary. You killed a bodyguard and took the eye of his young daughter as if this innocent child was a writing tablet for you to scrawl a memo! You left her half blind and screaming in the street to say to her father, 'I am better than you, Sergei Bilguun! I could have taken her life but I only did . . . *this*!'" Yuri rose. "And you did it for what? Did it bring Mother back? No. You did it for money. So you could shock the Marauder into momentary retreat, to remain standing long enough to sell your territories to other criminals and send me into hiding in one place, you in another. When I needed a father the most, you chose financial security."

"For you." Bolshakov's voice was weak, but it was all he had.

"How kind," Yuri sneered. "You see before you the result of your carefully wrought plan. For hate of you I could not take a wife or have children. I did not want to inflict this poison on another soul. So I chose work. Maybe that is your legacy, *Father*. Work above all else. You know the slogan the Germans had in their concentration camps? 'Work sets you free.' I saw it in photographs in our files. It was a cruel joke then and it is a cruel joke now." Yuri squatted suddenly in front of the older man. "You will take me to the site and you will help me get inside and then you can disappear again, I don't care. But you *will* do this for me."

Bolshakov looked into the hard eyes as his own gaze dissolved into tears. Yuri's expression did not change; his father did not expect it to. But he could no longer contain his own upset.

Yuri started to rise and Bolshakov grabbed his sleeve, held it tight.

"Nothing . . . nothing that you have said is incorrect," the older man sobbed. "And it may be that I deserved every word of it. But you have one advantage I did not possess. Hindsight. I would have traded myself for your mother, but I was not given that option. My only thought was to protect you, and that required money. Everything after that dark day—all of it was for you."

"You stayed away."

"So they could not find you. Your aunt changed her name at

great expense. I gave her almost everything I had. Even as she suffered the loss of her sister, you were her only concern."

Yuri glared at him. "And that is what you call 'hindsight,'" he said. "Here it is, Father. You chose that life. You got Mother killed. You forced me to hide. Your choices, your responsibility. I am sorry for you but I don't feel bad for you." He wrenched his arm free. "I am going to get the vehicle. Be downstairs in fifteen minutes." He rose and headed toward the door, turned back. "I'm sorry. That was the Bolshakov in me. Here is the Kochnev: 'Will you be downstairs in fifteen minutes?'"

Bolshakov nodded once and his son grabbed a shoulder bag and slammed the door behind him. Alone, the older man cried into his open palms, feeling the kind of shame only a son or father could inflict on one another. Not everything Yuri had said was as simple as he made it out to be. But that didn't matter. The hate— that was very real.

His shoulders heaving, Bolshakov released what he had kept inside for decades as he prayed quietly to the soul of his dead wife not just to forgive him but to give him guidance.

CHAPTER TWENTY-ONE

Evin Prison, Evin, Iran
July 2, 12:29 A.M.

When Evin Prison was built in 1972, it was designed to hold 320 prisoners—most of them political enemies of the shah. Here, they were incarcerated, tried, and disposed of in the execution courtyard—often on the same day, which was why the ruler did not need a large number of cells.

The number of persons incarcerated under the Islamic regime reached fifteen thousand at its height. The idea was to gather up everyone who did not support the Republic and keep them here until they did. The process not only stopped the depletion of useful citizens, the horrid conditions discouraged others from dissent.

The tactic was so popular at Evin and in nearby Qasr Prison that it was necessary to construct a third facility, *Fashafoyeh*, the Great Tehran Penitentiary, the central prison of Tehran. That lessened the crowding at Evin, allowing for the incarceration of not only dissenters but foreign troublemakers.

Having spent a week here, Dr. Parand Ghasemi actually

found the location in northwestern Tehran, at the base of the
Alborz Mountains, quite relaxing. When she wasn't making videos
in a cell, she had comfortable rooms adjoining the courthouse. A
cot had been set up for her, she had Wi-Fi and a computer, and
the judges' bathroom was down the hall, complete with a shower.

Not that any of that helped her with the work at hand. She
needed on-site photographs for that. After three years of contem-
plating, of research, of meetings, of planning, she hoped to have
them soon.

The woman looked at the time on her computer. It had been
six hours. She reached for the bottle of painkillers, shook out a
pair of tablets, slapped them in her mouth, and poured water from
a carafe. She swallowed carefully, since the tip of a lash had also
caught the front of her throat. Parand did not want to pop that
gauze bandage.

She shifted uncomfortably in the tall-backed wooden chair.
The doctor had redressed the cuts but the cushion she'd placed
there didn't entirely protect her back. It was her own fault she was
in pain, and she did not regret it: she was the one who had insisted
on being whipped. It gave the scenario plausibility, more than just
being held in front of a camera and threatened.

But the bloody beating made it difficult to sleep these past
few days. The cot itself was like an ancient instrument of torture,
a rack, where pain awaited. She preferred working and dozing in
the chair.

Fortunately, she found the work fully engaging. It was a
puzzle—or rather, a series of puzzles: what to bring on a long journey where you must travel relatively light, when you don't know

what you'll be required to do, and where your time might be extremely limited in an environment for which you have no description, other than that it is brutally cold and most likely quite dark. And, of course, she was learning Russian—the relevant words, the Cyrillic expression of the scientific language, the names of tools.

It was certainly unlike anything she had experienced in academia. And there was still the larger issue, of greater concern than *what* to do: what if they found nothing? What if her information had been wrong? How would she survive the prosecutor's disappointment, his embarrassment?

Her father had used to tell her, warn her, "*Those are the risks at the heights.*" He rose, but that was not his doing. He sought nothing. He instigated nothing. As his experience was needed, superiors came to him.

But to have no ambition was to be dead while alive, she thought. As the daughter of a Christian, her opportunities in Iran had been limited. Even though she did not practice the faith, the only way to rise in the Islamic Republic of Iran was to take bold chances like this one. She felt, she *believed*, that the prosecutor saw her as a patriot above all. If not, he would never have supported her plan.

Her plan.

Aware of the potential for failure, but with pride of ownership, Parand was the one who had initiated this operation. It had begun when she returned from the symposium in Moscow in 2015. Her superior, Dr. Sadeq Farhadi, had been there, too, and they worked together on a project that had been triggered by an offhanded comment by that cigar-smoking Cuban, the chatty old woman with the sun-leathered skin:

"They must still be out there, the other weapons," she had said. "I saw the manifests—the Russians hauled them around with no more concern than if they were sugarcane headed for winter storage."

There were just two Iranians in Cuba at the time, and they immediately got to work with the Russians trying to figure out just what the physicist had been referring to. They asked her, from time to time—without tipping their hand why they wanted to know—about Cuba's nuclear arrangement with the Soviet Union in the early 1960s. Finally, enough actionable information came together: Cuba had not been the only site where the Soviets placed a secret nuclear missile installation. The other was in the Arctic: an underground bunker containing two medium-range R-12 missiles with a range of 1,200 miles and two medium-range R-14 missiles with a range of 2,800 miles. All were armed with warheads containing plutonium-239.

"Good for twenty-four thousand years," Professor Christopher Pike once quipped at Oxford, "though for those of you into longer-term planning you might consider uranium-235, which has a half-life of nearly 704 million years."

Professor Pike had joked about it because all the commercial and military applications seemed either unrelentingly grim or preposterously dangerous. Yet there was an insatiable demand for both, and more—a demand that Pike and his team were helping the world to fill.

Parand reviewed her requisition list again. She had to find a way to make her own gear more compact since she would be flying commercially under an assumed identity, ostensibly to study the ongoing radiation leaks at Fukushima. The equipment she brought must be equitable with that assignment; she had to find things to leave behind—

But not now, she thought.

The oxycodone she had taken was starting to make her drowsy. Her chin came forward on her chest, her eyes shut, and her brain started to swirl with a blissful lack of focus.

Perhaps, she reflected, *it was good that all Iranians were unaware of these side effects, or there would be a nation of flagellants.*

The last thought Parand had was not of the mission but of her father, whom she hoped very much she would see again. . . .

CHAPTER TWENTY-TWO

Zagan, Poland
July 1, 10:40 P.M.

When the JSOC cell team leader Mike Volner was a kid, he used to watch his older cousin Elvis play Pac-Man at the local arcade. Elvis didn't mind bringing the boy along, since he was an orphan living with his maternal grandparents in the Germantown section of Philadelphia. It wasn't the safest of neighborhoods, then, and the sixteen-year-old high-school wrestler watched out for him.

It was always interesting but frustrating to watch the teenager play. Mike stood there, on the little stool that Elvis did not need to reach the controls . . . and he watched. Once in a while, when he had a quarter, Elvis would let him use it. He'd pick him up and help him manipulate the buttons. That was where the future military man first learned about teamwork.

For the twenty-nine-year-old, NATO drills were a lot like the Pac-Man games where he just watched—albeit, these games were like thousands of Pac-Mans being played at one time. This was the second year in a row that the alliance was putting on this kind of a massive display: eighty-eight tanks, 140 armored vehicles, and over three thousand troops moving across a field with temporary observation towers on four sides. The tower where Major Volner was an observer was stationed nearest the pummeling, thundering tank rounds of the "Iron Brigade" of the Fourth Infantry Division. To conceal their movements from drones as they moved toward an engagement, the tanks were covered with dark green foliage to hide them against the thick grasses and leaves of spring and summer. During the winter, when the last drills were conducted, white cloth had been slung around the tanks here and there so that, from above, they'd look like snowy fields.

The difference this year was that the simulations were not only occurring in warm weather, they were being conducted at night. That was in case the sneaky Russians decided to cross the border under cover of darkness. Moscow had recently survived a near-showdown in Ukraine of which Op-Center had been a part, which was the only reason an obscure officer like Volner had been invited.

"You have sex appeal," Chase Williams had told him when the Department of Defense had forwarded Volner's orders.

What Williams meant was that he was briefly a darling of the media, especially after taking down an assassin in New York. Sex appeal? That was not a phrase Volner applied to himself. Standing five feet ten inches tall and weighing a lean 160 pounds—none of which was body fat—the officer had short-cropped brown hair, brown eyes, and a serene bearing that came from his strong Lutheran faith.

The booming of the tanks roared over the relentless *phut-phut-phut* of the 25mm M242 chain gun and 7.62mm M240C machine guns of the Bradley Fighting Vehicles moving alongside. Volner listened to the tumult, observed the flashes, felt the explosions. Like Pac-Man, the drills were invigorating to start, then ultimately somewhat dull in their noisy patterns. It was muscle-flexing more than actual combat simulation, though it was probably useful to give the troops experience with live ammunition and a crowded field in darkness. Volner remembered a training drill at Fort Bragg where a Humvee containing Major General John Kuhl of the First Theater Sustainment Command ran over and into a deep foxhole while observing midnight maneuvers. His driver had been asked if he had problems seeing at night; he had never been asked if he'd driven through a field at night.

Beside Volner was a pair of much older Polish flag officers who were watching through night-vision goggles. Like the major, they were buttoned up in their best military uniforms; unlike their young American colleague, they were openly enjoying, and often reacting, to each pop and boom and magnesium-white burst on the field below.

Volner understood their enthusiasm . . . and relief. Over four years ago, when Putin seized the Crimea, the United States did not have any tanks in Europe. The situation was quickly remedied, which was one reason NATO was staging these displays: to discourage any further territorial grabs by the Russian leader. These career soldiers were potentially very much in the crosshairs.

And I have no doubt they grew up on stories from their parents or grandparents what happened the last time a dictator blitzkrieged his way into Poland, Volner thought.

The tower shook alarmingly as the Iron Brigade churned by.

They refrained from firing here as, in the dark, they executed masterful, very quick reversals.

The older man, a divisional general, turned to Volner, his long face and white moustache lit from above by the single, suspended light bulb. "You are not from mechanized," he said in fair English.

"No, sir," Volner replied.

"Do you know what we learned from Hitler and his invasion?" he asked. "That the tank must engage as a unified . . . ," he sought the right word, ". . . a unified *mechanism*. No individual deployment. That is especially so in the battlefield today because there is so much . . . real-time. Real-time information. The tank platoon must fight and communicate and shield, with its armor, the troops behind it. But," he said, turning back to the field, "each tank cannot survive on . . . on the plating, the armor, alone. The crews must understand the full scope of a fight. All around them. Above them. Below them, with mines. They must read the moments of quiet, the rising intensity, the slower pace, then faster. To do all of this at night—I am very proud of these people. Very proud."

And suddenly Volner was, too.

He had come here not wanting to get away from Bragg. After the killings in New York and Russia, he had just wanted to get back into his routine: preparedness drilling, survival training, field-testing new weapons. He hadn't wanted a long plane ride when he could *think* about those now-frozen moments when he looked at his targets, and his targets looked back, and the last thing that those targets would see in this world was the cold face of a man who had to take their lives. Volner's actions had saved lives. He would not have done anything differently. But it did not stop him from compulsively revisiting—*Hell, savoring?* he was forced to ask himself—the moment when his finger moved and a life was terminated. Drill instructors used to seem apologetic when they uttered the cliché, but it was true: each time you kill, there are two victims. The more the twenty-nine-year-old did *this*, remained an active duty officer with notches on his gun, the more he evolved into some other Mike Volner. He was not just older and more experienced, that was to be expected of any man. He became someone who was simultaneously, paradoxically, more than and less than other people . . . god and devil, both in one, with less and less in the mortal middle.

And here we are again, he chastised himself for revisiting every thought and emotion he had chewed and re-chewed since he left Bragg for Poland.

Volner turned his mind back to the war games. He raised his eyes from what was below to take in the entire field. It was a spectacle of fire and noise with a tactile component few people got to experience: the rumble of the floorboards, the heat of the explosions, the shock wave of the nearest blasts—a little too near in some cases, but that was what they were here for, to let the crews hone their skills. This was killing, too, but it was faceless. The simulation was not that different from the reality.

Stop! he told himself yet again.

He had two more days of this, then back to Bragg to begin preparing for what he was especially looking forward to, being part of an eight-week "mega-drill," scheduled to begin in mid-August.

Code-named Pacific Broadside, the "highly realistic" drill would involve special forces troops belonging to the Navy SEALs, the Marine Corps Special Operations Command, the Air Force Special Operations Command, and the Army Special Forces Command—the fabled Green Berets. These Special Operations Command commando teams would be air-dropped, at night, on the Hawaiian islands of Molokai and Lanai where they would be supported by 1,200 conventional military units culled primarily from the Army's Eighty-Second Airborne and the Marine Corps Expeditionary Units. SOCOM's stated goal was to explore new visions and tactics in warfare, which would involve everything from infiltration to extraction to assassination.

Of course, there was another saying he'd learned very early in his military career: "Fate does not favor the dreams and desires of the soldier." Volner himself had a saying at JSOC: "The world and Williams will always interfere."

With a crooked grin that was different from the big, proud smiles of the Polish officers, Volner's angel and demon made a private wager:

How much do you want to bet you don't get to go to Hawaii?

CHAPTER TWENTY-THREE

Op-Center Headquarters, Fort Belvoir North,
Springfield, Virginia
July 1, 4:49 P.M.

"The word you're looking for is 'nowhere.'"

Chase Williams did not say that with malice or even impatience; it was simply a fact.

He was standing in Aaron Bleich's office in the Geek Tank with Anne Sullivan, Paul Bankole, and Op-Center's operations director Brian Dawson. The three had just seen everything Bleich and Kathleen Hays had pulled together on the Ghasemis, the Bolshakovs, and Operation Anadyr.

"We're still working on Corps General Heydar Najafabadi," Bankole reminded his superior. "He was part of the Iranian team buying secondhand Russian guns for anti-Saddam Iraqis in 2001, and one of those suppliers may have been this man Bolshakov."

"Bolshakov did not deal internationally," Anne reminded him, looking at his tablet.

"He may have sold to Russians who sold to Tehran," Bankole said.

"All of that may be true," the director agreed, "but that doesn't tie these threads together now." He shook his head, not at the team but at the situation. "How is it possible that we know so little about so much?"

"Because we've gone digital on a world that was still largely analog," said Brian Dawson.

The forty-year-old operations director said it matter-of-factly, which was how the six-foot four-inch charmer said everything. Nonetheless, the former West Pointer and Fifth Special Forces Group commander had the training and field experience to be taken very, very seriously.

"Anyone have a suggestion as to next steps?" Williams asked.

"Kathleen is going through digitized newspaper microfilm files now," Bleich said. "She's looking for anything on the Russian or that Cuban physicist."

Williams sighed. It wasn't a criticism; it was a logical step. But it was most likely a very, very small step. Anne looked at Williams with her every-scrap-helps expression but he wasn't buying. It was why they made a good pair at the top: impulse and patience in balance. Right now, though, Williams did not like the idea that he felt—*felt*, did not know for sure—that Tehran had time to play a waiting game but Washington did not. Despite the efforts of four top officials, there was no guarantee they'd gotten any useful information from General Ghasemi. A stalemate made it a win for Iran.

"How about—" Dawson said, thinking aloud, "—how about bringing General Ghasemi here?"

The four other people crowded into the office stood quite still. It appeared, to Dawson, as if he'd triggered some kind of conservation of energy equation: the body must not move so the brain can.

"What does that get us?" Anne asked.

"Ghasemi's reaction to something unexpected," Dawson said.

"I like it," Bankole added thoughtfully. He looked at the others. "If the general's here to defect, as he says, then this will just be another place he's being shuffled to, held, interviewed at. But if he's here to try and figure out what we know or suspect, how we work, he may be as inquisitive as we are."

"It's not bad," Williams agreed.

"You realize that January Dow would come with," Anne pointed out.

"We get along fine," Williams said.

"That's not what I meant. She's going to leap at that opportunity."

"I know," Williams said. "First, let's see if we can make it happen. Brian?"

"Sure. So who do I ask, Dow or Harward?" Dawson asked.

"January's got jurisdiction," Williams said. "Call her, sell it. Harward won't oppose her."

Dawson hurried off. The rest of the group left the Tank, Bankole following Dawson, Anne and Williams walking together.

"She'd be the first outsider to come here," Anne said.

"I know."

"Even Paul Hood kept the doors locked when he ran the show."

"I know that, too. Maybe it's overdue."

"We are invisible for a reason, Chase."

"Budget," Williams said. "What they don't know, they can't downsize."

"That's right. I know you don't like to think about these things, but January and Allen Kim and all our other associates are fishing for bucks in the same shrinking pond. She will look for fat."

"Are we fat?"

"You know we aren't, but she'll ask for a tour, find nits to pick. It'll become uncontested truth from one end of town to the other."

"And we'll stay above it," Williams said. "As long as we deliver, no one will touch us. If we don't deliver, then we deserve to be touched."

"You know, sometimes I really hate your sense of fairness. This is not the military where there are codes and ethics."

Williams stopped in front of his office and looked down at her. "It isn't just the military, Anne. Honor is us, it's America— the one I know and love. I didn't get that from the Navy. 'Always do right. This will gratify some people and astonish the rest' and 'If you tell the truth, you don't have to remember anything.'" He grinned. "They're both Mark Twain quotes and I learned them in junior high. I figured if they were good enough for the author of *Tom Sawyer*, they were good enough for me."

The deputy director made a face. "'And you, *Señor* Quixote, will take such a beating. . . .' I don't remember what part of Cervantes that's from, and I'm probably paraphrasing, but Washington is a windmill that keeps on spinning, fast and hard."

"All of which is good to keep in mind, and I hope you'll continue warning me when I should duck. In the meantime," he said, glancing down at his buzzing smartphone, "it looks like we'll be saddling up."

CHAPTER TWENTY-FOUR

FBI Academy, Marine Corps Base, Quantico, Virginia
July 1, 5:30 P.M.

"Long haul, sir?"

The sentry saluted Allen Kim as he pulled his Prius up to Gate 4, the back gate of the base. The comment was a pleasantry; the young woman already knew the answer to that question. Scanning the sticker on his windshield to check him out, she had seen that he had not left since the small hours of that morning. She did not know that his early visit had been to convey General Ghasemi to the base; that was need-to-know. The Iranian had simply been listed as "Guest A" on the pass, which Kim had signed. The scanner showed that "Guest A" was still on-premises.

"Have a good night, sir," she said as her companion inside the booth raised the bar.

Kim nodded pleasantly as he drove into the still-warm daylight. He kept the window down, allowing the scent of the new foliage to waft in as he turned onto U.S. 1 toward historic Dumfries. He wanted the traditional group hug from his wife and six-year-old son and the vegan dinner—complete with details about his wife's day in the EPA press office, and his son's latest efforts to conform to the first grade—followed by something light on TV, then early bed. As he'd climbed into his car, he'd received a screaming text from Harward that Chase Williams had asked January Dow to bring General Ghasemi over to Op-Center for the next phase of questioning; Kim had texted back that he was all for it:

`If nothing else we get tomorrow off`

That was true, and welcome, and Harward wasn't amused. With only Dow having a reason to accompany Ghasemi to Op-Center, Harward was out of the circuit. Kim himself didn't care; he was a long-time colleague of Roger McCord, had been to Op-Center, and shared domestic intel with the group. Even if Williams and his team were just spitballing, they did it better than anyone in the intelligence business. He was damned curious to see what Williams and his team would come up with.

So simple, the young man thought. *And smart.* During this first session, Quantico had been neutral territory for the main interrogators and their subject. His team and Dow's behind-the-scenes advisors hadn't come up with anything here, nothing to "crack the safe," as the FBI put it. *Give yourself a home court advantage and change the dynamics.*

Traffic was typically light along this stretch and Kim punched up his iPhone. Dixieland jazz . . . Al Hirt. That and the breeze and the scents and the sunlight flashing through the white pine and white oak should keep his tired eyes open and alert—

Kim heard the crack and felt the hot whizz under his nose and saw a gouge appear in his dashboard, all at the same time. His reflexes processed "gunshot" before his brain did. As one, his foot crushed the gas pedal, he shrunk as low as he could and he leaned to the passenger's side—the last two to create as low a profile as possible, as he'd been trained to do.

A second shot slammed into the window on the passenger's side, blowing shards in all directions. Kim's brain finally took control and he swerved to the side of the road, jammed on the brake, and put the car in park. He flopped on the seat, on the glass, reached into his blazer, and pulled a new 9mm Sig Sauer P320 duty pistol from the shoulder holster. He knew that he was being targeted by a rifle from the north; he did not know if that was the only weapon. He lay there as a third bullet *thunked* into the driver's side door; as soon as it hit, he risked reaching up and grabbing his phone, which was incongruously playing "Sugar Lips." He did not bother calling 911; as cars behind him screeched to a stop, he called Gate 4.

"Deputy Director Kim, under fire," he said sharply when they answered. "Three shots, sniper—north side of US1, quarter mile east of back gate."

"Shots heard, sir, CIRG teams on their way," the guard replied.

The Critical Incident Response Group unit was the rapid-deployment unit in that quadrant. He had overseen some of their training. They were good and they were fast.

"Are you injured, sir?" the guard asked.

"No—not sure if intentional or lucky."

He was trying to provide as much information as possible in case he died here. Forensically, every detail was potentially vital.

As he spoke, Kim heard a chopper take off behind the southern tree line and race toward him, undoubtedly in support of the ground team. The Bell 407 flew to the left of the car, over the trees; about a minute later he heard the vans come to a stop from behind and ahead—the latter having exited by the main gate. He heard the shouts of the agents as they emerged on the southern side of their vehicles. Kim prayed this wasn't an ambush by someone who knew the FBI's response pattern; he didn't think so, since it was all Marine property east of his position.

Agents, crouching low, came along the side of his car.

"Can you pop the lock, sir?" someone asked after trying the handle.

It was incongruous that a Prius safety feature held back the CIRG team. Kim was facing in that direction and cracked the door. One agent pulled it open and helped him out on his belly. Another rose slightly, inserted the barrel of an MP5 submachine gun through the broken window, and sited the opposite side of the street. As he emerged, Kim saw agents behind the trunk and hood doing the same.

When he was on the ground, the agent who had pulled him out examined him for wounds. One of the agents manning the hood reported that Kim was safe and apparently not seriously injured. It was only when he heard the "not seriously," and noticed the agent quickly examining him, that Kim realized his chest was spattered with blood—most likely from the glass.

Kim knew that the goal would be to extract him back to the

base for a more complete medical checkup, but that would not be done until the area had been secured. And that could not be done until the sweep of the forest had been completed using high resolution and thermal aerial scans. A second chopper joined the search, though none of their crosstalk came through the agent's radio. While they waited, that agent had kept a gloved hand flat on Kim's shoulder to make sure he stayed where he was—but also to reassure him. He knew that tactic, too. After events like this, individuals were frequently in a mild-to-severe state of post-traumatic stress. The physical presence of another human being, especially one who had rescued them, was extraordinarily healing.

By now, Kim could see the flashing lights of police cars that had sealed the road and joined in the hunt for a sniper. It was about fifteen or twenty minutes before the agents moved from behind the car and across the street. An EMT team arrived to confirm the agent's initial assessment, after which Kim was moved to a gurney and into an ambulance.

"My phone," he said, before they took him away.

One of them went and retrieved it from the front seat of the Prius.

It was only then that Kim began to consider, in earnest, who had been shooting at him, why—and whether it had in fact been their intention to miss. He had rarely been involved in any high-profile matters, and no one other than Ghasemi had been interrogated at Quantico for over a year.

Someone had to have seen me bring him in, or at least seen the car, he realized. *Someone who had been in that very spot since early this morning.*

The only call Kim made from the ambulance was to his wife, Eva, who would have heard about the gunfire outside the base and would have been concerned. He waited until he was at the Marine infirmary before he sent a text to Roger McCord:

```
That was me being shot at. Let's talk.
```

CHAPTER TWENTY-FIVE

Anadyr, Russia
July 2, 10:44 A.M.

It was fitting that in this frigid, crystalline-ice region of the world, that time should be frozen as well.

Yuri had been gone for nearly an hour before calling up and telling his father to join him in front of the hotel. Once Bolshakov and his son left the town center, the world outside the modern, olive-green Ulyanovsk UAZ-452 off-road van looked little different than it had when the old man had viewed them through young eyes. The flat, two-lane road had a name now, Kolkhoznaya Street, and it was paved now—though the road retained the boundaries established by the convoy whose wheels had defined it in 1962. The landscape, too, still had its flat, earthy sameness, an unchanging mixture of rock, frozen brown soil, and lifeless dark green moss that somehow survived on sunlight and ice.

After picking up the van, Yuri had resumed his stubborn silence. Maybe it was punitive, heartfelt, or both, but Bolshakov was determined to at least try and find a way around it.

"I am going to talk," Bolshakov said. "You need not listen,

of course, but we have an hour's ride ahead of us and I'd rather have words rattling around in my head. For instance—I will talk to you as someone who himself had a military career. If the weapons were left behind, it was because someone intended to claim them going forward. That is how things were in the Soviet Union, at the end. Everyone hiding things." He made tiny, mole-like digging motions with his hands. "But so much time passing . . . 'Why now?' I ask myself. And the Konstantin Bolshakov who answers is the one you detest. The answer is: 'Someone wants them. More to the point, someone wants to *purchase* them.' And that raises the question: 'Why is the GRU involved?' The answer to which would be: 'Because the military, even if it is aware of this, cannot be involved.'"

Yuri did not react to his father's monologue. He lit another cigarette.

"Perhaps you know this, but the GRU ran more rogue operations, more assassinations, than I or any—"

"Stop!" Yuri shouted.

"Why?" his father asked. "If it upsets you, let me out, right here. Continue to your destination—you have a general idea where it is and I'm sure you can figure out how to open it." He unwound his scarf as sunlight warmed the van on top of the purr of the heater. "Since you arrived, I have tried to be sensitive to what you went through, what you are still feeling. I don't discount any of it. But not everything I did was sinful."

"Compared to what?" Yuri barked. "You sold death. It brought death to our family."

"If I hadn't done it, someone else would have. I know, that's not a justification. But it is an explanation. You judge me with hindsight. Then, the future was uncertain. We did not know what would replace the Soviet Union, whether Russia would stand. In my mind was a scheme, a larger plan: if the military conducts a coup, what chance do the people have? None, unless they had weapons."

"Oh, now you became an arms dealer out of patriotism?"

"Nothing is clean, Yuri. Nothing is ever just one thing arising from one cause."

Bolshakov felt it was a personal triumph when Yuri did not respond to that. The older man took a breath, sat back, said no more. He felt—or at least hoped—that a low, low base camp had been established on a very high mountain. For the first time that day he felt he'd achieved *something*.

The countryside rolled on, the Gulf of Anadyr sparkling behind Yuri. Beyond the gulf was the Bering Sea and past that—America. It had been such a mystery to Bolshakov back then. Alaska, Canada, the United States. The enemy.

In a way, he had been convinced, the way Yuri was, that something was monolithic in its monstrosity. Now, whether it was age and wisdom or the relative ease with which international news was available, or both, things were no longer so clear. He remembered the Voice of America broadcasts, which were heard in Russia in 1947 and were discussed in town—quietly, since Stalin had ears everywhere. While Bolshakov was stationed here, officers would listen to it for a laugh. Americans were not as good at propaganda as the Soviets were. Maybe because they did not have the interests of the people at heart, only the interests of their *interests*.

But things were no longer so clear. Or rather—and perhaps this was the case with Yuri when he was younger, lost, angry—things were clearer when someone else made the decisions, crafted the policy.

Bolshakov had intended to ask about family members whom Yuri might still be in touch with. His aunt and uncle were gone, that much he knew. But there were cousins, and a branch of the family in Lithuania. He must have been curious enough to look them up.

Not now, Bolshakov had already decided. *Let it all rest now.*

Sections of the coastline had fallen away over the years, eroded by freezing and refreezing. Most of that had tumbled into the gulf where it was washed away. In some places, the road passed within just a few meters of a sheer drop without a guard rail to protect them. A few areas had been scooped out as small jetties for naval ships—now long gone. Only the rock and hardened soil and a few rotted moorings remained. It seemed curious to him that the navy had carried construction materiel and the missiles themselves from Anadyr, but then he remembered that while there were no flyovers then, American submarines routinely plied these waters. They might very well have seen, and heard, and gleaned what was going on.

Bolshakov was certain that if he opened the window the smell of the air would take him back, the intervening years would vanish. He wished he knew the great Russian novelists and poets. They would have had thoughts, lines, perspectives for what he was suddenly feeling. It was much more than he'd felt in Anadyr, where much had changed. This was exactly as it had been.

After a long, straight ride the coast curved outward roughly two hundred yards to form a mini-peninsula. Erosion had taken the stone seawall but old concrete barricades about four feet high remained upright on all four sides. Brittle-looking barbed wire was strung along the top, some of it sagging over the edges. Here and there hardy vines had managed to ascend to the top. A single wide path broke from the main road and ran up the center of the artificial finger of land. Once there had been gravel on the roadway; it was gone and the road was deeply rutted. Whatever signage had once stood here had fallen and been carried off by the winds.

Yuri slowed as they approached. "Yes?" he asked.

"Yes," his father replied almost reverently as he looked out. "Was this how I looked to you today? A ruin?"

Unexpectedly, something approaching a half smile touched Yuri's lips but he said nothing. Bolshakov took that, too, as a little victory.

An iron bar, once emphatically yellow and red striped, now mostly rust, lay across the entrance to the road. Bolshakov noticed dozens of pockmarks in it and in the stanchion that supported it.

Target practice, he knew.

Signs and abandoned structures were often used by locals not just for shooting but to express displeasure with the government. So far from Moscow, the northern and northeastern regions had never been fully engaged in the Soviet Union. This was one way to show it.

Yuri parked a few feet away, in a clutch of grasses that half concealed the car from the road. He looked around. They had not passed another car for miles, and there was no sound but the wind.

"Tempting booty, out here," Bolshakov said, looking around the isolated spot.

Yuri walked to the front of the vehicle. He used a pocket knife to push down on the pin in the valve stem of the two tires, then did the same in the rear.

"You have a pump," Bolshakov said knowingly.

Yuri retrieved a key ring from his shoulder bag and got out. The cold sea air was a shock, white puffs of breath coming rapidly as the young man raised his collar against the chill and walked with audibly crunching steps toward the gate. The earth was not soft, despite the summer thaw; but it wasn't as slippery as it would have been two months earlier. Removing a large padlock, Yuri swung the single, thick bar outward, the solid tip clearing the front fender by only two or three inches.

He has a good eye, his father thought proudly.

Yuri returned, pulled the van in, the flattened tires lumping, then got out and locked the gate behind him.

"Are you afraid of trespassers—or are we staying?" Bolshakov asked.

As he drove ahead, the younger man jerked his head toward the back of the long van. "There are groceries and bedrolls."

The road turned slightly toward one side of the narrow strip of land. To their right was a long, narrow stretch of heavy rocks piled layer upon layer. Bolshakov remembered this well. That was where they had made the excavation to lower the missiles inside. The area had been covered with a large canvas tent and the missiles and warheads had been brought over in trucks, in pieces, to be assembled below. When they were finished, a foot of concrete was poured over a metal and wood framework. Once that had hardened, boulders were brought over by bulldozers. After that, the only way in or out was by a long, vertical passageway, which was covered by a heavy iron door.

There were two other iron doors set in the ground, both of them round, like manholes. Bolshakov could no longer see them but he knew well where they were. Those were the covers on the two silos and they could only be opened by explosive bolts triggered from inside the silo. Two keys were required for each detonation. At the time, after the construction crews had left and there were just Rear Admiral Merkassov and his small crew, all three doors bore the ironic label: bomb shelter. In case anyone happened by, they would naturally presume the more common meaning.

"You know, I'm sure, about the safeguard," Bolshakov said.

"The interior door won't open unless the hatch is locked," Yuri replied. "We have that information. Behind the interior door, however—all that information has been lost."

Because the rear admiral burned the blueprints, as did his counterpart in Moscow, Bolshakov thought. Neither man was reckless. The fact that they left the missiles behind, disassembled, was evidence of that. The two warheads were not documented, anywhere. To have brought them from here, decades later, would have invited them to fall into the hands of arms dealers. Bolshakov knew that because for all the times he had been asked to acquire nuclear material, he had never once mentioned this place. In its own perverse way, he had always taken that as a good deed—

even as he was selling Kalashnikovs to diamond smugglers in Volgograd. His justification was that the South Africans were no better than the émigrés from Kazakhstan and for all he cared they could shoot each other into oblivion—

The van stopped with a little skid, which Yuri handled adroitly on the deflated tires that helped minimize slippage. Once again, that told his father that he was accustomed to more than just Moscow's icy streets, which were quickly and thoroughly plowed. The young man got out and his father followed. The ground was a little muddy here; this close to the water, the salty sea mist prevented it from freezing, even at night. That sea air, that throaty mud smell, the unchanged horizon all took Bolshakov back.

Yuri had his key case out. He had turned a shoulder to the stiffer wind as they walked to the bent-over grasses that described a perfectly circular bare patch in the middle. Bolshakov remembered the rear admiral having planted them so that the hatch would not be visible from the road. They were knee-high and covered the little peninsula, then. Now they were beaten down and spotty, no longer golden but deathly pale. Yuri stepped over them and waited for his father. Bolshakov had paused to clear away a patch of tawny scrub.

"We'll want to breathe," his father said as he cleared a vent.

Yuri nodded. "I was told I could lift this," he said, looking down.

"We used two men," Bolshakov replied. "So should you."

Yuri looked up. The oblique offer to help once again drew the hint of a half smile—fleeting but present.

Squatting, Yuri slipped a large key into the opening, between two handles. It entered halfway. It took a pocket knife and several tries before he could work through the collected, crusted grime, but Yuri eventually got the key inside and the lock turned with squeaking disagreeability. . . .

CHAPTER TWENTY-SIX

Op-Center Headquarters, Fort Belvoir North,
Springfield, Virginia
July 1, 6:20 P.M.

"Either the sniper was a really awful shot," Paul Bankole was saying to Chase Williams and Anne Sullivan, "or he didn't intend to kill Allen Kim."

The three were in Williams's office; except for stepping outside the building to get a minute of sun and air, he felt like something of an automaton, wet-wired to the world through this place. For a man accustomed to being out in the field, it was the one part of this job he truly disliked.

"Kim suspects that whoever took the shots recognized the car," Bankole went on. "The shooter also had to have known that Ghasemi wasn't in there since the window was open and there was no vehicular entourage."

"You referred to the shooter as 'he,' not 'they,'" Anne remarked.

"The three shots came from the same rifle," Bankole told her. "It was a Nakhjir sniper rifle—a knockoff of the Russian Dragunov.

And there was only one set of footprints out there leading to a path where they vanish. No security cameras out there."

"So the spot was carefully selected and the shooting was a message," Williams said. "Saying what?"

"On the surface, an Iranian was telling us not to help Ghasemi or next time the shots wouldn't miss," Bankole said. "But I'm not buying it."

"Why?" Anne asked.

"Because how did they even know Ghasemi was there? How did he know to watch Quantico?"

"They may have been watching all likely locations," Anne said. "Jim Wright reports that thirty-six hours ago there was a big uptick of people coming and going at Pakistan's embassy, folks we ID'ed as members of the Interests Section of the Islamic Republic of Iran based there."

Jim Wright was the domestic crisis manager, former FBI, and a close friend of both McCord and Kim. One of his responsibilities was to keep track of the comings and goings of hostile personnel from embassies and the nations harbored therein with which Washington has no official diplomatic relations.

"Watching several facilities suggests standard operating procedure," Anne said. "Whereas . . ."

"If they only watched Quantico, then they had to know where we were taking the general," Williams said.

"And we would have known they knew, meaning there's a leak," Bankole added.

Williams looked from Anne to Bankole. "When Ghasemi gets here, we're going to ask him about that. And we're going to ask January what access he has had to any devices."

"You think he's a plant," Anne said.

"I haven't a clue," Williams admitted. "All I know is that the Iranians like to chew up resources by wearing them down on the wrong target. They tied us up in Iraq and Syria and Afghanistan, consumed countless hours and personnel by forcing us to deal with improvised explosive devices instead of the Taliban or ISIS. And the IEDs themselves forced us to move slower. General Ghasemi could be all of that in one person."

"But there could be a twist here," Bankole said. "He could be exactly what he says he isn't. A spy."

"'The Purloined Letter,'" Anne said. Off the questioning looks of the others she explained, "Classic Edgar Allan Poe story about everyone searching for a letter with compromising information. The whole time it was out in the open, in a card rack. Same thing here—hide in plain sight. The general tells us his mission, the one he supposedly scrapped, then fulfills it anyway."

Bankole shook his head. "We don't know that. The sniper may have gotten the information some other way."

"Not through ELINT," Anne said. "Pakistan's Attaché Defense Procurement Bhutta has assured the DoD that Tehran only has personnel at the embassy, nothing more."

"And they believe him because . . . ?" Bankole asked.

"He is Punjabi, wisely mistrusts Iran, and wants naval upgrades from the U.S."

Williams sighed. "All right. We've got"—he looked at his computer—"about an hour until January gets here with our guest. Anne, make sure Aaron and Kathleen stick around, and let's make certain Jim and Brian are available."

"I don't know that we'll have a lot of time," Anne told them. "January said the general hasn't gotten much sleep."

Williams considered that for a moment, then replied, "I don't think we'll need a lot of time."

"You have an idea?" she asked.

"Working on one," he replied.

Anne knew better than to press the director; when he had something to share, he would do so. She also did not see Williams and Bankole exchange a look, one that was charged with decades of hard-won military experience—and wisdom. There were two schools of thought about sleep deprivation. First, the traditional and obvious view, that it lowered the resistance of prisoners undergoing interrogation. But the second, more modern view—espoused by trained military psychologists—was that it was easier to determine when a rested captive was lying or probing for information himself. One could see the captive listening. What they responded to, what made them alert, what made them leave one topic and go to another—all were valuable indicators of what an enemy knew or suspected. Both men also knew there were third, fourth, and fifth approaches. Torture was frowned upon in Washington, if not elsewhere on the globe. Two rounds of waterboarding or electric shock, a few hours apart, and information would flow. If the prisoner were lying, they rarely remembered what they said to make the torture stop and invariably told two different stories. If they were telling the truth, the stories were the same. Neither Williams nor Bankole had ever gone that route—not for the sake of a prisoner but for their own postwar state of mind. Combat was dehumanizing enough without adding willful abuse to the list of activities branded on their souls.

Psychoactive drugs were a fourth option, but the data recovered was often disjointed falling into narrow windows of opportunity between three categories: cloudiness, calmness, or amnesia. Initial dosages varied from person to person and the effects lingered in the system, making subsequent injections even less reliable.

But there was the fifth option, and with that last remark Williams had just let Bankole know he might be willing to take it.

"Anne, I'm going to go see Aaron," Williams said, already heading out the door.

"Anything in particular you're looking for?"

"I need him to find me something," he replied. "Let me know when the chopper touches down."

Anne looked at Bankole who wore a search-me expression as he followed the director out, headed to his own office. Anne lingered a moment to check on both Ghasemi and the status of Roger McCord's trip to Cuba. Ghasemi was being transferred by helicopter, not only in the interest of time but for the sake of security. Until the Quantico shooter was found, watches would be placed along the roadway to secure traffic going to and from the base. Matt Berry had been able to get McCord on a diplomatic flight leaving from Reagan International at eight P.M. The United States was making two trips daily, firming political and economic ties with the island nation. Though McCord would have to wait for his paperwork to be emailed over, at least he would be in the country.

As she headed back to her own office, Anne thought of another Poe story that suddenly seemed relevant: "The Murders in the Rue Morgue," also featuring sleuth C. Auguste Dupin. This one was about a bank clerk who is interrogated for crimes to which he has no connection, other than knowing the two victims. The same might be true with the general.

But it was also true that the work they did here demanded several different approaches to a problem, which spoke to the point about the resources consumed by intelligence operations. One reason Chase Williams had proven to be such an effective force here—*and the bête noire of bureaucrats elsewhere*, she thought—is that whatever he came up with invariably cut through a lot of budget-swelling, effort-duplicating waste, and achieved what they were all here to do:

Protect the nation.

CHAPTER TWENTY-SEVEN

SIGINT Base, Lourdes, Cuba
July 1, 7:17 P.M.

Adoncia Bermejo was always extremely happy when she was able to apply the principles of her work to daily life. That used to happen a lot, with Castro—particular Newtonian physics such as a military action against them creating an equal and opposite reaction or nature abhorring a vacuum—typically an open space that proved too tempting to Batista's soldiers.

In nuclear physics, fission was the splitting of an atomic nucleus into lighter nuclei, thus emitting energy. Today, her unexpected guest Enrich Sanjulian was about to allow another foundational concept to be put to use.

Pulling on a kerchief and leaving the apartment after an hour, she walked through along the side of the building away from where the fire had been. The concrete sidewalk and adjoining grasses were wet with runoff from the infrequently used hoses that did not fit very well on old, rusted hydrants. The air had the taste of charred wood and burned paper: the smoke had begun to settle to the ground carrying the odor of the most combustible materials with it. She covered her mouth with the neckerchief—odd, she thought, given how much she loved cigars and yet found a similar smell so unpleasant. She passed the parking lot where she kept her old Rambler.

Adoncia's destination was a small office that still had the old sign that read *JUNTA DE PLANIFICACIÓN CENTRAL* above the door. Even though that central planning board had been dismantled in 1993, there was nostalgia for everything-Revolutionary among the small team of Lourdes's Cuban managers. So the sign stayed. And it still applied: anything that was needed from Havana, by Russian or Cuban workers, was sent through this office.

"Good evening, Chano," she said as she greeted the sixty-two-year-old clerk. "Exciting day."

His expression told her he would have been happier not to have to fill out forms on his laptop—a daunting enough task for someone who disliked paperwork in general, more when it wasn't on paper at all.

"Is there something you need, Dr. Bermejo?" he asked impatiently. "I have to requisition—it's too much to explain," he decided. "But we need upgrades in our equipment."

"So the little rivers told me," she said.

It took him a moment to understand, part of that distraction because he hadn't stopped typing. "Not just the hydrants and hoses but what was burned. They're still sending me emails."

"Then I won't keep you long," she said. "I need a pass for someone to visit."

Chano Rodriguez was immediately wary. It was his job to be careful. "Who?"

"You must not tell anyone if I tell you," she said.

He stopped typing. "Who?" he repeated. Now he was more interested than wary.

"Alberto Guevara." She waited for the name to register before adding, "A cousin."

If there were a sign of the cross for heroes of the Revolution, Chano would have made it. Instead, he just continued to stare. "I didn't know he had surviving family."

"Few do," she replied. "Which is why I'm reluctant to ask for this but he wishes to see me and as you know he cannot enter—"

"He can, and will," Chano said. "I will call the sentry. But only if you permit me to meet him."

"I will try to arrange that for you," she said. "He is extremely protective of his kinship."

"Of course, I understand," Chano said. "What time?" he asked as he picked up the landline and punched in the number.

"I am going out to get him at the bus station in about a half hour."

Chano made the call, referring to the individual only as "a very distinguished visitor," then actually thanked Adoncia for having made him a part of the great story—"Even a little bit," as he put it.

Adoncia thanked him and allowed him to return to his work. As she walked back to the apartment, she thought, *And just like that, a new Guevara, a lighter nucleus, has been created.* Now all she had to do to get Enrich out was use some of that released energy to manipulate the guard.

As darkness fell, she put on jeans and pulled on a gray fleece vest—more to hold cigars than to protect her skinny frame from the chill sea air. Then she drove her car to the street in front of her apartment and Enrich got into the backseat. He had put on the woman's raincoat—which was too small, but looked all right in the shadows, worn over his shoulders. Then she lit a cigar.

"The boy will know me," Enrich said. "He sees me every day."

"That is why you are in the back. As long as he doesn't look, we are okay."

"Russians are still out searching," he said as he peered into the darkness.

"And they will be looking after we are gone," she said confidently.

Adoncia steered the short distance to the gate, which was just east of the field where she had been walking earlier in the day. *Was it just today?* It was a new iron gate beside an older wooden guardhouse. Except for Wi-Fi, the latter not been had been upgraded in over sixty years.

The young guard in a sharp blue uniform, Mauricio, seemed perplexed when she stopped. "Doctor, I was told you would be *arriving* with a guest who was to be welcomed discreetly."

"Clearly, that is not correct," she said, patiently blowing smoke. "Chano was very busy when I saw him—things have been going on, yes?"

"Yes," the man agreed.

"What he had *meant* to say was that I would be *leaving* with a distinguished guest. Please let us pass—we are late."

The young man seemed confused. "But how and when did he get here, then? I am required to check him out against the entry log."

"He came this afternoon, during the fire." She picked up her cell phone. "Mauricio, we are in a hurry. Do you want me to phone Chano and clarify?"

"I will, if you don't mind," the young man said contritely, turning toward the booth. "It is my job, you know." He reached for the phone on the small desk that sat against the opposite wall.

"Hold a moment!" Adoncia snapped. "You have a flashlight?"

He turned. "Of course."

"Get it."

"Doctor?"

"I said bring it here! Shine it on the face of royalty, into the eyes of a Guevara. An old friend and fellow Revolutionary who, after having dined with me to discuss how we will honor the fiftieth anniversary of the *murder* of his cousin—who I am now bringing to the residence of the president of the Council of State. Let your light illuminate your own indiscretion and see if you *ever* leave this guard booth, Mauricio. *Ever!*"

The young man had one hand on the powerful flashlight that sat on the desk, and the other hand still on the phone. He also had a mother, grandmother, and great-grandmother, all just like this woman. He peered into the darkness of the car, hesitated, then turned back to the door and pressed a button and the metal arm swung up.

"Please forgive me," he said. "A mistake, surely. I—I have been on duty since this morning. I am not thinking clearly . . . did not understand."

Adoncia bit the cigar to express her indignation and drove on. As she turned onto the small main road, steering around a vegetable stand in the back of a truck half on the grass, half on the road, she heard Enrich's labored breathing in back.

"I would have run, but I was too afraid to move," he said. "How will you go back, now? He will talk."

"I do not think so," she said. "He will log my departure with a guest who had been validated by Chano Rodriguez. Chano will never check. If he asks me, I will tell him we had a wonderful visit."

"You are incredible," Enrich said. "I owe you . . . as much as the nation owes you," he added, when he couldn't think of anything less than majestic to apply to this woman.

Her own heart was beating hard. Adoncia had not experienced that kind of excitement for a very long time—and fittingly against a Cuban figure of authority. It was an incomparable feeling, and she would not have missed this for anything

She drove the man into town, which was a loosely defined suburb of Havana that had grown up around the SIGINT station. There were police outside the room he rented on Mantua, so they couldn't go there for his belongings.

"I'll tell you what," she said. "We'll drive on to Havana proper where we will pick up a few things and you can leave by bus. I wouldn't go to family—when you don't report for work, they will check."

"I used to work at a hotel in Guardalavaca," he said. "The owner liked me—I will go there."

"Fine, fine," she said. "Clothes, bus ticket, then a quiet meal, eh?"

All he could do was thank her as they set off on the short

drive to the north. She had finished the cigar and, tossing it from the window, pulled another from her vest pocket. She lit a match with her thumbnail and lit it triumphantly.

It felt good to be back on the side of the angels.

CHAPTER TWENTY-EIGHT

Op-Center Headquarters, Fort Belvoir North,
Springfield, Virginia
July 1, 7:34 P.M.

"Sorry I'm late," Chase Williams announced as he strode into his own office. "General, it's good to see you again," he added, barely pausing to shake the man's hand.

With Williams's okay, Anne had decided to bring General Ghasemi and January Dow there instead of the small conference room. Simply exchanging one conference room for another was not good tactics, encouraged similar patterns simply to repeat themselves. And that was not what anyone at Op-Center wanted.

Paul Bankole and Anne were present, along with the general and a visibly unhappy January. Ghasemi was drinking the water Anne had provided; January was seated beside him, on the sofa, her crossed leg impatiently tapping to some unheard beat.

Williams shut the door behind him. He did not go behind his desk but leaned on the edge only a few feet from the sofa. Anne was standing on the other end of the room. She shook her head slowly, once. Bankole was in an armchair across from Ghasemi.

"I was getting an update about a Dr. Sadeq Farhadi," Williams said. He was looking squarely at Ghasemi. "Do you know him, General?"

"I have never even heard this name."

"He works with your government's international counterintelligence division. You know them?"

"I know the department—"

"The team Dr. Farhadi works with tags individuals with low-level radiation so Tehran can track them. You've never heard of anything like that?"

"No, Mr. Williams."

"You never met him?"

"Not that I am aware."

"He knows your daughter."

Ghasemi did not immediately respond.

"General?" Williams said.

"I'm sorry, I was thinking," Ghasemi said. "I know very few of my daughter's friends, and I cannot recall meeting any of her colleagues."

"All right," Williams said. "The sniper who fired at Allen Kim. What can you tell us about him?"

"Also, nothing." He added, "I was as deeply disturbed as everyone else. I like Mr. Kim."

"Did you ever work with snipers?"

Ghasemi was quiet again and January's leg stopped moving. Anne smiled to herself. She didn't know what the opening salvo regarding the Iranian doctor had been about, but this was good. If Ghasemi answered no, he'd most likely be lying. An Iranian officer in Iraq would have exactly that kind of experience. If the general answered yes, he would open a line of questioning where there was little room to fudge, any lie would be detected.

"I have," he replied.

"Will you provide us with names, units, weapons so that we can see if any of them have come through our airports?"

Ghasemi hesitated. "I'll do my best."

Williams reached around and picked up his own tablet, thumbed it from slumber. He handed it to the general.

"It will take time," Ghasemi said.

"Whatever you can do, and while you think I'd like to ask you—why would anyone have wanted to intimidate Kim?"

January rose suddenly. "Chase, can I see you outside?"

Williams didn't move and the two or three seconds of stalemate were, to the others, like a world war. The woman suddenly understood why. She quickly added, "While the general thinks."

"Sure," Williams said, and left with her.

Out in the hallway, Williams walked her toward Anne's office. They stepped inside and he shut the door behind them.

"You almost gave him cover in there," Williams said angrily.

"I understand and I'm sorry," she said. "But you're all over the map with him," January said. "Anne told me you'd be questioning him, not fishing."

"I'm not fishing."

"No? Is there an actionable connection between this Dr. Farhadi and Parand Ghasemi? Because we know all about TAG and we scanned Ghasemi in Iraq. He was clean."

"I know your protocols and, no, I don't think Ghasemi

knows Farhadi. Tehran does not have that kind of vertical integration."

"Then—?"

"I wanted to see him in a new environment," Williams said.

"The kid in a candy-store gambit?" she said. "I did that at Quantico, Chase! I'm not a novice at this."

"We'll get to that in a moment," Williams replied, causing her to start. "I wanted to know, firsthand, if Ghasemi was going to ask questions, look around—"

"And how do you know he didn't? We were there ten minutes before—"

"Anne told me," he interrupted, not bothering to explain about the headshake. "As to the other point, I have a very good idea how Tehran knew where he was."

"How? He hasn't been alone and he hasn't had access to any electronic devices, if that's where you're going."

"He didn't need any of that," Williams said. "Two names, January: Abū Khan and Pak Dai. Defectors from ISIS and Kim Jong-un."

She seemed more mystified than thoughtful.

"Both of them went to embassies last year, Khan in Afghanistan and Dai in Seoul, and both were brought to Quantico." He nodded in the general direction of the Tank. "We just hacked that from internal communications at State. Took five minutes. Tehran probably already had that information on file. Helluva way to find out our weaknesses, but at least we have."

January was now openly concerned. "Why do you think they shot at Allen?"

"My guess? It fits Tehran's SOP. If they'd killed him, it's international news. A big spotlight on Ghasemi's defection. This way, it's still localized. We waste time asking about it, looking into it, trying to find a connection instead of investigating what's really going on. How many people have we got searching for one man?"

January didn't have to answer. They both knew the answer: dozens. "So where does this leave us?" she asked. "As important as this is, there are still rules of asylum—"

"There is still a soft target instead of the hard ones," Williams answered, cutting the lecture short. He'd heard it before many times, in many forms. "I think Ghasemi told us the truth about everything in there. That's why I asked, to get a baseline reaction. Now we go back and I finish."

"With what?" January asked.

"The interrogation," he said. "Then you can take him and go."

It was less a peace offering than a battle plan, but January accepted by extending her hand toward the door.

They returned to Williams's office where the director resumed his previous position. January closed the door and stood with her back to it. Williams did not think she was there to bar the general's escape or to hover protectively. Bankole handed Williams the tablet and nodded: Ghasemi provided an overview of information that he would reasonably be expected to know. There was no point delving deeper, now. Williams glanced at the device and set it on the desk.

"General, I only have only a few more questions for you," Williams said. "We all believe what you told us in Quantico, that Tehran asked you to come here in search of information. Thank you for being honest about that, too," he said, indicating the tablet on his desk. "There's just one thing we haven't discussed."

The general was silent, still. He seemed very much alone on the sofa.

"Sir," Williams said, "when was the last time you saw your daughter?" Everyone in the room, including January, noticed a change come over the man. He had been sitting forward and now he leaned back, crossed a leg, put his hands in his lap. He swallowed.

"It was several weeks before I left," he answered, his voice characteristically steady.

"How many weeks, General?"

He appeared to be thinking, not hedging. "Three."

"And when did you last *speak* with her?"

Ghasemi swallowed again. "Then," he said. "When I saw her."

"This was before the video was recorded?" he asked.

Ghasemi nodded.

"The video—was not recorded for your benefit, was it?" Williams asked. "It was made to convince us that you had something to risk by defecting. It was designed to make us trust you."

"I-I truly do not know. You may be right."

"What was the last thing your daughter said to you?" Williams pressed.

Ghasemi shook his head slowly as if to say he did not recall.

Williams pushed his butt from the desk and stood. "Think hard, General."

January took two stops forward, stopping behind the sofa. "Chase—" she cautioned.

Williams ignored her. "General? What was the last thing she said to you?"

The officer looked at Williams. "She—" he said, then stopped again and breathed.

"Back off, Chase!" January said, moving between them.

"Not yet," Chase said, moving around her to lean on the arm of the sofa. Now she was going to have to push him off. "General— what did Parand say to you?"

"She was the one who asked me to come here."

That stopped the room.

"On whose behalf?"

"Prosecutor Younesi," he said. "That . . . that was true."

Williams did not move. January came up behind him.

"General, are you all right?" she asked. "Do you want your water?"

"Nursemaid," Bankole said under his breath.

"What?" January shot him a look.

"Just talking to myself," Bankole replied.

Williams barely heard the exchange. Anne's tablet pinged. He didn't hear that, either.

"Please do not hurt my daughter," Ghasemi said. It was the first spontaneous remark he had made. Williams believed it was sincere.

"We would very much like that result," he said non-committally. "One more question," Williams said, still looking at Ghasemi. "Why didn't you go through with the plan, General?"

Ghasemi took a long breath, almost a sob. "I intended to," he admitted.

"But?" Williams pressed.

Ghasemi looked up at Williams for the first time. "You have to understand, sir. I-I didn't know what else to do. But I tell you, her eyes were not my daughter's eyes. They were something, some-*one* else. I did not"—he began, choking now—"I did not see my girl's soul there. I do not know what happened, how any of this came to be."

"I think I do," Anne said.

Once again the room fell silent. She handed Williams her tablet. There was a text from Aaron Bleich flagged MU in red—most urgent. The director read the text, his expression implacable. He looked at January and Ghasemi.

"Our team analyzed the video of Parand," he said. "They believe the man in the cell with her was Dr. Sadeq Farhadi."

CHAPTER TWENTY-NINE

Outpost N64, Anadyr, Russia
July 2, 1:14 P.M.

The site was designated for the latitude on which it was constructed: N64° 44′ 11.9623″. The Kremlin had specifically wanted the name to reference the purpose of the bunker and twin silos: to Khrushchev, the east-west lying line pointed directly at the target, North America.

That was what Bolshakov had heard, anyway. Back then—and today, now that he considered it—gossip was a more reliable form of information than news.

The hatch had been constructed with a spring-action hinge. Turn the key and the two-inch thick iron plate was supposed to rise. But decades of disuse and as many years of freezing had left it unable to move on its own. Yuri removed three large keys from a case and inserted one. Bolshakov heard the lock turn but nothing more. Yuri returned to the car, rummaged through his gear, and returned with a thermos-sized jar. He held the narrow strawlike nozzle over the edge of the plate, pressed a button, and directed a high-powered jet of polyalphaolefin extreme cold-weather synthetic oil around the rim. The lubricant foamed as it seeped through the caked ice and soil frozen in the opening.

"Step back," Yuri instructed his father, who had put his hands on his knees and was leaning over, watching.

Bolshakov did as he was told. A moment later he heard the hinges squeak and then erupt with a loud metallic scream. The hatch wasn't open but it was unstuck.

"Some things we make very, very right," Bolshakov said admiringly.

Yuri returned to the car, stowed the lubricant, and returned with a crowbar and a flashlight. Bolshakov would have brought them all in one trip, but his son obviously had his way of doing things. At least this way he would probably never leave anything behind—which could be a key to survival on GRU missions.

The young man worked the crowbar around the edges to make sure it was entirely free. He inserted the edge, pressed tentatively on the other end, and the hatch came up slightly.

"I'll use the bar," Bolshakov said, reaching out.

Yuri handed it to him and in less than a minute, with a maximum of pushing down on the bar and pulling on the lip of the iron plate, the hatch was fully open, the disc locking firmly upright. Yuri swept the interior of the narrow shaft with the flashlight. Other than around the edges, where there were jagged patches of discoloration stretching down three or four inches, the charcoal-gray metal showed little sign of distress.

"Some things we make very, very right," Bolshakov repeated softly.

Yuri retrieved the key. He put the crowbar back in the car

and returned with two large backpacks and a Geiger counter, which he activated. It ticked, but at an acceptable level for where they were. There was a ladder almost beneath Yuri. Handing the Geiger counter and flashlight to his father, he climbed down. When he reached the bottom, the older man passed the two items plus the backpacks down and followed him in. The two men were a snug fit in the shaft, which rose roughly a foot above Yuri's head.

A submarine-style hatch was located behind where Bolshakov was standing. It had a two-key lock, top and bottom opposite the hinges. The seals appeared undamaged by the elements. Yuri climbed the ladder, his father following him with the light. The top hatch was lowered and relocked, clanging loudly in a way that felt painfully familiar to Bolshakov's eardrums. Then Yuri came back down and inserted the two other keys in their respective locks.

"I'll take the lower one," he said. "If you wouldn't mind—?"

"Of course," Bolshakov said, and walked to the top lock. He tucked the flashlight under his arm so that both men could see. That, too, was second nature, recorded in muscle memory. He put his fingers on a key he knew well.

"On three," Yuri said.

He counted it out and the keys were turned, the locks snapping simultaneously. He heard Yuri exhale. Bolshakov stepped back, Yuri rose, and after recovering the keys he turned the round steel handle in the center. It operated a toothed-gear that, when turned, pulled back the bars that secured the door.

Bolshakov had to move to allow the door to swing into the

shaft. The dry atmosphere was not like he remembered it, but then the room had been shut, without ventilation, for three decades. Yuri knew where to feel for the light switch. A series of fluorescent lights sputtered to life.

"They weren't sure these would work," Yuri said.

"Six to sixty thousand hours of luminous flux," Bolshakov muttered. "We all read the manual." He stuck his head in and looked around. "Each of us knew how to operate most everything."

Yuri stepped over the lip of the doorway and entered the chamber. His father followed. The air was difficult to breathe, like being on another world. He immediately went to a panel along the far wall and pressed a blue button. It activated a fan that was below the vent. It did not turn on.

"I'll have to fix this," Bolshakov said, looking up. "Air will get in, but the vent was not protected."

Yuri was not listening. Accompanied by the gentle tick of the Geiger counter—its low beat reassuring—Yuri had moved to one side of the command center where he stood still and in what Bolshakov regarded as an almost reverent silence. Just before the younger man, its cylindrical white shell and pointed red warhead illuminated by the flashlight, was an upright nuclear missile. It rested, still, in the mobile launcher that had been raised to a fully upright position. After a few moments, he turned the light behind him and shined it on the other nose cone.

"The power to destroy a civilization," Bolshakov said. He made his way toward his son. "The power to destroy *all* civilization. Now that we are here, will you tell me why?"

The young man snapped off the flashlight and put the Geiger counter down. He did not answer his father. Instead, he went to the control panel, leaned over a section on the far left that was unrelated to the launch controls, and picked up a telephone receiver that hung from the side. There was no dial; just the ominous black handset. Bolshakov remembered when they had built the facility, patching a cable into the trunk line that ran from Anadyr to Tiksi 1,200 miles to the west on the Laptev Sea, and from there to Norilsk to Syktyvkar to Moscow. Originally, since this was Khrushchev's private enterprise, the line terminated in the commissar's office in the Kremlin. The terminus had obviously been rerouted.

"N64 to KA1," he said, then repeated it.

Bolshakov suspected that KA stood for Khodynka Airfield where the GRU headquarters was located.

Within the heavy walls of the room, sound carried. Bolshakov could dimly hear a voice reply:

"Go ahead."

"Coordinates correct, objective achieved," Yuri said. "Please inform Iran that the contents are safe and secure."

CHAPTER THIRTY

Havana, Cuba
July 1, 11:01 P.M.

There was a time, until some sixty years before, that nighttime in Havana would have carried with it an image of bright lights outside the casinos, laughter inside, and the promise of sinful distractions in the rooms above.

After the Revolution, with the flight of the Mafia and American interests, Havana had sunk rapidly into a torpor of unfulfilled dreams—which had been vaguely envisioned to begin with and was utterly unrealized in reality. Castro's form of socialism, financed by Russia and then Venezuela, propped up the necessary social services while jobs and the quality of life slowly decayed.

Roger McCord had not had time to research the city much, and knew only what had been reported in the history books, news media, and more thoroughly and accurately in the intelligence community white papers. Like Russia writ smaller, it was a nation that subsisted on a black market economy, as a conduit for the drug trade and money laundering, and as a lucrative base of operations for nations intent on penetrating American borders. Planes, ships, and even submarines were constantly shuttling senior planners of terror groups to Florida and the Gulf Coast. Homeland Security knew about most of these trips and, for the most part, let the men and women through; the best way to know their plans and strategies was to watch and listen rather than apprehend.

Go-bag in hand, a phone call to his wife and daughters en route to Reagan International—they were accustomed to his sudden comings and goings, mostly the latter—the intelligence director had been able to make the eight P.M. plane from Reagan International in good time. The nonstop flight was just shy of two hours and forty-five minutes, after which he sat in a small cubicle beside Customs waiting for his paperwork to be validated. The documents had been emailed to Op-Center, printed, and signed en route; that required an extra level of confirmation with the Cuban Embassy in Washington.

While he waited, McCord checked his messages. There was a carefully worded text from "CW," which had arrived only minutes before:

```
Tank: Doc used ATM, 10:22 p.m., Centro
59 Bar, Avenida del Puerto
```

Lively octogenarian, McCord thought.

One reason that McCord was so successful when he was running the MARSOC intelligence operation for the Marines was that he had learned to wait.

As certainly as flawed information could cost lives, hurried efforts to obtain information were equally dangerous. There were times when the risk was necessary, as with an imminent attack or the escape of a high value target; and there were times when even the appearance of haste could cost information and access to that information.

This was one of those times when agitation would raise red flags, cause an even longer delay. He brought up the photo of Dr. Bermejo that Kathleen had found from the Moscow symposium, studied data the Tank had worked up about her height, five-foot-two; likely jewelry and shoe preference—a cross, flats in a formal setting suggested the same for casual; personal habits—enhanced analysis showed skin discoloration on the third finger of her left hand, suggesting a cigarette or cigar smoker; and similar observations.

McCord's documents were approved with surprising speed. After his bag was examined and passed, he hurried curbside and provided the address to a bored-looking cabdriver. Or maybe he was just tired of sweating; it was still in the low eighties and the sun was long gone. Whatever relief came from the sea was not felt here, sandwiched between the José Martí International Airport terminal and trees of various sizes that lined the roads.

McCord settled into the yellow cab, an American classic—a Galaxie from the late 1950s, right before the Revolution. The car felt refreshingly solid. He gave the driver the name of the bar and the street and hoped he could find Dr. Bermejo before she left. He knew from the translated symposium program that she spoke English and Russian, and McCord had done a few years of Spanish, so communicating shouldn't be a problem.

If she were there, he thought. *She could have been paying and leaving.*

That turned out to have been the case. The drive took ten minutes on streets with light traffic. The bar was a white brick building, old and halfheartedly refurbished. McCord gave the driver a generous tip, then asked how long he was on duty.

"Until nine A.M.," the man replied. "But I will stay longer if needed."

McCord thanked him, creating a contact on his cell phone for the company and the driver's name. Then he went inside the bar. It had more indoor palm trees than clients at the moment, most of them men—a bus driver, a policeman, other civil servants, it appeared—who were sitting under slow-turning fans and drinking beer with late-night tapas.

McCord debated whether to take a stool, order a drink, and tell the bartender he was looking for his friend Dr. Bermejo. He decided against it, figuring that anyone who knew her would know where she worked and want to know why he was asking. He couldn't very well show the photograph for the same reason.

He walked over to the restroom, found that it was empty, and decided to look around for where she might have parked. Avenida del Puerto was a very wide street on the coast, a collection of white buildings with worn façades brilliantly lit with modern, trendy signs. He watched the few women who were out; like the men in the bar they seemed to be workers who looked like they were headed toward a bus stop after a long day. As he walked, McCord was also busy formulating Plan Bs. He had a hotel room, also in this old section of the city, but he could not afford to spend days trying to catch the physicist outside Lourdes. For all he knew she did not leave very often.

That would mean getting inside, which would require planning—and time wasted.

Or—

In the distance, toward the water, he saw the fortress-style structure of the *Comandancia General*. He stopped, thought for a moment, then grabbed his phone and texted Williams:

```
Missed her. May be en route to office.
Need car deets.
```

Williams texted back less than a minute later that he ordered the Tank to check. Lourdes had been under satellite surveillance since Op-Center had opened a file on it, which meant that they might be able to pick up workable images by satellite. Then he asked McCord what he intended to do with the information. The intelligence officer replied:

```
Tell cops she struck me leaving the
bar.
```

CHAPTER THIRTY-ONE

Evin Prison, Evin, Iran
July 2, 7:34 A.M.

Parand was woken by a respectful knock on the door. She had slept fully clothed in her black *abaya* despite the summer heat and the meager relief that came through two open windows. It was essential, however, that she be ready, since she did not know when she might be summoned. Quickly pulling on her black *hijab* and slippers, she hurried to the door.

"They have found it," said the visitor, a man in his middle sixties. He was smiling. "The two missiles appear to be intact."

The woman did not realize how tense she had been until the joy of those words filled her body. The face of Dr. Sadeq Farhadi beamed even more when he saw her reaction.

"The helicopter is waiting to take you to the airfield," he said. "You leave at once."

"Yes, of course," she said, recovering and embracing the urgency of the moment. She had been told—not in detail, but enough to sharpen her mind—that even though the numbers of people involved were small, the Americans or Europeans might get onto the undertaking somehow. "*The numbers of their people watching is vast*," the prosecutor had told her.

Parand grabbed the small suitcase with her clothing and a large, solid briefcase with her equipment. The gray-haired Far-hadi took both from her as she came to the door.

"I am most proud of you," he stole a moment to say. "The prosecutor sends his personal greetings."

"Thank you, Sadeq," she said, flushing as she walked around him. Parand did not want compliments until the job was done. And even then, when the warheads were safely in Iran, her work would just be beginning.

The two left the room and hurried from the courthouse. As they stepped onto the asphalt of the parking lot, headed for the waiting helicopter, it was already ninety degrees at least. The wash of the rotors provided some relief, and it was cooler inside the small cargo area of the Italian-built Agusta-Bell 212. Farhadi helped Parand inside, then passed her luggage to her.

"'Travel through the land and observe how He began creation,'" Farhadi said, reciting the twentieth verse of chapter twenty-nine of the Quran. "'Then Allah will produce the final creation.'"

With a final smile of encouragement, he slid the door shut and ran off, as the helicopter took off toward Doshan Tappeh Air Base, southeast of Tehran. It was a unique experience, to rise and bank as they did, and Parand found it not entirely to her liking. She had intended to look back at the prison that had been her home for these many weeks, but the shifting patterns of sunlight and shadow were nearly as disorienting as the movement. She also felt the drumming rotors not just deep in her ears but along her spine. Other than a rickety lab stool, Parand's world was solid and predictable.

No more, she thought as she tightened the chest harness and sat back hard against the seat. Now her entire body felt the propellers turning. Fortunately, this leg of the journey would only last a few minutes. From the military field, Parand would take a thirteen-hour flight on a military cargo jet to the remotest regions of Russia, where the temperature would be refreshingly at the opposite end of the scale. She had not experienced cold weather since she was a student at Oxford, and even that was nothing like what she'd find in Anadyr.

That is not all which awaits, she reflected contentedly as the helicopter leveled off and her insides settled and her thoughts turned to her father. She did not think he would understand. He was a patriot, to be sure, but he was also a Christian. Parand had come to see how the two were incompatible and how figures like Dr. Farhadi and Prosecutor Younesi were ultimately the true lamps guiding Iran into the future—

Not into the past.

In the end, whether or not she ever saw him again—and she hoped she did—Parand would pray for the general, that he not be among the unbelievers or the ungrateful, and that he would attain the forgiveness of Allah and the entrance to paradise. . . .

CHAPTER THIRTY-TWO

Op-Center Headquarters, Fort Belvoir North,
Springfield, Virginia
July 2, 12:11 A.M.

January Dow had taken General Ghasemi to a new location, a safe house in Georgetown, to await further developments. Additional debriefing was not deemed necessary: either he had told the truth and it was everything he knew, or he was lying and would continue to lie. In either case, events would determine how and when he would be called upon.

Chase Williams sent Anne home, though he asked Aaron and Kathleen to stay after they finished looking for Dr. Bermejo's vehicle; support in Cuba was virtually nonexistent and he did not want McCord out there alone.

A tired-looking Kathleen walked into his office with a hazy green image on her tablet. It showed a Rambler headed to the SIGINT station at the correct time.

"A Rambler?" Williams had said, more from astonishment than to clarify.

"That's right," she said. "And you'll like this—it's self-verified."

"I don't follow."

She replied, "It's a Rebel model from 1959."

Williams grinned. "A sentimentalist," he said. "Color?"

She flipped to a screen that compensated for the night-vision view. "Silver," he said. "Get a glimpse of the tags?"

"First letters P3," she said. "Rest in shadow, bad angle."

"That should be enough," he told her. "Great work. If Mc-Cord is planning on going to sleep, you'll be able to head out."

She thanked him, shutting the door behind her as Williams contacted McCord and texted him the information. It was ten minutes before he received a single word in reply:

Done.

He waited a few minutes more and then got in touch with McCord by phone rather than text. He didn't think they'd be saying anything that would help the Russians. And if they were listening, part of him didn't care. They had probably figured out, when diplomatic relations were restored, that the gauntlet for the hearts and minds of the Cubans had been thrown down.

"Safe to talk?" Williams asked. He could hear the roll of wheels, knew that McCord was likely out on the street, on concrete.

"Just left the police station," he said. "Big place. Impressive. And they actually seemed interested in helping me."

"Because they want Americans to come or Russians to leave?" he asked.

"I'd say both," he replied. "Especially when it comes to

athletics, which they seemed to respond to. I told them that I am here to row and could not afford to be injured."

"Have you even contacted your colleague there yet?"

"Time enough in the morning," McCord replied. "He wasn't expecting me to come by until then anyway. The plan is for *la policía* to track the vehicle I described—the *P* stands for personal vehicle; that and the *3* should fix the specific Rambler Rebel. I'll know in the morning when I come back."

"That was good thinking," Williams said.

"What happened while I was away?"

Williams told him—again, in the broadest terms—that Ghasemi had not leaked his location, but cracked and admitted that his daughter had been "Svengalied" by a theocrat.

"That's a shame for him," McCord replied. "The timing of his arrival—suggests something imminent?"

"That's my takeaway. Even his escort was concerned, once she got past my playing bad cop with her boy."

"Ivory tower chalk in her veins," McCord grumped.

"True, but it keeps us honest," Williams remarked.

"You still have no idea what this is about, other than where everyone's profession points," McCord went on thoughtfully.

"That, plus the fact that we have a nation very actively in the market for what we don't want them to have," he replied. "Listen, we'll talk more tomorrow. You rest, I'll think. You earned it."

McCord was ominously quiet.

"You are going to the hotel, yes?" Williams pressed.

"Yeah, yeah . . . best to let this sit."

Williams agreed. He ended the call and lay the phone on his

desk. He walked back to the Tank and told Kathleen she could go home. She slumped, releasing the pressure, then grabbed her bag from under the desk.

"You did exceptional work today," he said as she began closing her station down. "You made some impressive connections with this data. Others will notice."

"Thank you," she replied. "But the computer did the heavy lifting—"

Even as she said that, there was a ping. She and Williams exchanged looks. She sat down, switched the monitor from slumber mode, and had a look.

"Well, this is interesting," she said.

"In a good way?"

"Not sure," she said. "When I set up the scan to report on Dr. Bermejo's financial activity, I wrote an add-on to give us information about anything that involved her."

"Well, Roger reported her car to the police. Maybe they just ID'ed the owner and have a notice out for—"

"It's not that, sir," Kathleen interrupted. She was waiting for the computer to translate the police report. "They've arrested a custodian from Lourdes wanted in connection with a fire intentionally set at the SIGINT station. Seems a guard from the facility was on a bus going home, smelled smoke on the man, recognized him, made a fuss, and the police came."

"How is Dr. Bermejo tied to this?"

"They found her home phone number in his shirt pocket," Kathleen read. "In her own writing." She looked up. "They've just gone to collect her."

Williams had to get McCord on this. He hurried back toward his office. "Do you mind not going just yet?" he asked over his shoulder.

"I didn't really think I was," Kathleen said pleasantly to herself as she sat back down.

CHAPTER THIRTY-THREE

Havana, Cuba
July 2, 12:11 A.M.

Adoncia had parked and shakily lit a cigar. Her face illuminated by the match, she realized she should not have had one Bucanero, let alone three cans.

But how often does one get to celebrate the successful evacuation of a fellow freedom fighter? she thought.

"*¡Viva la revolución!*" she said to the skies, her teeth on the cigar limiting the volume. She was glad for that; the other former SIGINT workers who lived her were old in spirit and body and rarely awake to see in a new day.

Tired but feeling utterly fulfilled, she had just unlocked the door when the phone rang. She considered not answering it until she realized that it might be Enrich. She couldn't imagine why he'd be calling her since she had only recently left him. Now that he was safely away, perhaps he wanted to thank her again.

"Hello," she said, surprised that her voice was so low, so gruff. Was it always?

"Dr. Bermejo," a voice said, "this is Alejándro at the main gate. Two police officers are on their way to see you."

It took a moment for her brain to process the message. "Are you certain they want me?"

"They asked for you by name, and for directions to your apartment."

"Ah," she said. Then she uttered something that was a cross between a *hmmm* and a sound of self-reproach. "My driving. Can't you just tell them I'm sorry? I rarely imbibe. Not even in the old days. *Especially* in the old days. Fidel would not—"

"Doctor, they are already on their way."

"Well, fine. Fine." She half replaced, half dropped the receiver. "Police do not frighten me. They *cannot* frighten me."

She fell into the nearest chair, the one in which she had been sitting to talk to Enrich. The cigar plopped to the carpet and she quickly retrieved it, put it in an ashtray on the table.

"No one ever visits except Russians," she said. "Now in just a few hours, a Cuban arsonist and police—"

Through the buzzing haze of the beer she wondered whether this was about the janitor. She swore.

I hope it is my driving, she thought, suddenly sobered as she saw the twin beams of car headlights play through the window on the opposite wall. They were followed by a single blue light and the loudly audible squeal of brakes. Old, forgotten sensations returned from her student days, meeting in classrooms to discuss politics, Marx and Engels, sedition, Revolution—

There was a hard knock on the door. She grabbed the cigar for moral support, blowing smoke as she rose.

"The dragon is unafraid," she slurred around the cigar as she walked to the door.

Two older officers waited for her on the other side. Her eyes dropped to something glowing-white in the obliquely shining headlights, held at the side of one of the men.

"*La mierda*," she said softly, recognizing it as the slip of paper she had impulsively given to Enrich.

"Dr. Adoncia Bermejo?" the other officer asked.

"Who else would be at her address at this hour, and looking like her?"

"We request that you accompany us to the station," the man said, ignoring the impertinence.

Adoncia sobered further. She was not accustomed to anyone speaking to her so formally. It carried menace. She didn't like it.

"Why?" she asked.

"We want to ask you about your activities this evening," he said. "We would appreciate if you would come willingly."

She nodded, unsure herself whether she was acknowledging that she understood or that she had agreed to go.

"You will arrest me otherwise?" she asked.

"Doctor, we would hope that will not be necessary," the man said. His tone showed respect for her title, his quiet manner for her age. She appreciated that.

"All right," she told him. She extended her arms at her sides. "After all, I'm still dressed for a nighttime outing, yes? Not like blessed Christ near naked on his cross."

The men flinched visibly at that, but stepped aside to let her through.

"And now, like Moses, you are parted!" she went on as she shut the light and closed the door. "I have helped to free us all yet I am not free."

The voice was still foreign to her ear and the bravado was false as she stepped into the lights of the police car suddenly feeling naked and vulnerable.

"I shouldn't," she blurted, suddenly stopping on her heels.

"Please, Doctor," the same man urged.

"I am not a collaborator."

The officers took her arms and gave a firm but respectful tug and Adoncia went along. Somewhere along the way she lost her cigar. She saw lights go on in other apartments and felt angry, then mortified in quick succession.

And then she thought about poor Enrich and began to sob. He hadn't given her up—her own stupid overconfidence had—but in a way she was glad to be joining him. He had the courage to do something important, and a man like that should not face this alone.

"*¡Viva la revolución!*" she said again, only this time the phrase was muttered, not to the sky but into her vest as her chin drooped to her chest.

CHAPTER THIRTY-FOUR

Op-Center Headquarters, Fort Belvoir North,
Springfield, Virginia
July 2, 1:00 A.M.

"Miss me already?"

"I wish it was that," Williams told him. "They just picked her up for abetting an arsonist at the facility. She's probably on her way to where you were."

"I did see a patrol car leave after we spoke," he said. "I'm going back. Without her, we've got nothing."

"I agree," Williams said. "I'll get whatever I can on this end."

The director called Kathleen to watch for any updates, then headed to the Tank. As he arrived, she was just bringing up a file from MacDill Air Force Base.

"Since it had to do with Lourdes, they followed the fire," she told him.

"You have a name on the accuser?" Williams asked.

Kathleen returned to the police report. "Mauricio Modesto."

"Get me everything you can on him," Williams said as he texted McCord:

Working on plan to help her. Talk before executing.

The director leaned over the back of Kathleen's chair. "What was the timeline of events, starting from the fire?"

Kathleen provided those, along with the two cash withdrawals Dr. Bermejo had made, the first at 7:33 that evening.

"So according to Mauricio, she left the compound with Enrich presumably in the car. Then she drove to Havana, withdrew money, and probably bought him a bus ticket and whatever he'd need because he obviously couldn't go home. After that she hung around until he left—on what bus?"

"I don't have that information but the first cash withdrawal was near the Havana Zoo. There's a bus kiosk there which services the route to Varadero, which is about seventy miles to the east. There are stops all along the coast."

"He obviously bikes there, maybe motorbike, or he wouldn't need a bus to get home."

"Bicycles are the number one mode of transportation among the populace," she said. "Happened between the end of Soviet oil and the rise of Venezuelan imports."

Williams was impressed and said so with a "*Hmmph.*"

"You start collecting intel, you have to at least scan related links," she said. "All right. Mauricio Modesto. Age twenty-six, and—here we are—trade school auto mechanic, was a motorbike repairman during his stint with the *Fuerzas Armadas Revolucionarias,* the Cuban Revolutionary Armed Forces. Undistinguished career, two disciplinary reports—"

"Where are you getting this?"

She grinned. "His police record."

"Oh? Then how the hell did he get work as a security guard at—"

"Like this," she said, bringing up a social media item.

Williams read the automatic translation that appeared beside an online photo album belonging to Modesto. He nodded with understanding.

"He married a Russian girl," he said. "Iya Firsova."

"Want to bet that if I looked her up I'd find she's related to someone at the facility?" Kathleen said.

"No doubt," Williams said.

It was an old Soviet tactic, marrying an ordinary man and planting him in a position to provide pillow-talk on unrecorded activities of those around him. There were some intelligence officials who said the so-called Red Wedding program reached its zenith with Lee Harvey Oswald and Marina Nikolayevna Prusakova in 1961—two years before he allegedly assassinated President Kennedy. He doubted it would be any consolation to Dr. Bermejo, but even without the incident on the bus, Mauricio would probably have said something to Iya that would eventually have implicated the scientist.

"This is great," Williams said. "Do we have access to any security cameras in the old section of—"

There was an alert that sounded simultaneously on the computer and on Kathleen's secure smartphone. If she had gone home, she would not have been able to access the data, only the case reference and FPCON assessment—the Force Protection Condition assessment, ranging from "Normal" through "Alpha," "Bravo," "Charlie," and "Delta."

"OA Bravo," she said. That was her intelligence file for Operation Anadyr with the potential risk-threat that requires attention. "We have an aircraft anomaly leaving the airspace of Afghanistan headed northeast and entering Tajikistan—an Iranian military jet off the normal flight paths."

"They operate there illegally all the time," Williams said. "What's this about?"

"An algorithm," she said. "The aircraft is a 707, long range. Given our current intelligence search parameters, the program is letting us know that the plane, the timing, and the direction indicate a possible destination of interest." She looked up at the director. "Anadyr."

CHAPTER THIRTY-FIVE

Havana, Cuba
July 2, 1:07 A.M.

Feeling highly visible and self-conscious about the *clack-clack-clack* of the suitcase he was dragging behind—*Spies are supposed to be invisible*, McCord reminded himself only half-jokingly—he hefted it up and carried it at his side. It was the last thing his tired arms or equally cranky right-side hip wanted, but at least the effort brought renewed life to his tired eyes.

The streets were relatively empty. Workers on graveyard shifts across Havana were already at or en route to their destinations, daytime workers were home, and mostly late-night drinkers and their dates were afoot.

As he returned to the police station, McCord was reminded of most of the third world cities he had visited, from Beirut to Manila, from Jakarta to Pyongyang: dispirited activity moved sluggishly through a metropolis that once knew or flirted with greatness. The old buildings weren't historic so much as they were wreckage, decaying structures patched and repurposed over the centuries as new leaders attempted to jumpstart prosperity in fractured societies.

It was a tragic scenario that played out from without and within. As imperialist nations were ousted, local tribes or clashing political ideologies or religious hatreds fed on what was left. What emerged, without fail, was a city that resembled one of those zombies on cable TV: something in motion but not really alive.

The danger to McCord throughout his twenty-three years of service was always to *not* enter these places feeling superior. Like the tiny mammals who survived as the big dinosaurs began dying off, there were always rodents and insects in hiding to pick on the flesh. So he remained alert, and now he was silent. He weaved as he walked, avoiding cones of light from streetlamps or the occasional automobile or still-lit neon signs.

All of this was both training and intuition. It freed his mind so he could actively concentrate on the matter at hand: within the next five minutes, coming up with a way of seeing Dr. Bermejo, discrediting the accuser, and somehow getting her out of prison.

If this were Ramadi, he would be going in with a unit, weapons, tactical and intelligence support, and backup. He could stage a clean and quick rescue and evac. At military-civilian meet-and-greets, the "unenlisted" as he called them always remarked about McCord's résumé, about the courage and skill his special intelligence operations demanded. He smiled and very politely accepted the compliments, but there was invariably a knowing look at a fellow soldier or officer. They knew that success depended on training, teamwork, intelligence, and a solid plan. Once you pulled the "go" trigger, you were part of a machine that was driven by purpose so absolute that it steamrollered fear.

Walking alone, in the small hours of the night, in a city where your only map was on your smartphone and you only just passably spoke the native tongue; that was not a military operation. That was—

What? he asked himself as he eyeballed the police station, reminded himself of the layout that he had instinctively noted, remembered the faces of everyone he saw. *What do I call this?*

He grinned in spite of the urgency of the moment, or perhaps because of it. He grinned because he had once tried to explain it to his wife with whom he could never discuss these occasional missions.

That is Op-Center, he thought. And within that there was always a crunch point that was at once daunting and exhilarating, what he called the Thomas Paine moment—

The smartphone hummed in the vest pocket of McCord's white shirt. It was a call. He didn't think Williams would be calling him with more halfheartedly coded communiqués; not this close to the station.

"The accuser has been married for seventeen months to a Russian national, a niece of the associate director of the foreign office at the station," Williams said without preamble. "He has a bank account considerably larger than his salary would suggest."

McCord suspected that many Cuban government workers had that as well, graft being extensive. Turning Enrich in had an added benefit, however. Cuba undoubtedly had a deal with the Russians that included hiring a large percentage of locals, similar to what nations did with embassies around the globe. If those locals could be proven to be untrustworthy, if each could be forced to reveal the names of one or two accomplices, they could be replaced by Russians or Russian sympathizers. That sealed security even tighter but that was only part of the objective. To make up for the loss to the local economy, Russian investment would be welcome. That was how governments were co-opted. That was how the Mafia came to own Havana under Batista.

"So we play it as a plot against the lady," McCord said.

"Affirmative. Enough to create doubt, but you'll also need to get to see her tonight."

"Got it," McCord said as he reached the station. But then he replayed something Williams had just said. "How essential is the timing—"

"Very," Williams said bluntly. "We have a convergence of elements that indicate a fast-developing situation. We need more intel ASAP."

"Understood," McCord replied. "I'll contact after," he said, thumbing off the phone as he reached the wide, sloping walk that lead to the main courtyard of the *Comandancia General*.

That was something else civilians didn't understand, not the way he and Williams and many of the Op-Center brass did. Most police officers he had met knew it to: how difficult it was to shift from by-the-book to seat-of-the-pants. Not in terms of heroics; most of the service personnel McCord had known and served with had a strong streak of cowboy in them. If they hadn't, they would have been in military maintenance or communications or some other support position. That wasn't a knock, it was the nature of the man or woman who served in the field. What was difficult was reconciling the needs of the nation versus the rules of the bureaucrats. And that, in the end, was why a bureaucrat at the top of the food chain, President Midkiff, had reactivated Op-Center. That was what earned it the nickname, the Ranch.

The weariness in his limbs left him, and the alertness in his eyes and ears sharpened, as the Thomas Paine moment was suddenly, vibrantly upon him:

"*These are the times that try men's souls. . . .*"

CHAPTER THIRTY-SIX

Zagan, Poland
July 2, 7:15 A.M.

Mike Volner was told that it was a respected custom for first-time observers who were about to depart.

One of the Polish officers had taken Volner aside after the previous night's meal and told him that hand-to-hand combat between officers of equal standing was not only expected, it was honorable. The major didn't believe it, not for a moment, but said he would never be one to break with tradition. The suggestion had the earmarks of being a game of "Embarrass the American," which was common among the NATO officer ranks. But the major's celebrated action in New York had preceded him and, setup or not, he didn't care. He was happy for the challenge after days of standing in a tower or on a gunnery range and—the word that had stuck in his gullet—*observing*.

"Observing what, sir?" he had pointedly asked his CO before he was sent over.

General March had responded with the schedule, but that wasn't what Volner had meant. Informing Chase Williams that he would not be available to command any JSOC operations for the duration, at least the director had a frank answer for him:

"You are being sent there to *be* observed, Major. Not only by the troops but by the press military and international press. Get used to that, at least until the next soldier makes headlines."

And so Volner did his duty with as much stature and dignity as he could muster. Now, he got to shuck that in a showdown that probably wasn't even legal. Why else would they be holding it before breakfast?

That, too, didn't matter. It had been a week since Volner had been able to do any rock climbing back at the base, and it had been a month since he last had a Combat Karate workout. The hard-hitting, hard-kneeing martial art was now the preferred form of hand-to-hand combat at many bases, created by Johnny Kuhl in the 1970s and replacing the decades-old over-the-hip Judo throws and Jujitsu fists and elbows. The objective was not to toss or kayo an opponent. The goal was to destroy him.

The rules were mixed martial arts. The term was a misnomer, as "MMA" had none of the finesse of the sharp, elegant, centered kung fu and Wing Chun forms Volner had studied. It was a mishmash of punching, kicking, throws and everything in between, a metaphor for the modern world: everyone learned to fight, and fight violently, typically without honor. Soldiers were not like the WWI pilots in the *Enemy Ace* comic books he had read as a kid, saluting fallen enemies as their burning planes spiraled to the ground. Today you clashed, just that; hard and kill-oriented. If you were losing, you went for the concealed knife. If it were a knife fight, capture-and-interrogate was an afterthought. The field was a slaughterhouse and the aim was slash and gut.

The site for this engagement was a boxing ring and it did not escape Volner's notice that the doors of the small gym were locked once the ten officers plus one other combatant had gathered. Volner's opponent was a Polish major named Marek Ziobro. Volner had been informed shortly after he arrived, and for no apparent reason—probably as a form of psyops, to unnerve him at this moment—that "Marek" meant "warlike." The description fit. The man was a good four inches over the American's five-foot-ten, and at least thirty pounds heavier. His thighs were as thick as the barrel chest they supported and his arms were a brutish match.

The men wore trunks, their own athletic footwear, and an ungenerously padded red head guard. There was no mouthpiece to protect the teeth. They wore matching red sparring gloves, which covered the backs of the hands but not the palms. The two entered the ring without corner men. The only "official" was the man who would ring the bell and then join the others watching. There were no rounds, Volner had been told.

"The fight is over when one of you says it is," one of the three English speakers had advised him adding, with what sounded like a prediction, "or when one of you is unable to say it is."

They met in the center where they tapped knuckles in a traditional fist-bump and backed away several paces. The canvas had too much give and the ropes even more; the American knew he could not rely on either of them for support. The bell sounded with a hollow gong that needed more than a screwdriver to fix. If any part of the ring were younger than NATO itself, Volner would have been surprised.

The essence of Combat Karate was to move forward in as straight a line as possible, releasing as much firepower as possible along the way. With the six-pack his opponent was showing, Volner knew not to bother hitting there. He was already breathing protectively, the major noticed: tongue to the roof of his mouth to regulate breathing. That would prevent him from hyperventilating and, with a quick, explosive exhale, would also tighten his already formidable abs. He held his arms kickboxer-style: forearms upraised, parallel, fists by his face, elbows just above the belly. The man had done some homework, knew how Volner had trained. Everything "straight ahead" was guarded.

Offensively, the stance also favored the Pole. He could jab straight out with either fist and bring it back to its protective position quite literally in the blink of an eye. The way he was staring, that was obviously what he'd been trained to do: wait till his opponent blinked, then piston the big arm outward.

Volner did not expect that for an open gambit, however, and he stayed just out of reach of the gloves. He wanted to coax the Pole into leading with something else.

There were two places where Ziobro was open. Volner kept his eyes on them while Ziobro advanced—slowly, cautiously, unwilling to underestimate his smaller adversary. Volner retreated tactically, not from fear, and also watched how his opponent walked. Ziobro's size and the ailing canvas made him somewhat flatfooted. If the man intended to kick, he would announce it by shifting his weight to one leg. The bare muscles of that thigh would tense. His upper torso would begin to list in that direction. All of that would take a second, but that was more than enough time for Volner to respond.

Before the fight, Volner had observed Ziobro, knew he was right-handed. He would probably kick with that side, too. Volner began to circle the big man counterclockwise, one leg crossing behind the other. He wanted to be moving in the opposite direction from a right-leg kick. Nothing obvious . . . just enough to give him a head start—

The kick came as Volner had expected: a stiff, roundhouse swing toward his left hip accompanied by a loud *kiai*. The shout was intended to frighten a foe and also marshal one's own energies. Ziobro not only kicked but pivoted perfectly, swinging the leg faster than Volner had intended. He leapt to his right but the foot caught him in the hip, sending him stumbling to the right. Volner ducked as he regained his footing or the powerful left jab would have landed squarely in Volner's face—which even the glancing foot-blow had put within range.

Bent at the waist as the first passed overhead, Volner regained the target he had been eyeing before. He had to move quickly while the momentum of the punch still had Ziobro off balance.

The big Pole's exposed left side was briefly facing Volner. It did not have the muscular protection of his abdomen. It had ribs, which the American could see clearly through the skin. Volner did not hit them with his padded knuckles. He opened his fingers and swung his right arm like a scythe. His long ridge-hand struck halfway between the man's armpit and waist. There was a sharp intake of wind and Ziobro bent to that side. While the man was momentarily distracted, Volner moved in with a left uppercut. He brought it practically from the mat to the man's chin. In strikes like these, a fighter did not aim for the target but at someplace beyond—in this case, the ceiling of the gym. The gloved fist connected with an audible *thump* that straightened the momentarily breathless man and caused him to stumble backward on his heels.

Ziobro's arms were wobbly and his head was shaking. He did not see the knee that flew like a cannonball into the perfect abs. The Pole did, however, see Volner standing over him a few moments after he struck the canvas.

Ziobro smiled up. "Well done," he said on an exhale, wincing from the pain in his side. "We—*we* are done."

Volner was pulling off his gloves but did not offer a hand-up; the man would need at least two big men to get him on his feet and would need to be bandaged before heading to the infirmary. From the wheezing quality of his breathing, Volner was confident that one, possibly two ribs had been broken.

There were a few thumbs-up from the other Europeans, especially those who had obviously been given favorable odds in the betting pool and were in the process of collecting.

Returning to the locker room, Volner saw that he had missed a call from Chase Williams. Flopping on the wooden bench and being painfully reminded of his own wounded hip, he returned the call.

"Sorry I wasn't available," Volner said. He glanced at the time. "It's late there. Something up?"

"Seems likely," Williams told him. "You're scheduled to leave at noon."

"C-130, just me and a bunch of prototype loaners from the Missile Defense Agency."

"You're not riding shotgun, are you?"

"No."

Williams was referencing the fact that when prototype weapons were loaned to NATO, officers often babysat them coming and going. That was conceived as a deterrent to keep them from being photographed up close.

"ETD is still a couple hours off," Williams said distractedly. "We've got a situation developing on the Bering Sea, Russia side. Looks like a mini-convention of dangerous players."

Volner knew the director wouldn't say anything more on an open line. "I'll wait to hear from you. Meantime, I'll familiarize myself with the region. What about JSOC?"

"I'd like you to have them on standby," Williams said.

"That dangerous?" Volner said.

"Very possibly," the director replied.

The remark hung there, full of portent, which could not be addressed. Volner hung up and sat in the room, which was rank with the musk of decades. It reminded him of so many periods of his life: high-school track, boot-camp barracks, gyms, changing facilities adjacent ready rooms. Not really pleasant, yet in a strange way the place was home. It reminded him of something a priest had once told him when he signed up: "*Go into a church anywhere in the world and you will be home.*"

"So it's a locker instead," he said, chuckling as he pulled off the trunks, grabbed a towel from the rack, and headed to the shower.

As he turned on the hot spray, he couldn't help but wonder what the hell a locker room would be like in a place that was probably below freezing 365 days a year. . . .

CHAPTER THIRTY-SEVEN

Comandancia General, Havana, Cuba
July 2, 1:23 A.M.

Roger McCord didn't know why the phrase came to him as he reentered the police station: "Now is the time for all good men to come to the aid of the party."

He had always thought it was a wonderful, earnest, team-building expression, and he had used it himself when he had a command. It was about ten years ago he learned that someone had coined it as a typing exercise—nothing more.

Still, the sentiment was no less true for its origins, and it probably came to him because somehow he was going to have to put aside the story he'd concocted, that Adoncia Bermejo had glanced him with her car, and come to her rescue. Not just for her but for that greater good: to learn, and then help stop whatever was going on in the Russian Arctic.

The police station had been built in 1939 after the style of a classic fortress like the one that had stood on this spot, the *Bastion de San Telmo*. The main room had a high, arched ceiling and was filled with benches. Footsteps echoed in a way that must create a constant, hollow drone during high volume hours. There was only one corridor leading from the main hall and it was located in the back, opposite the desk. Ahead, a door opened to the parking lot. Behind was the ramp by which McCord had entered. Many of the locals still held the Castros in very high regard, but McCord could not help but think of the countless political prisoners who had been dragged down that corridor, and probably just one way.

The room was no longer harboring the few drunks and brawlers McCord had seen earlier. He saw a clutch of men who had just arrived for duty, private citizens who were members of *la guardia*, a volunteer force that walked the streets making sure that women and now tourists were safe. Coincidentally, McCord had heard about them a few weeks ago when it was suggested that, being unpaid, they might be open to payments for information. Confidential informants remained one of the chief intelligence-gathering sources around the globe.

There was a high wooden desk with beefy *Sargento* Carlitos Garcia still sitting behind a computer monitor on top of it. There was a white mug with the chain of a tea ball hanging over it. McCord had formulated generally what he was going to say. The trick would be not saying too much; he was not supposed to know what had happened with Enrich, the guard, and Dr. Bermejo.

"Did you forget something, *señor*?" the sergeant asked with exaggerated sincerity. It was a tone McCord recognized, one which many locals everywhere were forced to assume for needy, entitled tourists.

"I was just thinking . . . *remembering*, actually," McCord said with an intensely reflective expression. That was only partly a false front, however, as he struggled with his Spanish. "The driver . . . of the car . . . may have been very dark-skinned. I noticed that . . . when she passed under a streetlamp."

The sergeant registered genuine curiosity. "You forgot such an important detail?"

"Sergeant, you saw . . . I was not all right," McCord said. "But as I replay it . . . I remember."

"It could have been a shadow."

"It is . . . possible," McCord admitted. "But I thought I should mention it."

"Well, whatever you saw or thought you saw, we have the woman in custody," the sergeant said.

"Oh? That quickly?"

The jowly man nodded. "The car you described was located nearby."

"Very impressive," McCord said, then stood there mutely, waiting.

"Was there something else?" the policeman asked.

"Would it not help for me to identify her? To be sure?"

"We have this under control," he assured McCord. "She is wanted on other matters."

"I see," McCord nodded knowingly. He turned to go, muttering, "I suspect the young man she was yelling at."

Now the sergeant showed genuine interest. "Just a minute!"

McCord turned back as the officer leaned forward, swiveling away the computer screen. "What young man?"

"It was . . . let me think, I was not really . . . engaged. She said he was a . . . traitor, married to a Russian woman. No," he corrected himself, making a show of thinking hard, of reliving the moment. "She called him . . . *el espía*, I think. That could have been why she was distracted and grazed me. She was angry."

The sergeant motioned for McCord to stay where he was and picked up a landline hanging behind him. He spoke quickly, urgently, saying something about a possible new development.

"I will want a statement," Garcia said to McCord, covering the mouthpiece. "But briefly, can you describe this young man?"

Williams had not provided a name or physical details. But they would have been too much in any case. The description had to be sketchy, but just enough.

"I did not get a good look, but I heard her say something about being fit to guard only pigs," McCord replied. "But I thought she might have been . . . drinking. Looking for . . . some insult."

"An insult with some truth," Garcia remarked.

He got back on the call and repeated what McCord had told him. Then he said to bring Mauricio out front.

Garcia listened, then said, "His statement may be a lie! The doctor's phone number? Sanjulian said she gave it to him so he could ask about the old days. How do we know that isn't the case?" He was silent for a moment. "I do not know who to believe, but bring Mauricio out front. I want this man to see him!"

The sergeant hung up, then turned back to McCord. "I'm sorry for this delay, but you may be able to help us clear this up. This woman, Dr. Bermejo—she fought beside the Castros. I want to be very sure we do not dishonor *la patriota*."

The police officer said it as if he were suddenly very proud to know her and less smug to be entertaining her in a prison cell.

McCord stepped back from the desk, listening. It wasn't long before he heard heavy footsteps echoing in the darkness. They drowned a soft but agitated voice speaking quickly.

". . . to see me about?" he was saying. "I came of my own accord, I'm very late for dinner, and I just want to leave!"

The man McCord hadn't seen, but said he had, was walked into the main room by a pair of guards. Though off-duty he was wearing a blue uniform, the jacket of which was still buttoned; on the streets, military-style dress ensured a degree of respect. The officers were not holding him but they were on either side, just behind him. The young man's arms swung large, like he was on parade, his step equally big and impatient.

One of the guards directed him toward the desk. He was already moving in that direction, down the aisle between the benches.

"I was expecting a ride home, not further questioning!" he said to Garcia from halfway across the hall. "You already have my signed statement!"

Garcia picked up a pen and tapped it head-down on the desk. It, too, echoed. He waited until he was nearer before responding.

"We have your account," Garcia agreed affably, "but is it accurate?"

"What are you talking about?" Mauricio demanded, his face souring as he approached. He did not appear to notice McCord.

"We have had a report that you and the doctor were arguing in front of Centro 59 Bar earlier this evening," Garcia said.

Muaricio shot broom-stiff. "What? *What?* I was nowhere near that place tonight!"

Garcia motioned him closer. Mauricio stepped toward the desk. The sergeant leaned forward slightly. "I smell drink on your breath. I have a very good nose." He sat back. "Where did you take your refreshment?"

"*El Misterioso Extraño*, where I always go."

Garcia shrugged. "Two doors away on the same side of the street."

"But I didn't talk to her—I didn't even see her!"

Garcia pointed the pen toward McCord. "This gentleman tells a different story."

Mauricio took a step forward and one of the guards grabbed his arm. "This 'gentleman' is a liar! Who is he, anyway? An American?"

"Who he is does not matter, other than that he has no stake in the outcome." Garcia looked at McCord. "Do you, *señor*?"

"I came here to scull, not to become . . ." he sought the correct Spanish word, failed to find it, ". . . become tied in a domestic fight."

Garcia nodded. "We can check that." He looked back at Mauricio, jabbed the pen toward the guard holding him. "Ernesto will drive you home. Marco—you will bring Dr. Bermejo here."

Still protesting as if the interview had not taken place, Mauricio was escorted to the parking lot while the other officer went to retrieve Adoncia Bermejo. He returned a few minutes later with a woman who was dressed in jeans and a gray fleece vest. Her gray-white hair was caught back in a black band; it reminded McCord of quartz. The hanging lights overhead threw a succession of long shadows down the aisle and she looked as unbowed as the era that spawned her. Unlike Mauricio—who was gone by the time she arrived—her eyes took in everyone. They lingered on McCord, someone who clearly didn't belong. Her eyes moved back to the desk as she neared. The guard had maintained a respectful distance and now Garcia shooed him away.

"Doctor," the sergeant said solicitously, rising and coming from behind the desk, "it appears the guard may have been in error—at least, there is reason to question the guard's account."

If Adoncia seemed surprised, she was smart enough not to show it.

Garcia held a hand toward McCord. "This man, *Señor* McCord, witnessed the exchange on the street, told us that *Señor* Modesto may have had other reasons for overstating the matter."

"What of Enrich Sanjulian?" she asked, plucking a cigar from her vest and holding it unlit in all five fingers.

"We will investigate this situation further, but there is no need for you to remain. Though," he glanced at McCord, then back at Adoncia, "I *do* ask that you drive with greater care."

"I can't drive at all with my car back at the base," she said. "I also can't light my cigar. You took my matches, as if I would burn my fellow Cubans along with this wretched place."

The sergeant fetched them, handed the crisp book to her. "We will give you a ride, Doctor."

"I don't want one," she shot back. She looked at McCord. "Do you have a car?"

"I have the name of a very reliable cabdriver," McCord replied.

"Most of those who interact with the public here are reliable," she said, a pointed barb at the police. It was also a statement reflecting the pride she felt in the working men and women of her home. McCord should have worded that with greater sensitivity.

The two walked out together, McCord thanking the sergeant who stood watching them go.

The physicist had been drinking, he could tell; it was on her breath, in her walk. Perhaps she wasn't fully cognizant of what he knew: that they'd been borne from the station on the wings of a big lie. The intelligence director felt a familiar desire to run and he tamped it down, hard. McCord did not know how long he had to get information from Dr. Bermejo but he did know this much:

It had to be very, very soon.

CHAPTER THIRTY-EIGHT

Outpost N64, Anadyr, Russia
July 2, 6:30 P.M.

There was no wind, no sea smell, no sound, no sunlight. And after those initial, seemingly hopeful exchanges, there was no further conversation with Yuri.

Part of that was due to the fact that once he had made his report, Yuri rested. It had been a long, tiring flight and Yuri had not yet gone to the hotel. Bolshakov slept as well, each man in one of the four cots that was still in the facility. The blankets were folded exactly where they had been left on an overhead shelf. All were dry and intact.

The older man awoke first, his sleep untroubled—as it had always been—by his proximity to a pair of nuclear warheads. He lay on his back in the near-complete darkness, which was lit only by a handful of lights on the one active panel. He felt as if time had folded on itself and it was once again 1963. The smells, the ominous silence, the absence of human activity bringing it all vividly to life. The only difference was the fan, which refused to work. He had removed the blades and the grate to allow more air in, but the place was still stuffier than it had once been. Climbing the ladder to get to it had brought back one strong sense-memory: the way his hands smelled of perspiration and iron when he was done.

There was, however, one major difference between "then" and "now." He was not here for Mother Russia. The weapons were "safe and secure" for Iran.

When he first heard that, Bolshakov told himself it was not his concern. He was here for his son, would have come whatever the reason. But the more he reflected on it, the less willing he was to let it pass. Yuri had spent decades blaming his father's profession for the murder of Vavara. Now, the CRU agent was apparently in the same business with an even more dangerous client.

How can he reconcile his judgments with his actions? Bolshakov wondered.

The older man got up. The air was warm down here, as it always was, stirred gently by the fan. He walked to the panel, to the grip containing the food and water, and selected a snack bar of some kind. . . .

That's what comes from traveling light, he thought as he peeled off the wrapper. *Malnutrition.*

He looked back at his sleeping son. He tried not to think of the hypocrisy of the man. Then he looked at the warheads. He'd passed through them, obliviously, to get here. Had he been in this business for so long, from boy to octogenarian, that nothing murderous affected him anymore?

As he chewed, he turned to the panel. There was no destruct switch. The Kremlin had been concerned about a single poorly paid soldier being bribed to shut the missiles down.

"Get away from there."

Bolshakov looked back. Yuri was standing beside the cot, a 9×18mm Makarov held hip-high. It was pointed at the older man. Bolshakov turned fully and faced him.

"I can do no damage," the man calmly assured him. "But if you want to shoot me, please go ahead." He smiled faintly. "It would be fitting. That was the same handgun I had here."

"I want to shoot," Yuri said, stepping forward. "I want to very badly. I want to scream. I want to do *something* to get rid of this hate."

"Do both. They're easy."

"No. None of that would help. It would only add patricide to this corrupt scenario you created. So just move away and stay away."

Bolshakov did as he was told. There was a time, down here, when he and the other seamen practiced knife fighting in the event of an invasion by American troops. Now, that fist held a snack bar. The scenario wasn't just corrupt, it was surreal, comical.

Yuri lowered the weapon.

"Do you really intend to turn these warheads over to Iran?" Bolshakov asked.

"Those are my orders."

"Simple orders, part of a clean plan," his father said thoughtfully. "We sell to Iran and make a great deal of money. The United States is forced to move against the ayatollahs, which means that they buy more weapons from us. The generals take bribes, arms become a profit center, and you, Yuri, are complicit in a large-scale program like the one I ran. The only difference is that you are selling to a foreign power and it is all government sanctioned. Morally, it's no better . . . arguably worse, if you consider the scope of the destruction."

"*We* form alliances to protect Russia. *You* sold weapons that killed Russians. You have no moral standing. You have only— and this remains to be determined—only a slight chance at redeeming your honor in the eyes of the Kremlin."

"And in your eyes?"

Yuri was utterly cold and still, as if he were an outcrop of the bunker itself.

The gun was still pointed down but his face began to contort— to Bolshakov it happened so slowly that it appeared to be clay melting in the hot sun. And then the young man screamed, a high-pitched cry that sounded more boy than man. Bolshakov wanted to go to him but remained where he was, squeezing the bar so tightly that it crumbled.

When it stopped, Yuri panted and stared and looked like he wanted to jump at the older man—but sounds coming through the air vent stopped them. Both men were instantly free of the past; they were present and alert.

The van, Bolshakov thought. *Someone has seen it.* The voices were too muted for them to hear what was being said, only to determine that there were at least two individuals above.

As quickly as Yuri had gone from man to child and back, he turned into something else—something feral. He grabbed his heavy overcoat, and moved toward the hatch.

"You will let me out, and then in," he quietly ordered his father.

"Yuri, think about this—"

"About what, the mission? Is this it, then? Your patriotic return?"

"Son, if you chase them away others may come. If you kill them, others *will* come. They cannot move the van, you saw to that. And they have to know someone will be returning—"

"Let me out. Then let me back in."

"Please, don't go out like this. What if they are police—?"

Yuri went to the hatch and opened it. He glared behind him as he buttoned his coat and slipped the gun in his right pocket. "Now."

Bolshakov had nothing vested in the mission, only in his son. He did not agree with what Yuri was doing but the time for being a disciplining parent was dead. Bolshakov had killed it. Guilt and yearning were compelling him to be the supportive father. He knew that neither, however, was right. There was another way.

He came forward, stepping halfway into the shaft and lightly taking Yuri by the arm. The younger man looked as if he wanted to hit something.

"Yuri, I have a better idea," Bolshakov said quietly.

He then proceeded to explain something Rear Admiral Merkassov had taught him decades before: how to undermine an enemy.

CHAPTER THIRTY-NINE

Havana, Cuba
July 2, 1:32 A.M.

"Who are you and why did you lie back there? About everything?"

As soon as they left the station, Dr. Bermejo hooked her hand in McCord's free arm. He did not know whether that was for support or to keep him from running off. She also asked the question in English. McCord wondered if that was for his sake or so that the occasional passerby might not understand what they were discussing.

He hefted his bag with his free arm, buying himself a moment to consider his answer. He did not want to scare her into silence. He also did not want to flatter her; she did not seem like someone who needed or would fall for that.

"My name is Roger McCord," he said. "I lied to get into Cuba, said I was here to scull with rowers I know, and I saw no reason to change course."

She was silent for a moment, then laughed a single, explosive "Ha! An honest liar!"

"I did not just happen to be there," he said carefully, but also aware of the investigation that would continue at the *Comandancia General*.

"Of course not," Adoncia said. "Who would be?"

"I would like to help your friend Mr. Sanjulian."

"Do you know him?"

"Never met him," McCord admitted.

"How would you help him?"

"I'm not sure," he said. "But I *am* sure I can do something."

"I see. I gather, Mr. McCord, that you don't want the Russians here any more than he does," she said. "Though not for the same reason."

"That is correct," McCord said.

She squeezed his arm in a small show of affection. "I appreciate what you did for me back there, but I am not interested in swapping one taskmaster for another. The Russian conscripts—they are here for women and drink. The Americans I have known were here for money and a military footprint. What are you here for?"

"Help," he said. "With a word."

She looked at him for the first time. "A word? What word?"

"Anadyr," he replied.

Adoncia stopped walking. They were within sight of McCord's hotel. "How did you hear of it?"

"It keeps showing up in people's—in their travel plans," McCord said. "Not Cubans, just Russians and others."

Adoncia considered this and resumed walking. She was still holding on to McCord.

"It is a very funny coincidence, if you think about it that way," she said.

"What is?"

"This is the second time today a man has come to me with something that I did not ask to be involved in," Adoncia replied. "That's a lot to ask of a woman who is eighty-three and very set in her ways."

"The first man was Cuban," McCord observed. "That made it easier for you to help."

"Very much so."

"I'm sorry to impose on you," he said. "Truly."

"But you do so, reluctantly, because your cause is righteous," she said, raising her unlit cigar with a flourish.

"Dr. Bermejo, tell me it is not, tell me there is nothing to be concerned about, and I'll leave you," McCord said.

The woman lowered her arm. "I have lived in the shadow of 'concern' for most of my life. Not enough to eat, not enough ammunition, too much ammunition in the wrong hands, America imperialists, Russian imperialists, my personal safety. . . . Why should I take on your problems, Mr. McCord? You only took on mine because you needed me, yes?"

"That's right. But I didn't do it for me."

"No," she said as she considered his answer. "You did it for—your government? Your military, which still occupies a corner of my land? Both?"

McCord was not going to debate her points. She wasn't wrong and there wasn't time.

"Dr. Bermejo, I can't answer for the past or the future. All I'm concerned about is the threat facing the present."

"So, you are an altruist?"

McCord didn't know what was talking here: her anti-imperialism, the alcohol, or just inherent stubbornness. There wasn't time for him to weave through that, either.

"No," he replied. "I'll tell you what I am. I'm a retired U.S. Marine. I was a company commander in Fallujah and a battalion exec in Ramadi. I was wounded twice, the second time with a leg injury so bad it ended my combat career. The people around me in the hospital? Many were worse. Most were. I'm sure you've seen that in your career."

She was silent, listening. Remembering.

"That second time I was laid up for months and decided to read *Ivan Denisovich*. I wonder if you can figure out why."

"Solzhenitsyn was a bitter soldier," she replied quietly.

"And a political prisoner," McCord said. "It was irrelevant to me that he was Russian. Or that Boris Pasternak was Russian. Or that Ernest Hemingway was an American. That novel is by a man who was still a patriot but not a nationalist, if that makes any sense. His home was still his home but his vision had been broadened." McCord laughed sincerely. "I'm no Solzhenitsyn, Dr. Bermejo. For one thing, I can't write a passable sentence. For another, I am not quite so jaded. Not yet. But I will tell you that if it is possible to save any life, anywhere, at any time, I will do so. Even if you choose not to help me, if you ask, I will walk back in there and help you free Enrich Sanjulian this minute. I also believe in the words of another author, Mark Twain, who wrote, 'Do what's right.'"

"How precious to know what 'right' is," she said quietly. Her shoulders relaxed in a way that silently signified trust. "I'm still searching. But, yes. Life first. If we do not secure that, there can be no further discussion." Her eyes, which had been fixed on some elusive vision, came back to McCord. "This has troubled me, too, if you must know."

"What has?"

"What you ask about. Perhaps you're right." She took a moment to retrieve the matches from her hip pocket and lit her cigar.

McCord used the delay to remember the woman's face. The face of a humanist, not a Cuban. Unlike him, she was about to betray a trust.

"All those years ago," she said, over smoke, "not all the missiles were sent to Cuba. And none of those other warheads was recalled."

"Anadyr," McCord said, his fears made real.

"Anadyr," she repeated.

CHAPTER FORTY

Outpost N64, Anadyr, Russia
July 2, 6:36 P.M.

It was not a weapon of mass destruction that emerged from the hatch. It was Konstantin Bolshakov, his face immediately feeling the drop in temperature and passing it along to his chest. His arms shivered as he stepped out, the nighttime sun contributing little warmth.

"Hello," he said, his voice cutting through the brittle cold.

Two men stood on either side of the car, near the front. One was tall, one was short, both wore heavy parkas with hoods. The hood of the car was upraised.

Neither man answered his greeting. He stepped to the surface, careful not to make any sudden moves. Their pockets bulged ominously. Both men were wearing gloves but he knew, from experience, that those could come off in an instant.

"My name is Konstantin," Bolshakov said. "My team and I are doing maintenance here. That is our car."

From the corner of his eye he saw their own truck on the road, behind the gate. Bolshakov recognized it immediately, an

old four-by-four two-ton GAZ-63. Produced at the Gorky
Automobile Plant, it was the workhorse out here during their stay.
He suspected it was sold when the military departed, marked
officially as scrapped.

The men conversed in low voices, then came toward him
around opposite sides of the vehicle.

"No one comes out here anymore," the taller man continued.
"Why are you here?"

"As I said—"

"We know what you *said*," the shorter man cut him off. "But
what would need 'maintenance' in an abandoned military facility?
There have always been rumors about this place. Talk of weapons.
We'd like to go down and see."

"That won't be possible," Bolshakov told them.

The taller man pulled back his hood so he could get a clearer
look at Bolshakov. He was bald with a tattoo on his scalp. He was
most likely a gang member, one of the many pro-Russia thugs
who operated with the consent of Moscow and the local com-
munities.

"You're a grandpa!" the man marveled.

"I'm not alone, I assure you," Bolshakov said.

"Then maybe we can all help one another," said the shorter
man as they cleared the rental van. They were now just a few feet
from the hatch. "You let us see what is down there, then perhaps
we can help with your 'maintenance.'"

Bolshakov shook his head sadly. "Even if you go down there,
you cannot get in."

"Why is that?" the taller man asked.

"You don't know how."

"You'll tell us."

Bolshakov shook his head again.

"I think you will," the shorter man said, drawing a 9×18mm Makarov handgun from his pocket. That, too, was a remnant from the bunker's past.

"We know this place," the taller man said with a sweep of his arm. "We have been coming here since boyhood. We figured that this is the only way in or out, which means that no one inside will ever *get* out unless you cooperate. Either you let us in or we close the hatch and roll your car over it. Then," he warned, "we set a fire over by the vent that is deep in the grasses—"

He turned and jerked a thumb toward the grate that Bolshakov had uncovered. Yuri was standing in the opening, his 9×18mm Makarov held straight ahead, his left hand supporting his right.

The shorter man turned to see what had stopped his companion. Both men stood very still, twisted backward at the waist.

Bolshakov stepped out of the line of fire. He knew that the next move was a purely tactical decision, not a moral one. Kill them and they would be missed; others would come. Release them and they would certainly return with fellow gang members. Take them prisoner and security would be breached when the Iranians left.

"Drop your gun and turn around," Yuri told them.

The men obeyed. Bolshakov collected the shorter man's gun, patted the other man's pocket and removed a second weapon. He tossed them aside. He did not look at the two men. He knew which course his son would choose.

Yuri walked over and shot both men in the back of the head in quick, accurate succession. Bolshakov's shoulders sagged as the shots were swallowed by the wind. The shooting was execution-style, the method preferred by gang members. When the bodies were eventually discovered, this would be considered an attack by rivals.

"Go back inside," Yuri told his father. "I will take care of this."

"What will you do with the truck?"

"Over the seawall," Yuri replied, tucking his gun in his pocket and grabbing one man by the top of his blood-spattered hood. "With luck, they won't be found for several days."

Bolshakov nodded and went back into the hatch. It felt good to get out of the wind, though he felt colder now than he had before.

The art of distraction, he thought. He wondered what Rear Admiral Merkassov would think, knowing that his student had used it to kill.

"You are on assignment for the motherland," he could hear the man's voice in his head. *"Nothing is a higher priority than success."*

But the Russia of today was not the Soviet Union of 1962, and tasks blindly followed when he was in his twenties were fiercely questioned now that he was in his eighties. This mission was a fuzzy version of patriotism. Iran wasn't Cuba, it was a powerful nation that could one day threaten Moscow. To provide them with operational nuclear warheads—

The tone Bolshakov had taken during the ride out here was perhaps too belligerent. He would try talking to Yuri one more time—not to change the young man's mind but to understand it.

Killing—he never had a problem sleeping after that. He always slept better, in fact, after debts were paid in blood. There was nothing halfway or uncertain about a bullet to the head. The calculation was ethical as well as logistical. But murder, mass destruction . . . that was something else.

Especially, he thought, *when you have the power to prevent it.* . . .

CHAPTER FORTY-ONE

After his last conversation with McCord, to tell him about Mauricio's Russian wife, Chase Williams had eased onto the leather sofa for a quick nap. The phone was on the coffee table; when it woke him, he had no idea whether one minute or one hour had passed.

A half hour, he saw. Enough to take the edge off.

"Yeah, Roger," he said.

"Nukes," he said.

"At that location," Williams said.

"That's right. Fifty-six years old, apparently still functional."

With, it appeared, a Russian arms dealer and possibly an Iranian military representative headed to that location.

"What are you going to do?" Williams asked.

"I had to lie to the police to get the information—they'll probably come looking for me. I'll have to lay low somewhere."

It was over five hundred miles to Guantanamo, so seeking

sanctuary there was probably out of the question. "Did you make any friends there?"

"Possibly," McCord told him. "I'll be in touch."

Williams hung up. He reluctantly pushed McCord's situation from his mind to deal with the larger issue. While he brought up a map on his tablet, he put in a call to Mike Volner.

"Yes, sir," Volner answered at once.

"I need your team at Elmendorf AFB." The base was located in Anchorage, the nearest staging area to whatever was going on in Anadyr.

"Roger," Volner replied. "I'll have Moore airborne ASAP. My orders?"

"I'm looking up commercial flights; I don't see how I can get you there in time." A military flight over Russian airspace was out of the question.

"Is there an ECP?" Volner asked.

An exit choke point was the place where leaders fled a failed operation, typically a public airport or train station; it could also be a safe haven, such as a friendly city where they could become lost in a crowd. It was always easy to spot a player who was running for his life: he was the one weaving and running faster than everyone else.

"Tehran, probably. Moscow, possibly. No place that helps us."

Williams knew that Volner would never stall a mission just so he could be at the controls. He looked quickly at the last month of JSOC drills.

"Then let me do this," Volner said. "I'll stay put and work out the plans for the team, get it to them soon after takeoff. Are we looking at land or sea?"

"Not enough intel to say," Williams informed him. He shut the file. "You're confident that Moore can handle this?"

"He's ready," Volner said.

Special Forces Operations' Sergeant. Charles Moore was the Brooklyn-born "whip-cracker," as Volner described him, a tough and thorough drill instructor. Williams was referring to his recent actions on the Ukraine-Russia border in which his lone wolf qualities shined, not any command ability.

"All right, Major," Williams said. "Get 'em flying."

Volner said he would text when they were up and had an ETA. In the meantime, Williams was going to have to inform the president through Trevor Harward. JSOC could be detached on request by Op-Center 24-7 but the *Posse Comitatus* statute precluded the use of this team in the continental United States without a presidential waiver.

He put in the call. A groggy Harward heard him out, then asked, "Does General Ghasemi figure into this?"

"I don't know," Williams said.

"Should we talk to him again?"

It sounded more like the groggy national security advisor was thinking out loud rather than soliciting an opinion.

"That can wait until we know where the Iranian aircraft is going," Harward went on. "I'll brief the commands at Elmendorf, Clear, and Eielson in case something goes active before your team gets there."

"What are you prepared to do?" Williams asked. "These are viable warheads we're looking at . . . and an Iranian nuclear physicist on her way."

"I'm prepared to tell my superiors and colleagues just that," Harward said, "and to advise them it'd be a bad idea to let Tehran get those nukes."

Williams frowned. In other words, he'd pass the buck. "I'd keep this information local, at any rate," Williams cautioned.

"Of course."

Williams was concerned that the Russians had highly sophisticated satellite eyes and ears on these Air Force bases so close to their shores. If word went out from high command, any preparations or unusual activity might be picked up and additional Russian resources would be brought to bear.

"I've gotta tell you, Chase—and this may be just two hours sleep talking—but ever since you guys were pulled from the mothballs, I've been getting less rest than I used to. If it isn't calls, it's reports. If it isn't reports, it's flags on someone else's reports. If it's none of that, it's the president asking me to find out what you think. It almost seems like there's been an uptick in hostile activity just to welcome you back."

"Nothing's changed out there," Williams said. "We believe in sweating the small stuff before it becomes big stuff. If Iran is going to collect Russian nukes, what's the point in kicking that can down the road?"

Harward snickered. "Because it's not a direct threat to us?"

"'First they came for the socialists, and I did not speak out . . .'" Williams began.

"Right, right," Harward said. "'Then they came for me—and there was no one left to speak for me.' You can't reduce the world to a poem. But the president agrees with you, so off we go again."

Harward told Williams to call only with urgent developments and said he would brief the president in the morning.

"I don't know what scares me more," Harward said. "The fact that we may need a waiver to protect our shores up there . . . or that we won't because we will be operating again on foreign soil."

Williams ended the call glad that his team, his location, and his personal interests were all outside the Beltway. If he had to deal with this kind of thick inertia every day he would—

"Be as miserable as Trevor Harward," he muttered as he set the phone on the table, lay back, and threw his arm over his eyes to catch what sleep he could.

CHAPTER FORTY-TWO

Pope Field, Cumberland, North Carolina
July 2, 2:00 A.M.

The Joint Special Operations Command was a platoon-sized unit that trained at Fort Bragg and could be detached on request by Op-Center, 24-7. When he was assigned to the team, Sergeant Moore thought it would be "bridesmaid detail": all dressed up but never quite making it to the altar.

He was wrong. But that was to be expected. The men were the same age, with birthdays a week apart, but he was the cynic to Major Volner's optimist. In fact, the two were utterly dissimilar, which is what made them such a good fit. Moore was the product of a tight—and outspoken—Irish family while Volner was raised by a very proper grandmother; he was a satyr in contrast to Volner's one-woman approach to dating; Moore embraced the regimen of repetitive free weights while Volner preferred the asymmetrical challenge of rock climbing.

And now, in the warm predawn hours, with the smell of jet fuel not yet heavy on the tarmac, the JSOC team lifted off from Pope Field. Formerly designated Pope Air Force Base, the complex is still utilized by the Air Force but is now a U.S. Army asset that is an extension of the Fort Bragg Garrison. Absent the major, the eleven-man JSOC contingent, with their five-man support team, had the cavernous belly of the 174-foot-long C-17 more or less all to themselves. The aircraft was designed to hold 102 paratroopers and equipment; the team was fairly lost inside. There had not been time for supplies or ordnance to be designated and loaded; Moore got the call from Volner, the team got the wake-up from Moore, and forty minutes later the team and their gear were onboard. This included a compact but highly capable communications suite, cots that were functional but little more, a field kitchen, and a variety of cold-weather operational gear. The team also carried large and small arms, grenades, C-4, and ordnance packed with the stable, highly potent explosive IMX-101. They were a self-contained operation, prepared to do just about anything and to wait for as long as it took.

Included in the load-in was each individual's secure tablet which, during flight, would be loaded with mission details. Seated in the inadequately cushioned seats along the interior walls of the fuselage, constantly rattled by the four fully reversible F117-PW-100 engines—each with a thundering 40,440 pounds of thrust—Moore would review the details first, discuss the plan with Volner, make whatever tweaks were necessary, then share with the rest of the team.

With its range of 2,400 nautical miles, the big Globemaster III would take two aerial refuelings en route. Once the aircraft landed, the JSOC contingent would be directed to a storage hangar in a remote corner of the base. There, they would unload their gear and either make themselves at home or saddle up—events, and nothing else, would determine that.

Moore hoped there would be no waiting. He would try and catch a little sleep before Volner made contact. After that, once the plan was in his head, he did not want to stop. It wasn't just a question of adrenaline, it was a matter of muscle memory. The plan would invoke training and that, in turn, would bring up the hours the team spent executing those specific drills-and-skills that were about to be called upon. Every member of the team liked for the particular drills-and-skills to be alive and active when they set out. Sustaining that over a prolonged sit-down was difficult.

As soon as the monster jet was airborne, Moore shut his eyes and hunkered into the seat as best as possible. He might have an hour or two to rest and he wanted to take advantage of that. To him, the engines were white noise that lulled him into a contented rest. All he knew was where they were headed—Joint Base Elmendorf-Richardson in Richardson, Alaska—but not why. But the location gave him a pretty good notion. The United States was not likely facing hostiles in Canada, which left only the Bering Sea.

Or the frozen Russian lands beyond.

I've never been to Elmendorf, he thought as he began to doze. *Sunshine at night, this time of year. Outside o' Brooklyn it's a weird freakin' world any way you look at it. . . .*

CHAPTER FORTY-THREE

Cargo Ship Nardis, *The Bering Sea*
July 2, 9:01 P.M.

Captain Ahmad Salehi stood on the bridge wing, just below the wheelhouse of his vessel. The wind was sharp and the sun was low in the sky yet he was not cold. He was like a chameleon: wherever he went on the sea; he immediately adapted. He was also ready, prepared to begin the most important nautical adventure in the history of the Islamic Republic of Iran—perhaps in all of Persian history.

Below him, the twin helicopters were being prepared for takeoff. One was a Mi-171, among the first delivered by Russia, a medium twin-turbine transport vehicle. That one was going to Yelizovo Airport, Petropavlovsk-Kamchatsky, Kamchatka Krai. The other—

The other, Salehi thought admiringly.

That was a Boeing CH-47 Chinook tandem rotor heavy-lift helicopter. That was going to a location outside of the Russian city of Anadyr. It was being sent to collect "the twins," as Prosecutor Younesi had named them. Even if Dr. Ghasemi determined that they weren't functioning—which was unlikely, given the environmentally safe state in which they had been stored—the nuclear material itself would be pristine. It would be an easy matter for Iranian scientists to reconstruct the damaged operative workings.

And like the Roman empire that had succeeded great Cyrus, he thought, *those young twins would suckle on a wolf and give rise to unprecedented global conquest.* He did not know the specific plans, or the timetable, but he knew that an Iran, finally nuclear, testing just one of these weapons in the desert, would shake the ground on which all of civilization rested.

Lieutenant Commander Chitchian arrived to inform the captain that the aircraft carrying Dr. Parand Ghasemi was an hour from landing. Salehi told him to order the Mi-171 aloft, and then the CH-47.

The powder-blue helicopter rose and banked toward shore. It was followed by the ivory-white Chinook, and only then did Salehi finally feel a chill—not from the cold but from excitement. He offered a quiet prayer of thanks for this honor, then turned toward the wheelhouse so he could be at his post when they reached the coast off Anadyr.

CHAPTER FORTY-FOUR

Yelizovo Airport, Petropavlovsk-Kamchatsky,
Kamchatka Krai
July 3, 2:34 A.M.

Parand emerged from the aircraft, down the steps to a tarmac, like an electron that had been knocked from its orbit: free and explosive. She had not slept at all during the flight, she had ingested information. Electrified, she moved quickly, carrying her bags and the language books she had been studying, her eyes seeking a sign with the words she had been taught to recognize in Cyrillic: Dr. Ghasemi. There was no need for secrecy; any foreign agent who might be watching for her would not only be inside, they would not have seen any Muslim-attired women emerge from the aircraft. Parand had not embraced Islam but she understood the need to respect the men who did, the men she would be working with. Nor would it have been possible for anyone to follow her in any case. Her ride was there: she saw the sign—written in red, as she'd been told—among a small row of livery drivers waiting for other passengers.

After months of planning, she was eager beyond anything

she had anticipated. The environment helped. Pulling up to the terminal she had seen Russian military aircraft, mostly steely-gray fighter jets, parked openly in front of their own, dedicated hangars. Families with young children waited inside the boxy, two-story structure; latent death lurked not far away. It was almost religious in its orderly completeness, from birth to death.

She met the tall man in black military attire and uttered what she had been told to say: "N6."

The man replied with a single numeral: "4."

Then they were off, toward a motorized cart waiting near the building. The man wordlessly took her bags. He said nothing, walked efficiently, and within under two minutes they were driving toward one of the fortified hangars that had been cut in an adjoining hillside. The only words he said now were into a radio. She did not understand them; from his monotone, she assumed he was telling someone they were on the way. Each time they crossed a tarred-seam in the concrete she winced, every jolt hurting her scarred back. She forced herself to think of something other than the pain. It mustn't impede her.

She looked to her right, beyond the terminal. There were snow-topped mountains. From her reading, she recognized the titan in the middle from her reading: *Gora Moroznaya*, Frosty Mountain. To the left, now, she saw the space telemetry station, one of the most advanced in the world. She would like to have stopped there, to see Earth from another perspective. But just knowing it was there, and that she was close to it, gave her a rush of excitement. How Sadeq Farhadi would have enjoyed seeing that.

Perhaps one day we can return, she thought.

Dazed and starstruck, she allowed her mind to go elsewhere, to a place from which she had shielded herself.

Papa, papa, papa . . .

In her mind, she saw his face, her mother—

No! She would not be so *stupid*. This was no time for family or lovers, no time for sentiment. There should only be one thing on her mind, and she focused on the words she had studied, the scant blueprints she had been shown, the timetable—that was very important. She did not have a lot of time to do what must be done. Her countrymen had to be in and out with Parand and their cargo.

Nothing matters but that!

They had reached the impressive, comfortable-looking helicopter that was to take her to her destination. A fuel hose was being disconnected and the overhead propeller and the tail rotor were already spinning. A staircase was down. The cart swung around so that Parand was at the foot of the steps. An Iranian officer with a pleasant smile tucked in his neatly trimmed beard helped her out and inside while another man collected her bags. He introduced himself as Lieutenant Amiri and she replied with her own full name, as she'd been instructed. At the doorway she thought to turn and thank her driver with a wave but he was already gone. Even before she had been shown to her seat the staircase had been lifted and the door shut.

These men, too, knew they were on a strict timetable. In under a minute they were aloft.

Parand took just a moment to admire the rocky old man in

the distance—it reminded her of her father, accomplished but lost under ice and shrinking as she ascended. She was offered tea and gratefully accepted it. Then, as if to help order her mind, Parand tore through her materials and eliminated everything about the journey, everything Russian that was not about the outpost. Now she could actively forget those things and concentrate on the heart of the mission.

She knew from her reading that they would be making a brief refueling stop at a field in Korf, to the northwest, before continuing to their destination. The entire journey would take three and one-half hours, and when she had read and re-read everything until it started to blur—she stopped. She knew, from her university days, that now her brain would do the heavy lifting on its own.

Now it was time to rest.

She dreamt: of Sadeq, of her father, of the prison. Somewhere inside her brain, the beat of the rotors registered as a steadying drone. Energy did not like chaos, and hers had been chaotic; sound was a calming, homogenizing force, which was the reason she was able to sleep. When the sound finally changed, she woke with a start.

The helicopter was descending on a barren landscape. The sea was ahead, flat, sparsely grassed lands behind. Below—

There it was. She only thought what would be irreverent to speak: this was holy ground. Her breath came faster, her heart sped, her rested eyes sought the landmarks she had been told to expect. The main hatch, the air vent.

The twin silos.

Tears formed and ran warmly into her smile. She quickly went through the papers she would need below, the old Soviet manual she had been provided, and held it under her arm as tight and precious as if it were a child. The helicopter touched down with the gentlest bump and she was on her feet before the officer entered the cabin.

The warm air continued to circulate but she could feel the radiant cold already pressing against the exterior of the fuselage. It, too, was invigorating. With purposeful stride, she went toward him and waited while Lieutenant Amiri made his way from the cockpit with a large case that resembled an old-fashioned valise. She did not know, but assumed, that this was an uplink to the cargo ship. He set it down, opened the door, and dropped the short staircase. A young man in a great coat was hurrying toward them, bent low and holding his fur-lined hat on his head. He looked up without expression, offered helping hands. Parand carefully passed him her documents and he clutched them tight to his chest as he backed away.

She descended, followed by the officer who had greeted her. Then the steps were withdrawn, the door shut, and the helicopter powered down. The sea wind pushed hard against them, forcing them to turn their faces and preventing conversation. But even turned to the south, Parand's eyes never left the heavy open hatch just to the east.

The Russian moved adroitly onto the ladder, losing neither his balance nor the documents as he climbed down. Parand descended next, helped and then followed by the crewman. The Russian passed her belongings to the Iranian, went back up the ladder to wait for the Iranian officer. When he arrived after several minutes, he shut the hatch. For a moment, they were in a dark and timeless space, silent save for their own breath and scraping footsteps.

And then latches were moved, the interior door opened, and Parand humbly stepped into both the past and the future.

Behind her, Lieutenant Amiri did two things. First, he sent a test message through the portable comm.

"Site achieved," he said in Pashto—an Eastern Iranian language that might befuddle the Russians if they spoke modern Persian.

"Message received," came the reply.

The second thing he did was touch his finger to the stopwatch icon on his phone. Then he looked at Parand and said a single word:

"Begin."

CHAPTER FORTY-FIVE

Havana, Cuba
July 3, 10:30 A.M.

When Roger McCord spoke with Chase Williams in the midnight hour, he had hoped he was correct—that he'd made a friend here. Without one, in the vernacular of his old sculling instructor, he would be "AWOL": adrift without leverage.

Whether it was sympathy, pity, a touch of drunkenness, admiration, or some combination thereof, Adoncia had decided to help. She might not be a friend, but at least she wasn't an enemy. And her decision, made quickly, had come none too soon.

"You cannot go to the hotel," she had said after his call.

McCord told her he knew that, and was thinking of "borrowing" a motorbike to at least get out of the old part of Havana.

"They will find you," she assured him. "They are good at roadblocks and I do not think you know your way here."

"Why do you say that?"

"We just walked past your hotel," she said. She was thinking while she spoke. "But I have a place. We'll need a taxi."

"That I can provide," McCord said as he called the driver

who had brought him here. He was there within five minutes. Adoncia provided a destination: *La Catedral de la Virgen María de la Concepción Inmaculada de La Habana.*

"Havana Cathedral," she said. "Completed in 1777, built of coral mined from the seabed. You can see fossils in the walls. I—I, too, see the past."

That was all she said until they arrived. The Baroque-Tuscan edifice towered over the *Plaza de la Catedral* but McCord did not have time to admire it. They did not enter through the large rust-red doors out front but walked around the side. It was a very dark, narrow path; he sought and found signs, one of which said *TACÓN* and the other *EMPEDRADO*, in case he needed to inform Williams. To McCord's left was one of the two bell towers that buttressed the cathedral. On the right was a two-story structure that appeared to have been built at the same time as the cathedral.

"*Palacio del Conde Lombillo*," she said around her still unlit cigar. "Museum . . . city offices . . . I don't know, many varied uses over the years, I've lost track. But"—she raised a finger—"a sanctuary for the Revolution when we were not permitted to meet at the university."

Years peeled from the woman as they headed toward an iron gate that opened into an alley. There was a keypad and Adoncia input the code. The latch popped reassuringly and she leaned on the old ironworks.

"The padre," she said, jerking her head toward the cathedral. "One of us." Her voice lowered conspiratorially. "Doesn't like the Russians, either. He and a few others here keep the flames alive."

They entered the alley, shut the door, and went to a door at the very end. McCord did not like the fact that he was in a dead-end alley in a building whose layout he did not know. But a distant siren reminded him of his situation, and there was something else, something he *did* like: the strong smell of salty sea air.

Hidden in shadow, the woman opened a sturdy wooden door, ushered McCord in, and eased behind him to push it shut with her shoulder. There was a strong smell of musty rot in here. She felt for an overhead strip and pulled it. A single hooded light bulb came on.

The room was about four feet deep and six feet wide. It was filled with firewood.

"There is a trap door beneath the cords there," she pointed toward the back. "But I do not think we will need it."

"We?" McCord said.

"Sure. Yes. I'm staying." She settled on a pile of wood as if it were a familiar old chair. "There is an old chamber pot," she said, pointing to an area behind the door. "Just in case."

"Thank you," he said, settling onto his own pile of wood and finally, happily, setting his go-bag down. "I have water and granola bars, if you'd like anything."

"A match, but then the custodian might find us. He has no reason to come here during the summer."

McCord finally allowed himself to relax. It was one of those familiar situations where he did not realize how tense he was until he let everything go.

"You've been very kind," he said quietly, though the wood soaked up sound as if it were water.

"I've been—no, it's not that," she said. "I've been enjoying myself. No," she said again. "Yes, maybe . . . but it's more feeling useful. Yes," she finally agreed with herself. "Useful. And in the right way, for my people and not for invaders. It has been very long since I've had that feeling." Her dark eyes landed on Mc-Cord. She took the cigar from her mouth and jabbed it at him. "There are two things I have for you."

"Oh?"

"The first," she said, "is a use. I do not know what you are doing with the information I gave you, but I hope it is not a replay of what was done here. What do you call it? *¿La política arriesgada?*"

"I think you mean 'brinkmanship,' if you're referring to the old missile crisis."

"That's it, brinkmanship." She waved the cigar dismissively. "Not that."

"No," he assured her. "We just don't want those warheads running around loose or in the hands of people who might actually use them."

"I believe that, which is why I am sitting on a pile of wood with you," she said. "And probably because I had too much to drink. But my use for you is that I wish you to go home and use whatever little influence you have to keep America out. Not as tourists, or guests, but as conquerors . . . again."

"I don't have 'little' influence," he told her. "I have none. But I do have a boss who talks to the president on a regular basis. He's a good man and I will share your story, your ideas. He will do what he can, I can assure you."

"Good," she said. "I cannot ask for more. And it is a start."

She put the cigar back in her mouth and nodded quietly in apparent satisfaction.

"Dr. Bermejo . . . you said there were two things you have for me."

"That's right," she said, remembering. "It's been a long day, I'm sorry. It's beginning to catch up to me. The second thing is something you said before."

"About?"

She smiled. "About how you are going to leave Cuba without the police apprehending you."

It was a pleasant thought to go to sleep on. Using his go-bag as a pillow, McCord relocated to the floor where he awoke late the following morning—

Alone, except for a curious message.

CHAPTER FORTY-SIX

Globemaster III, southeast of Anchorage, Alaska
July 3, 5:34 A.M.

"They do Iditarods here!"

That was the takeaway of Private First Class Dick Siegel to the briefing file on the company iPad. A New Yorker, like Moore, Siegel was from Staten Island where he used to assemble his own winter mush-teams from a sled and the family's two German shepherds.

"Don't wanna break your heart, but you probably won't have time," Moore shouted down the row as the aircraft made its final approach. Any possible follow-through—and Siegel usually had something to add—was lost as Moore received a communication directly from Op-Center. It came through the aircraft comm system so that he could hear it through the headphones that sat in his lap.

"Yes, sir?" he said.

"Sergeant, it's Mike Volner."

"Sir."

"Director Williams is on the call and will be conducting this briefing. Mr. Director?"

"Sergeant, I'm having images sent from the Tank," he said. "There's a container ship one hundred and sixty miles south of Anadyr and two helicopters on the ground, on the coastline, northwest of the vessel. Preliminary satellite recon shows a CH-47 and a Mi-171."

"Cargo or personnel on the Chinook?" Moore asked.

"That isn't known. Based on additional intel, we believe the ship and choppers may be Iranian traveling without markings. There's also a van, Russian origin. We do not know if this is an officially sanctioned operation; the presence of one of the players, a Russian named Bolshakov, suggests an illegal arms transaction. We believe the purpose of this meeting is to transfer nuclear warheads that have been stored in an underground facility at that location since the Cold War."

"Iran's got Chinooks and Mil factory aircraft," Volner said.

"Correct," Williams said. "And a scientist who we believe is in-country, a nuclear physicist named Parand Ghasemi."

As the men spoke, the images began arriving on Moore's tablet. He looked at the installation locale first. The evening sun provided little detail in the long shadows, but the images did reveal something else, something that Moore did not find encouraging.

"You will note," Volner said, "there's a rocky sea ledge which suggests that any bunker built inside will be virtually impregnable."

"We suspect it was designed to survive not just a siege but a nuclear strike," Williams said.

A second batch of images arrived. They showed the ship. Two helicopter pads were plainly visible, even in the semidarkness.

"There are a number of operational options," Volner said, "none of them ideal. If the vehicles are disabled, no one and nothing leaves. But that entails an attack on Russian soil."

"They forgave us once," Williams said. "I don't want to press our luck."

The director was referring to the fight between JSOC and Ukrainian commandos in Sudzha, Russia, nearly one month before.

"We also have the ship, which is carefully in international waters," Williams went on. "That suggests they don't want to be buzzed by Russians, either—which lends support to the rogue operation scenario."

"We've got to stop doing the Kremlin's heavy lifting," Moore remarked as he studied the few images of the vessel. "I don't see any heavy artillery."

"Or cargo," Williams said. "The ship shows up in a few images. It was low profile all the way."

"Slip in, slip out."

"Officially, of course, we can't launch an attack that would sink her and kill Iranian sailors," Williams said.

"And they have doubtless drilled to deal with gunships or attempts to board," Volner added.

"We're obviously not equipped to box her in," Moore said.

"That's a Navy call," Williams told him. "And frankly, we know how it ends: Tehran whines, the ship sits at sea and pretends to starve, a U.N. party is allowed onboard, they find nothing, the vessel is released—with the nukes—and the U.S. ends up with more Iranian egg on its face."

"Disable her?" Moore suggested.

"Arguably less advantageous," Williams told him. "They send repair ships and then it's a shell game—we won't know where the warheads are."

Moore looked at the overhead photos of the landscape, covered with a fine grid and coordinates.

"They're obviously going to evac by Chinook," Moore said. "What if it goes down in the sea?"

"If the nukes are intact, Iran's still in the best position to recover," Volner noted. "And if they're not—we're the guys who poisoned the Bering Sea."

Moore was not immediately seeing a mission here. He was beginning to wonder whether Dick Siegel was going to get to run an Iditarod after all.

And then he was reminded of something Williams had said.

"What about this scientist?" Moore asked. "Parand Ghasemi?"

"Just missed her," Volner said. "We tracked her aircraft to Yelizovo Airport, well to the south. They probably flew her there so Anadyr wouldn't seem like a convention site. We tracked what is likely this same Mi-171 flying from Yelizovo to this location."

"How long has she been there?" Moore asked.

"Long enough to get inside, but not to do much more," Volner said.

Moore heard what the major had really just said. He exhaled, birthing a little smile in the process. "So we've got time to intercept the warheads. Pin 'em down or pick 'em up?"

Williams said, "I don't know yet. That will be the president's call."

Moore's smile evaporated. He was just as likely to let the transfer go as planned and have the diplomats hash it out. The net result, as always, was that Tehran would get what it wanted.

"Sirs," Moore said, looking at the cargo ship, "there's another option. Sea-to-sea. Not to disable or commandeer but to prevent the transfer."

"How?" Williams asked.

"No landing pad, no landing."

The other two were silent for a moment. Williams broke it.

"You come at them from above, you take fire," Williams said.

"We don't do it that way," Volner thought out loud. "We come in unmarked, by sea."

Moore was looking at the photos of the cargo ship. "We come in long shadow side after the Chinook takes off," he said. "Everyone will be watching that."

"You're talking about transferring from boat to ship," Williams said.

"We've done it," Volner said. "Borrowed our drill from the SEAL Team Six manual. Ran up along the side of a speeding cutter, hooked on, hauled ass onboard."

"You last ran it three weeks ago," Williams said, bringing up and reading the drill report.

"We *first* ran it three weeks ago," Volner admitted. "Ballbuster. But every man made it. Eventually."

Williams knew that nothing was guaranteed in any military adventure, though this seemed riskier than anything he'd heard.

"I don't like it but I don't have anything better," Williams admitted.

"It's not so bad, sir," Volner assured him. "In fact, we've got the easy job, sir."

"Sergeant?"

The major replied, "You're the one who has to sell it to the president."

CHAPTER FORTY-SEVEN

Op-Center Headquarters, Fort Belvoir North,
Springfield, Virginia
July 3, 6:40 A.M.

After hanging up with his commanders, Williams phoned Trevor Harward. Only as an afterthought, he checked the time. The president usually was not up before seven; he would have to make an exception.

To Williams's surprise, President Midkiff was not only awake, but his national security advisor had also briefed him. Williams brought both men up-to-date, after which Harward left the call at the president's request.

"Whatever you have planned, Trevor's of two minds about it," the president said.

"That's not surprising," Williams replied.

"Be kind, Chase. He's a career politician. And he cares about the country, but not in the same way you do."

"Reaction is preferable to action," Williams said.

"Something like that," the president replied. "But I think a part of him wants this to go forward. He thinks I give Op-Center too much freedom. He seems to feel that will stop if you fail."

"We're talking about the lives of my team here, sir," Williams said.

"Not at this height we're not," the president shot back. "Nothing personal but he's only interested in the big picture."

"And you, sir?"

"My interests are my concern, Chase."

The question was necessary; so was the rebuke. "Sorry, Mr. President."

"Trevor said you have a plan. What is it?"

Williams explained what he had worked out with Major Volner. Taking a page from the Russian flyby playbook, U.S. fighter jets buzz the Iranian ship to draw their attention portside, which was where the sun would be shining. While the crew was distracted, Sergeant Moore and his team would approach quietly from the shadowed side, board the vessel, and destroy the helicopter landing pads. That would force the Chinook to return to Russia.

"What happens then?" the president asked.

"The jets will have taken video of the action. It goes to Russia. If they fail to take action, it goes to the press."

"What if the Iranians fire at us?" the president asked. "You say there are no guns on the ship but they can poke a rocket launcher from a hatch."

"In that case, sir, the rules of engagement allow return fire," Williams said. "We will oblige and the hatch becomes a crater."

"Fine. Your team gets caught on the ship," Midkiff said. "What then? I don't want a repeat of Tehran trotting out ten captured sailors like they did in 2016."

"They're in civvies, no IDs," Williams said. "If they're caught, we don't know who they are."

"And you said that Trevor was cold," Midkiff said.

"Sir, I'd be sick if it came to that. I pray to God it does not."

The president sighed. Now it was Midkiff who had crossed the line; he knew Chase Williams, and the president also knew the difference between a steely command decision and "cold." They were equally aware that overstatement was in the nature of things when intelligence went from "actionable" to "action-enabled."

"Sorry, Chase," the president said. "Give me a minute."

Williams heard himself put on hold. Midkiff was either talking to Harward or, more likely, to the chairman of the Joint Chiefs of Staff, General Paul Broad. He went over to the single-cup coffee machine and made a cup while he waited. One thing about the plan that was sure to appeal to the president was deniability. Without uniforms or marked transports, he could always say that JSOC was just as unofficial as the Russian and Iranian teams.

Midkiff was back in under two minutes.

"I've authorized the plan with a pair of F-22 Raptors from the Third Wing," the president said. "The Fourth Marine Division will give you three FC580s. Work for you?"

"Absolutely," Williams said. "Thank you, sir."

"I know I don't have to ask, but I'm going to anyway," Midkiff said. "They've drilled for boarding. General Broad wanted to know which playbook you're running for the egress?"

That was a little dig from General Broad. The former Army Ranger was a very good man. And while he was impressed with the improvised tactics of the team's last mission, that was not his style. He liked to have plans, even if they were not followed exactly—or even generally. Before answering, Williams glanced, as he often did, at the signed photo of General MacArthur.

"Please inform the general that the plan, as far as we've worked it, is 'that elusive and deathless thing called soldiering,'" Williams replied. "I'm sure he'll understand."

Hanging up, Williams gave a few moments' thought to another plan of attack, one they would be able to use if the military option failed. As he had told the president, he did not want to think like that; as a commander, however, he had no choice.

He made the call.

CHAPTER FORTY-EIGHT

Joint Base Elmendorf-Richardson in Richardson, Alaska
July 3, 6:50 A.M.

The disappointments were typically wide-ranging for JSOC: the operational plan came together so quickly that General Broad did not get to see a plan and PFC Dick Siegel did not get to see a sled dog.

Before touching down, the men had changed into civilian clothes, no IDs, and Moore had divided the team into three groups: six-man Assault A, five-man Backup B, and six-man Support C. Upon landing, Support C immediately unloaded the weapons and gear the other two units would need to go into battle. Each of the eleven combat troops was carrying the Close Quarter Battle Receiver, a replacement for the M4A1 carbine—a submachine gun that fired rifle cartridges with enormous stopping and penetrating power. Three Assault A members carried grenades and were paired with members who would provide cover for their use. The arsenal—carried in compact waterproof backpacks—consisted of M67 fragmentation grenades, M14 incendiary grenades, and M8 colored smoke grenades. The green emission was designed to be distinguishable from the white and gray smoke of burning targets. PFC Siegel and Corporal Al Fitzpatrick would each be shouldering the backpacks with what Siegel lovingly called "the Bazook," an AT-4 anti-tank weapon. These would be used to disable the helicopter landing pads. Each man would also be wearing a Beretta 9mm handgun, a Mark 3 knife with a six-inch stainless steel blade, and a Strider folding knife. The backup was necessary since field conditions often called for the blade tip to be used for and dulled by prying, unscrewing, and cutting barbed wire.

Also included in their gear were a pair of TAIL systems: Tactical Air Initiated Launch guns. The tubes resembled rocket launchers. Propelled by gas, each fired a titanium grapnel attached to one hundred lines of Kevlar line.

As the team stood on the far end of the tarmac in the shadow of the Globemaster III bay, a Wilson Global Explorer was being prepped to deliver the team and their rafts within range of the cargo ship. The amphibious boat was over a quarter-century old and was used for remote search-and-rescue operations. It was also painted a highly reflective silver. This served two purposes: it could be seen from a distance, and it could not be identified from a distance. The glare would make it virtually indistinguishable from a vessel, Navy or commercial, passing on the horizon.

The fighter jets would not be dispatched until the WGE had reached its destination.

"Mountains, too," Siegel muttered as he knelt on the tarmac, checking his weapons. "I never get to see real mountains, with snow."

"You can come back here on leave," his partner, Corporal Fitzpatrick, said.

"Nah, honeymoon," Siegel replied. "That's how I'll know I have the right girl. She won't want to go to Niagara or Capri or some shit like that. She'll want to get a cabin in the Rockies."

"I'll introduce you to my cousin Major Tara Fitzpatrick," the corporal said. "She spent a winter at McMurdo in the South Pole before she enlisted in the Marines."

Siegel looked up from the Bazook he was repacking. "She on social media?" he asked eagerly.

"Yeah," said Private Cornelius "Corn" Scroggins of New Orleans. "Screen name: AssBFroze."

Moore let the men talk. It was what they did. He was on a call with Volner the entire time, alternately checking his gear and fine-tuning the emerging plan. It had to be ready by the time they took off at 0800: the men would have just under an hour to review it en route to the dispatch point.

As Major Volner had always told the team—as he himself had demonstrated in New York—it isn't the plan that makes a soldier. Drilling creates essential teamwork, an intuitive knowledge of what the other team members are going to do. The real benefit, however, was learning the muscle-memory skills that could be used off-plan for any given situation.

In that respect, though, the operation was one that the personnel at JBER had never practiced: the aircraft, the three rafts and portable GPS units, and the dispatch support team were all onboard and prepped at exactly H-Hour. Though each man had his way of dealing with these moments when a mission got underway, there was a singular sense of electric calm in the cabin. No one was overly agitated but everyone was alert and becoming more so by the minute.

It was here, and how, personalities submerged and mind-muscle skills came to the surface. Specific strengths were allowed to emerge, speed and reaction time quickened internally, senses sharpened dramatically. So doing, the team reknit in a way that was familiar from drilling. Without ego, they became a single entity. There was no New York, no New Orleans, no social media, no huskies or mountains.

There was only the mission, and in this order of importance: success and survival.

CHAPTER FORTY-NINE

Op-Center Headquarters, Fort Belvoir North,
Springfield, Virginia
July 3, 10:59 A.M.

Chase Williams sat at his desk writing on a small white pad that had his name on top in flat blue letters. He had a gift for conciseness, since coded messages often required that; he wished he had a greater skill for content. He had to communicate something without actually saying it. He wasn't entirely satisfied with what he had come up with, but it would do. It would have to.

As usual, by sidestepping channels and protocol, by making lateral moves instead of trickle-down from the Oval Office, Chase Williams had managed to piss off the people he contacted.

On the other hand, as President Midkiff had indicated, people were going to cooperate for one of two reasons. If Op-Center succeeded, there would be shared glory for everyone who took part. If Op-Center failed, Chase Williams and his team would go back into the dust bin.

It was with that win-win attitude that January Dow and her security detail had returned to Fort Belvoir North with Brigadier

General Amir Ghasemi. She did not know what this visit was about and Williams did not have the authority to tell her; General Broad had designated the mission as SCI—sensitive compartmented information—which was above top secret. That was a result of both the nature of the mission and the identity of the American players: DIC, disavow if captured, was in effect CYA. The fewer people who knew, the more covered was one's ass. At Op-Center, only Williams, Anne, and Paul Bankole knew what was transpiring. Bankole was informed when January and the general had arrived and he joined the meeting. Williams also asked Tank linguist Salim Singh to join them. Both men remained standing on either side of the big TV monitor. It was not intended to intimidate, but had that effect nonetheless.

Dressed in jeans, a white shirt, and a brown blazer—imperfectly fitting, pulled from the safe house closet so as not to leave hackable transaction receipts that would describe his attire—General Ghasemi looked wan to Williams as Anne showed him and January back into the director's office. It could be the fact that he had been indoors since he had arrived at the U.S. Embassy in Iraq; given a general dullness in his expression, especially the eyes, he suspected it was something else.

Anne was rested, concerned that Williams was not, and hovered protectively in the office as he welcomed the guests. He had briefed her when she arrived, but now he was learning details as she did. The JSOC team was nearly at their drop-off point and the operation was now being managed by Volner directly at a secure NATO command center in Poland. It was actually a somewhat efficient arrangement. NATO's communications tools were more sophisticated than those of Op-Center; this operation was little different from the way Houston managed flights launched from Cape Canaveral.

"Good morning, January . . . General," Williams said as they entered.

"Trevor Harward told me this is important," January said as Anne shut the door behind them. "But that was all he said."

The statement was actually a question, one which Williams left hanging. He introduced the newcomers to Singh—which told January that English would not be the only language spoken here this morning—then regarded Ghasemi, who eased onto the sofa at January's invitation. She sat beside him. Williams addressed the general.

"Your daughter is in the process of dismantling a pair of Russian nuclear warheads for shipment to Iran," the director said without preamble.

January looked as though she were stuck in a yoga pose, immobile but suddenly frowning. Ghasemi sat wide-eyed and slack-mouthed. January was savvy enough to say and ask nothing.

"We'd like you to text her," Williams went on.

"She has her phone—?" he started, stopped. "Sir, did they *beat* her into this?"

"No, General," Williams said. "I cannot get into the specifics just now, but I can assure you that the video was staged for your benefit."

The man shook his head. January just continued to stare at Williams. A barely perceptible nod told her that what he had said was true. She seemed only slightly less surprised than the scientist's father.

The man slid slender fingers into the vest pocket of the

blazer and withdrew his phone. As he unlocked it, Singh moved behind him. January immediately registered displeasure at the distraught general being crowded; Williams made a small gesture that told the Indian-born linguist to take just a small step back. It wasn't a real concession, but it had the appearance of compliance.

"I will say it aloud," Ghasemi said, obviously aware of what was going on. He looked up at Williams with sorrowful eyes. "What is the message, please?"

Williams looked down at his pad. He did not want her or the Russians to know what Op-Center knew. They might accelerate their plans or assume a strike was imminent, jeopardizing the security of the warheads or the safety of the Op-Center team. He had a specific objective in mind, one that was not aimed at a mission but at a daughter. One that would let her know a line of communication was open.

"Did you have a nickname for your daughter?" Williams asked.

"'Petals,'" he said, choking a little. "She was always covering our stoop with rose petals."

Williams said, "Then I want you to say, simply, 'I am well, Petals. Are you?'"

CHAPTER FIFTY

Gulf of Anadyr, Anadyr, Russia
July 3, 3:30 P.M.

The incidents of the flight and landing had occurred somewhere in the background. To Moore, who had led only a seat-of-the-pants mission, the weight of command settled quickly. Purpose and efficiency took over as if there had been a supernatural transformation. There was no "how" to the way individuals became a single unit. It happened, not simply but efficiently. There were months of hard training behind the transition.

Major Volner switched communications to the Single Channel Ground and Airborne Radio System, which was the charge of radio specialist Corporal Ben Adams. Because the men were in civvies there was no helmet for the placement of video cameras. The major would be listening only; his presence was more informational than tactical. He would not be engaged in the action.

The plane landed like a goose, tail-section first, followed by the echoing howl of the twin overhead props and slashing of spray as the rest of the aircraft settled down. The side hatch was popped and the rafts were deployed by two men in wetsuits. Shaped like arrowheads, the rigid black vessels were just over nineteen feet long. Propelled by ninety horsepower engines and carrying a maximum load, the rafts would top out at some twenty miles an hour.

Sergeant Moore quickly ushered the men into their respective boats, which were being maneuvered at first by the WGE crew and then by the team themselves. Moore was the last to board. They set out with the sergeant, saluting the captain while Adams established direct communications with the cockpit. The flight of the F-22s would be controlled by the base, acting on information provided by the seaplane.

The Iranian cargo vessel was a dark brownish sliver just under a mile away. It rested atop a shadow that stretched from it like a high-walled plateau, one that was gently undulating on the wind-rippled sea.

In "A" boat, Moore watched through binoculars from the point of the arrowhead. Corporal Adams was just behind him, to the right.

"Bees moving in on our position," Adams told him, leaning close to his ear so he could be heard over the engine and slapping of the waves. Every mission had its own more-or-less self-defining glossary so that there was no confusion in the field, and Adams had worked these out on the Globemaster III. The WGE was "Gull," the F-22s were "Bees," the Iranian vessel was "Orca" and the Chinook was "Albatross."

Moore looked at his watch. They were fifteen minutes away. "Buzz at will," he said.

CHAPTER FIFTY-ONE

Gulf of Anadyr, Anadyr, Russia
July 3, 3:35 P.M.

Captain Ahmad Salehi was seated on the bridge, doing what this job primarily consisted of—waiting—when Lieutenant Commander Chitchian turned to him.

"Radar . . . seems to be confused, sir," the younger officer said. "There are images . . . and then there are not."

"Stealth aircraft changing profiles," Salehi said confidently. According to Russian reports he had read, the Americans based F-22s up here. "Distance and direction?"

"They are 198 miles and closing on our position."

"Is this a drill?"

Chitchian went through regional data that had been provided by the Russian air force. It listed the American bases in Alaska and their aerial routines.

"This is not a routine flyover, sir."

"Are they communicating with any air bases?" Salehi asked.

"It's impossible to say," Chitchian told him. "There are too many channels to scan and our radar—it's very basic, sir."

"No need to apologize," Salehi said. "We do nothing. These pilots have no authority here and they will not enter Russian airspace."

But as he considered this, he thought back to the journey. There was no way the United States could have identified them. They had made no open communications and there were no external markings that other ships in the region did not carry. This was a standard run.

Still, while his operation had been extremely careful, he wondered if that were true of everyone else. Tehran had flown a scientist to the region and the Russians were running an operation that might have been airtight. He did not want to overreact but he did not want to take unnecessary risks.

He turned to a man seated at the end of the console opposite Chitchian. "Lieutenant Naqdi, on the established timetable we have just under an hour until the cargo is airborne?"

"That is correct, sir," the young man replied.

"Have the 171 return at once, prepared to run interference for the fighter jets," he said.

"Immediately," Naqdi replied enthusiastically.

Everyone on the bridge—everyone on the ship—understood the need for extreme care. The mission was too important. But everyone onboard also understood that the days of being economically and diplomatically bullied by America were near an end. It would be right and fitting for a small show of defiance to begin here and now. With a relatively fragile helicopter in the air, the jets would not dare to fly too close. And if there were an incident caused by wash from their passage, then the world would focus on the harassment of an honest, commercial cargo ship . . . and not on the true mission.

Still, it was a risk. There were the lives of the pilot and co-pilot to consider, as well as the safety of the ship. They were not prepared for a sea-to-air gun battle.

"The aircraft is aloft, sir," Naqdi informed him.

Salehi wished he possessed a deeper faith in the word of the Prophet, though he did believe that Allah defends those who are true. And he had no doubt in the works they had undertaken here.

The bridge faced land and he retrieved his binoculars from the seat back, walked to the observation post beside Chitchian. He saw the blue-gray line of the coast, even as he began to feel the faintest vibration in the floor beneath him—the approach of the American warplanes. From their suddenly alert posture and shared looks, the others felt it as well.

"We are all within our rights here," Salehi remarked calmly. "We will remain focused on the mission."

Suddenly, Naqdi turned his narrow face toward the commander. "Sir. Broadcast from 171—open channel."

That was a breach of strict mission protocol. It could not be good.

"Put it on audible," he said.

"Go ahead, 171," Naqdi instructed.

"Sir!" the pilot's voice crackled over the single speaker. "We've spotted three high-performance rafts to the southwest. They are closing rapidly on your position!"

CHAPTER FIFTY-TWO

Gulf of Anadyr, Anadyr, Russia
July 3, 4:08 P.M.

"You've got company—chopper from the northwest."

The message from the Wilson Global Explorer was not welcome news.

It meant that either the rafts had been spotted—or soon would be.

"Is it the cargo chopper?" Moore asked.

"Negative," the pilot replied. "Profile does not fit twin-turbo."

Major Volner cut in almost at once. "What's your status, Sergeant?"

"Five minutes or so from target," Moore replied. "We're in formation—suggest we separate and continue in. If they achieve their objective, we have a real problem."

"You are on open water and the Raptors will *not* be able to intervene," Volner said. "They are under a non-engage order. You attempt to board, you *will* take fire from the ship."

"Understood," Moore replied. He leaned on the inflated side

of the boat for stability and searched the horizon for the chopper. He found it. He did not imagine they were significantly armed and did not believe they would come close.

They were about a minute from the outermost edge of the ship's shadow, the one they had hoped would give them visual cover. No more. Through the binoculars, he could see personnel beginning to line the railing beside and under the packets containing the inflatable lifeboats, using them for cover. Presumably, they were armed. He scanned the rest of the ship.

"Director, are you still on?" Moore asked.

"I am."

"What happens if the ship is disabled?"

There was a short silence. "Coast Guard offers assistance out of Anchorage, or Russians from any number of ports. Tehran declines and dispatches a rescue operation. We have no right to board."

"I was thinking TAILs shot into the screws, damage the works, stop her dead."

"Buys us time for diplomacy, if we wanted to rely on that," Williams replied. "Likely to fail."

Moore continued to explore he vessel through the binoculars. He suddenly stopped at a spot and studied it.

"Sir, can you convince JBER to let the jets run interference?" Moore asked.

"Sergeant, they cannot—"

"No-fire, I understand. Just low passes on our side of the ship."

"How low?"

"As low as they can so I can change direction," Moore replied.

"To go where?"

"Our original target is forward," Moore said. "I think I have a secondary one—not propulsion, something better."

Moore told Volner the plan. The major was not able to endorse it.

"This is way beyond our mission parameters, Sergeant. I want this stopped but there will be repercussions."

"Sergeant?" It was Chase Williams.

"Yes, sir."

"If the major doesn't object, I'll take responsibility for this," he said.

"No, sir," Volner said—though his tone suggested otherwise.

There was no time to discuss the matter further. Corporal Fitzpatrick was piloting at the stern. Moore turned to him and signaled for him to change directions. He motioned for "B" and "C" to do likewise. Then he pointed to Specialist Noiret in "A" and Specialist Mastroianni on "B." Moore held up his forearm, then extended four fingers. Then he lay it flat. Both men nodded with understanding. He wanted the AK-4s ready to be used from a prone-position, side-fire.

"Schematic of the boat!" Moore turned and barked at the logistics man on his left, PV2 Berne Wright.

The young officer moved his bare fingertips across the waterproof tablet, handed it to Moore. The sergeant studied it for a moment then expanded the view, circled a section in red, then passed it on to Fitzpatrick. The corporal looked out at the vessel, nodded once, then passed the tablet back to Wright. Wright sent the information to the other two boats.

"A" boat swerved dramatically, the others swinging behind like a water-going centipede.

Moore returned to the binoculars. There was no gunfire—yet. The Iranians still had no justification to fire on the rafts. The captain, whoever he was, would not be provoked into an engagement that could involve the jets.

As they made their approach, the twin F-22s did likewise, flying at roughly the same height as the bridge. Though they came screaming in at well under Mach 1, the men used their palms to cover their ears against the still-significant shriek of the two Pratt & Whitney F119-PW-100 turbofan engines.

Moore circled his hand above his head to rev up, the three rafts charging toward the stern where none of the Iranians had yet gathered. It was a maneuver one might expect if an attack amidships were suddenly broken off.

Moore did not know if the jets would get another pass; the 171 was nearing, would be there in less than a minute. If the chopper got there, the jets would provide no further interference.

The sergeant looked back. Noiret and Mastroianni were nearly ready, able to manage loading on their own while the team made room for them to stretch out.

The rafts were slapping the surface hard as the sailors began to move toward the stern. Only two hundred yards separated them from the hull. The Iranians had obviously seen the anti-tank weapons; it would be seconds before the rafts came under fire. To the left, the helicopter was moving in. To the right, the jets were making a second approach. The 171 got there first; the Raptors were forced to veer off.

"Suppressing fire!" Moore yelled back.

Three men on each boat started firing at the ship, just below where the sailors were positioned. Most retreated, but not all. The boats were not yet at optimal range, but they had no choice.

He turned and motioned for Fitzpatrick to slow, then pointed at Noiret and swung his arm toward the target: the juncture of the stern cargo ramp and the hull. The weapon roared and flashed and there was a clanging explosion near the waterline. Almost at once, Moore ordered Mastroianni to do the same. Noiret was reloading even as the second explosive detonated.

Another round was not necessary. Through the binoculars Moore could see a bubbling below the surface. Water was beginning to seep through the crack they'd made.

"Go!" Moore shouted, circling for all the rafts to evacuate along the hull to the east.

Bullets pinged as the sailors found their range. "C" took several hits, including one crewman in the shoulder that knocked him well forward from his post at the engine, and another who took a bullet in the hip. "C" continued on until the drag of the deflating sides was too great; rather than repair it, they let the equipment go and the men transferred to the other vessels. The team medic did triage on the shoulder wound first—the more serious injury—before turning to the in-and-out side wound.

Behind them there was a great deal of activity as the Iranian sailors tried to determine the extent of the damage. The report from the helicopter must have settled the matter; almost at once, the lifeboats were inflated.

The jets did a higher-altitude flyover and then, without dipping their wings to acknowledge kinship with the remaining FC580s—the entire episode had no doubt been recorded—the F-22s returned to base.

No doubt they had already informed JBER, which had informed Major Volner, but Moore was pleased to report it anyway:

"Target will not be receiving cargo."

CHAPTER FIFTY-THREE

Outpost N64, Anadyr, Russia
July 3, 4:14 P.M.

It had only taken moments for the bunker to go from laboratory to madhouse, from careful precision to lunacy.

Wearing heavy work gloves and perspiring beneath the insulated garments she wore beneath a utilitarian white lab coat, Parand turned from the garishly red warhead and looked down at Vadik, the man who was in charge of this operation. He was shouting into his radio and listening to the scratchy voice that came back.

A specially designed, rudimentary aluminum scaffold had been erected atop the mobile launcher for each missile, from which Parand and two engineers worked to remove the warheads. The R-12 rocket was at its lowest threat level—readiness nr. 4. The gyroscopes and internal control systems of the booster were still in place, though they had been disconnected a half century before. Similarly, the explosive system inside the warhead was still intact though the hard-wiring had been severed. What took time was removing the ten-foot-high warhead from the rocket.

The engineers had rigged a rudimentary block-and-tackle above each silo, which would put on motorized dollies and brought to the helicopter for transport. Neither was going to be raised until both had been disconnected. Parand was in the process of completing the second removal when panic struck.

Yuri and Konstantin Bolshakov were below her, trying to find out what was happening.

"Attack," was the only word she could make out at first. Then one of the two men working with her climbed down to find out what was going on. He returned pale-faced with news of a "piratical American attack" on the *Nardis* that was causing it to sink.

"The ship is being abandoned," the engineer said urgently. "We-we may have to leave."

"To go where?" Parand demanded.

"They are talking about the airfield in Anadyr—we cannot be found here."

"Without these?" she said, indicating the warhead.

"I don't know," he said.

Both men stopped working and climbed back down. Parand stood there watching her life turn to ash. Perhaps this was only temporary—if a decision had been made, she would have been informed. She turned back to the warhead, her hand shaking. She tried to look at the schematics on the tablet propped in front of her but it was blurry. The woman pulled a sleeve across her moist eyes.

Blinking, Parand could see the entire bunker reflected in the metallic red of the warhead. She saw Yuri approaching. The scientist turned and looked down.

The Russian motioned for her to come. His movements were not a suggestion.

Still, she hesitated. There was no physical danger here. Whatever was going on, what was the worst that could happen to her if she remained—if she stayed behind with these works of art from a bygone age, mechanisms she had studied for months.

This was why you become a scientist. For the opportunity to serve your nation, yes, but also to be a part of this greater history—

Yuri yelled at a group of Iranians who were packing up gear. He gestured toward Parand. One of those men called to Vadik, who came running from the now-open hatchway.

"Come, Dr. Ghasemi! We are leaving!" he shouted.

This was not a decision she wanted to make on her own. Against all caution not to involve Tehran directly, she decided to try and contact Sadeq Farhadi. Her fingers still trembling, she fished her phone from her deep pocket.

Parand punched in her code. There was a text. She recalled the phone buzzing earlier, had ignored it as she worked, then forgot about it. She opened the message.

I am well, Petals. Are you? Papa.

A storm of emotions fell on her in rapid succession. The first was anger and suspicion: *Who was forcing him to do this, and why?* The second was shame: *He found out I was lying about my imprisonment, that we were using him.* The third—

Her fingers pressed the keys.

All is lost for me.

Vadik yelled at her and she looked at him critically, like Maalik on-high, the guardian angel of hellfire.

"We must go *now!*" he cried. "Leave everything!"

"Why?"

"The authorities will come . . . we cannot be here."

A message came back from her father.

```
Never, while I live.
```

Parand responded quickly and then put her phone away, grabbed the tablet, and climbed down the scaffolding. Vadik took her firmly by the arm and led her to the hatch.

"Get in your helicopter," the officer said as they walked. "You will go to the airfield with the rest. You were here to meet the *Nardis* and upgrade their power grid."

"I am not an engineer—"

"You are now," the man said impatiently and pushed her toward the table where they had left their outerwear. She removed her lab coat, remembering to retrieve her phone, and pulled on her cold weather gear. Then Vadik took her toward the ladder where two other men waited.

"I will be with you in a moment," he told the others.

Parand looked back into the bunker. The nuclear weapons remained where they were, yet the world seemed suddenly on fire. Though the fault was not hers, the failure would stay with her for the rest of her life. There would be no other opportunities like this, no sponsor like the prosecutor, and likely no further communication from Farhadi. Parand understood that: he had his own life and future to consider.

Vadik returned with a flashlight. The younger Russian shut the hatch and the Iranians climbed the ladder, Parand obediently following all but Vadik who lit the way.

A man . . . a missile . . . a mission, she thought. *Following . . . always following while you thought you were moving forward.*

The evening sun struck her eyes with painful brilliance and she shielded her eyes as she was run to the Mi-171. Vadik pushed her inside, shut the door, and the helicopter lifted off. It was followed, in less than a minute, by the Chinook. Other than the personnel, everything had been left behind. There were no markings, nothing written to track the materials to Iran.

Like the desert, our footprints buried, she thought as her eyes adjusted to the light and she looked back at a dream once again frozen in time.

She removed her glove and put her hand in her pocket, where the phone was. She felt it buzz and removed it. Angling the screen away from the sun, which was beyond the pilot, she scrolled to the last two messages:

Watch for Petals.

To which he had replied:

Every day.

CHAPTER FIFTY-FOUR

Outpost N64, Anadyr, Russia
July 3, 4:36 P.M.

Yuri Bolshakov moved through the bunker, shutting the air vent and the silo hatches. His father did not disturb him as he worked. He helped where he could, turning off console functions in the same way he once did—albeit slower, now. His muscles remembered what his brain did not, though they were brutally tired now.

The truth revealed by the hurried evacuation was not so much a surprise as a disappointment. The Russian government was not a homogeneous system where one division knew what another was doing, and that was especially true of the activities of the GRU.

This had been either an unsanctioned or deep-black operation. The goal was to get nuclear weapons into Iranian hands without official Russian fingerprints being on them. That was simply an extension, and corruption, of the secrecy by which these missiles first came to Anadyr. A natural evolution of the greed and megalomania that had pervaded the Soviet Union and now Putin's Russia.

What bothered Bolshakov more was his son's stupendous

hypocrisy. Perhaps Yuri did not even realize it, because there were more layers of responsibility now, more functionaries. But this was no different than what the elder Bolshakov had done.

When the young man had finished, he asked his father to go on ahead. Bolshakov entered the shaft followed by Yuri, who locked the interior door, lit a cigarette, and turned a flashlight toward the ladder so his father could see. Instead, Bolshakov turned to his son.

"So there it is," the older man said, his breath coming in long, white puffs.

"There what is?"

"When you no longer have a buyer, you go home."

Yuri sighed. "I don't want your analysis, Father."

He stepped toward the closed hatch. "Then go up without me."

"We don't have time for this. Just climb, please."

"Not until you've heard me out," Bolshakov said.

"Later," Yuri said. "The cargo ship radioed an S.O.S. There will be flyovers. They will see the equipment."

"The truck with the bodies."

"That too," Yuri said.

"Then I will be very brief," Bolshakov insisted. "You have hated me for decisions I made at a point in time, at *moments* in time, when results could not be foreseen. Had I been a wiser man, I would have opened a butcher shop or learned to drive a bus. But I thought . . . it would have been equal parts slow financial death and irresponsibility to deny what I could do, what would earn a substantial living. I chose expedience."

"You knew the people you were dealing with," Yuri charged. "You should have known it could not end well."

"Did you?" his father asked. "Because you have the GRU behind you, you assumed everything would function perfectly? It did not, Yuri, and now you are running." Bolshakov moved closer. "To what? You killed two men. That will be discovered. Justifiable, perhaps, and you will not likely be punished because then the operation will be exposed. Everything else, you did according to a plan someone else conceived. Do you think anyone will acknowledge their part? When a plan goes flawlessly, it has many godparents. When it fails, there is just one."

Yuri regarded him with something approaching—worry? Concern, at least. Bolshakov wanted to embrace him but restrained himself. That would have to come from Yuri, if at all.

"It should not have failed," was all the younger man said. "We did not plan for this."

"For discovery?" Bolshakov said. "You did not. The GRU did. The plan was: there were two men in the field, on site, and somehow they were discovered. That is likely the case, you know. Someone in the United States, for whose intelligence agencies the GRU has always had contempt, found us out. That was always a possibility . . . now a reality."

Yuri made little sweeps with the flashlight. "We have to go."

"I know," Bolshakov said. "And when we get to Anadyr, we have to talk. Because there is just one way you will come out of this without being stuck in a corner office without a window or future prospects."

Yuri waited a moment longer, looked at his father's face in the light. "How?"

"Don't fall on your sword, *use* it," Bolshakov replied, "I had knowledge. Information. I knew who to bribe, who to pressure.

If you convince others that their fate is tied to your own, that your fall is their fall, I promise you will rise."

"At what cost?" Yuri asked.

Bolshakov could not help but grin. "Like me, you murdered to protect your work, your life, your future. You are already on the carousel, the price of admission paid. Becoming a bus driver or butcher, now—is that really what you want?"

Yuri thought, but only for a moment. "We will talk," he said.

The older man turned then and made his way up the ladder. His step seemed lighter than it had since he had first met Yuri at the airport. He felt, he believed, he hoped that he had gotten through to his son: emerging from the safety of an unchanging, limited bunker, life was inevitably a riot of choices, challenges, and decisions. He could make none of those for Yuri. He would never try, for they had lead very different lives.

All he could do, as a father, was to help his son find his *own* way.

CHAPTER FIFTY-FIVE

Havana, Cuba
July 3, 10:33 P.M.

It was far from the best of times, but it was equally far from the worst.

Adoncia had returned shortly after two. A.M. with food and drink, assuming—correctly—that if she had left her smoke, she would be returning. She also brought more: news.

"The police are looking for you," she said. "So here is what you will do." She fished something from her pants pocket and pressed it in his palm. "I have written a map and a name. You say you are a rower; I hope you were truthful."

"I was. Why?"

"I have arranged for a rowboat," she said, planting herself gingerly on a stack of logs. "Another old friend, Camilio, is a custodian at the *Granma Memorial*—that's the yacht we used to travel from Mexico with our little army in 1956." She shrugged her bony shoulders. "We lost then, but won later. Sometimes you have to learn."

"You did that impressively," McCord said.

She smiled. "I believe you are being sincere. Because I have seen you when you lie. This is not that."

McCord grinned self-effacingly. He was embarrassed to admit respect for rebels who had ultimately caused so much pain. Too many revolutionaries and too many terrorists had caused too much suffering. But so had legitimate governments, like those of czars and ayatollahs. Ultimately, it was a judgment about individuals, not ideas.

Adoncia stood on creaky knees. She remembered the newspaper in her back pocket, handed it to him.

"You can practice your Spanish," she said.

"You're going?"

"I must, and I will not see you again. No one should be coming for wood, but if they do the padre will tell them to let you be. Go around ten thirty tonight, which is when police shifts are near their end and cars are returned to their garages." She offered her hand. "I thank you for a very exciting evening. One like this I have not had in many, many years."

"It's been an honor," McCord said. "Do I . . . pay Camilio?"

"If you have the funds, yes. That would be nice. He is losing a boat, after all."

"I have the money and I will pay. May I also leave this?" he asked, indicating the go-bag.

"There are always people who can use things," she said. "I will inform the padre to collect it after you go."

He thanked her again with a generous hug, which she returned. She departed in a flash of sunlight and then there was just the one bulb. McCord sat, texted Williams, and told him he would be needing a Coast Guard pickup or a ship from Guantanamo sometime between eleven and twelve P.M., depending on his point of departure. The director acknowledged with:

```
OK. YOUR INFO A1
```

McCord could only imagine what was popping to the north—and in the far north. And while part of him was sorry not to be in on the events, part of him was happy to be doing nothing.

Doing nothing in a tropical land with endless beaches where you are sitting in a woodshed.

But he did not lament too deeply. If the conceptual pieces of this fit as he imagined, JSOC would be having a far more difficult time of it.

The day passed slowly, his time divided between rest, memorizing the map Adoncia had drawn—which he shredded—and a struggle to read the news in Spanish. There appeared to be an item about a fugitive American—the description, at least, matched his own—but there was no drawing and it was only a paragraph on page seven. He used the wood instead of the chamber pot, and did so sparingly; it absorbed the odor, which he did not want clinging to him when he left.

He had shut the phone to conserve the battery. When he turned it on after nightfall, there was a text from Williams with time and coordinates and also a note:

```
Success
```

McCord looked at the coordinates on a map, saw where he had to be three miles out, and shut the phone again. He would need the GPS for later. He hoped that Adoncia had gotten him more than just an old wooden rowboat. For more than a half century, people who set out for the United States in those did not survive.

Several times during the day he had stood and walked around the tight little room, stretching his right leg. Ever since the second wound, the bad one, in Iraq, it got very stiff when he was inactive for long. He could not afford to let that happen.

A church bell told the time. Fifteen minutes before the appointed half hour McCord took a windbreaker from his go-bag, made sure he had his phone, wallet, and passport, then put the small suitcase under some wood. He shut the light and listened. Adoncia's map had shown direction but not distance, and he used the outside sounds to visualize the street, the plaza, the way they had come. Taking several calming breaths and once again shaking his leg to make sure it could take a brisk walk, he opened the door.

There was no one outside and, moving quickly, he exited and shut it behind him.

McCord's destination was literally due east, just a few blocks away past the *Plaza de Armas*. There was a series of old wooden piers in Havana Bay and he went to the first, where a tall man sat smoking a pipe, his feet over the edge, a fishing rod in his hand. As McCord neared he saw, bobbing gently in the smooth sea four feet below him, a white, fiberglass rowboat with two benches and wide sides.

"*Señor* . . . Camilio?" McCord asked tentatively.

"*Si, Señor* Roger. *No hablo inglés.*"

McCord came toward the man and noticed he was wearing sunglasses. The American removed all the cash he had from his wallet and held it toward the fisherman. Certain, now, that he was blind, he pressed the bills into Camilio's hand.

"*Gracias*, Camilio," McCord said. "*Muchas gracias.*"

"*Si, si*," the man said affably, finally turning toward McCord and adding a heartfelt, "*¡Que llegues bien!*"

Have a safe journey.

The older man then pointed toward the north, in the direction of what McCord knew was the underwater *Túnel de la Bahía.* Thanking him again and moving carefully and quietly—there was a slight wind and the wooden planks were slippery—McCord lowered himself into the rowboat. It was about thirty-five hundred feet to the mouth of the bay and then he had the extra three miles; for the money he had just paid—nearly one thousand dollars, American—he probably could have bought himself a motorboat.

But Adoncia was right. This was better. If he were caught, of all the flimsy stories he could have given, going for a nocturnal row was at least remotely defensible.

The operative word being "remotely," he thought as he set out.

The waters were still in the bay and he was in good enough shape to clock a steady three miles an hour. That put him over the tunnel in forty minutes. The waters were more challenging when he hit the gulf, since he was accustomed to rowing in rivers, not on a swelling sea. It took him a while to master the trick of going forward while the current insisted, sometimes strongly, that he should be headed toward shore. He had been chilly when he set out, wearing only the windbreaker; the effort warmed him and he was now sweating like he did back at Princeton. But with older, wearier arms.

But the cell phone compass kept his course true and, some ninety minutes later, he noticed an occasional white light flashing ahead. The intermittent nature of the light told him it wasn't a buoy of any kind but a vessel—a vessel that was holding its position just past Cuba's territorial waters.

McCord stopped long enough to shine his cell phone in that direction, then hurried toward a twenty-nine-foot Response Boat—Small II. Helping hands from two of the three crewmembers assisted him onto the side of the low, orange-and-black vessel.

"Mr. McCord?" said a welcoming voice as he came aboard.

"I am," he said.

The second man threw a blanket over his shoulders and assisted him into the small, glass-canopied area. He sat behind the pilot, who greeted him pleasantly.

"The boat, sir?" the first man called over.

McCord peered into the dark at the faint lights of the island in the distance. "Cast her off," he said. "Maybe she'll find her way home."

"That's a nice thought, sir," the young man said in earnest.

McCord looked at the man's nametag and then gazed north. "Petty Officer Song," he said, "it is very nice thought indeed."

CHAPTER FIFTY-SIX

Silver Springs, Maryland
July 4, 4:00 P.M.

It was a single family ranch house on Rosemere Avenue. It was commutable by Yamaha VMAX and Aaron Bleich lived there with his girlfriend of three years, Jacqui, a Realtor. They met when she sold him this house; he fell in love, he said, when she lowered her commission so he could afford it.

The holiday mood was festive, consisting mostly of the staff of the Geek Tank and those officers like Williams and Bankole who did not have family obligations . . . or whose families preferred to be with hipsters, like the Roger McCords. Anne came by, though she would be leaving to attend a gathering the nature of which she did not reveal. As always, no one pressed her.

McCord had slept on the flight from MacDill—where he had been briefed by Williams before boarding—slept when he got home, and got up to bring his wife and two high-school-age daughters who wanted to "be cool" like Kathleen Hays or Charlene Squires and now Dongling Qui. He was surprisingly alert, though, as he told Williams and Anne, "sore as an old orangutan" after his row.

He had noticed at once that both Williams and Anne were distracted, and did not know if this were the time and place to ask if everything were all right. Williams himself seized an opportunity after Anne had left and the others were giving their dinner orders—Gary Gold rushing out to the supermarket with Bankole to get veggie burgers and curry sauce.

"You did great in Cuba," Williams said, going to get a beer and handing one to McCord.

"I feel guilty," McCord said. "It was almost like a Caribbean vacation."

Williams smiled, but it was forced. "We didn't get out of this one clean," he said gravely.

"What are you talking about?" McCord said. "The injured troops—"

Williams waved his hand. "Volner is going up to see them— he spoke by Skype, said they were fine. Proud."

"They *should* be. They prevented Iran from obtaining nuclear weapons."

"We—me, Op-Center—also authorized an action that sunk an Iranian cargo ship," Williams said. "They're calling it an onboard explosion as they were going to Anadyr to drop off unspecified equipment—which satellite images would disprove— and pick up fish. Privately, they are demanding that we pay for the ship."

"Were any lives lost?"

Williams shook his head.

"Then they got off lucky."

"The White House doesn't see it that way," Williams said.

"That's ridiculous," McCord said. He realized he was becoming agitated when his wife looked over from where Aaron was making balloon animals. "The original plan called for an attack on the landing pads."

"And that was what was authorized," Williams said. "The upshot of that would have been Midkiff's ability to prove to Tehran he knew what they were doing. Harward called it 'a precision exposé.'"

"God, I hate newspeak," McCord complained.

"Anyway, by sinking the *entire* ship, the attack—which we deny was ours, of course—comes off as brutish, broad, and haphazard. Those were also Harward's words."

"So what do they want? Did no one thank us for picking this up in the first place, let alone pulling this off?"

"To the last point, the president's brain trust agrees that the Iranians would have detonated one for show, kept the other for leverage, and denied—correctly, as it happens—that they broke any treaties. But having that one nuke would not have given the Iranians a huge tactical advantage. Only headlines for a few days."

"Chase, I am so glad we have to wage battles at home *and* abroad," McCord said. "Really keeps us in fighting trim."

"As to the other question," Williams went on, "there's a chance JSOC may be benched and that I may follow." He raised his beer. "Happy Independence Day."

McCord was open-mouth aghast. "No one there would

stand for that," he said after lubricating his jaw with a swallow. "No one."

"Then they'd be replaced," Williams said. "It's not a fait accompli, but January Dow also weighed in and said we blew the opportunity to turn Parand Ghasemi by failing to push her father."

"What, is that possibility dead?"

"No, but it's January's baby now," Williams replied. "About the only thing we appear to have done right was ID an active GRU agent who wasn't on our radar, Yuri Bolshakov. He's been added to Kathleen's watch list. At least," Williams added, "one of my people made a friend somewhere."

It took McCord a moment. "Brightest spot in this," he agreed. "She was a gem. I'd have loved to sit down and talk to her. Is she going to be okay?"

"Bankole and Wright will be working on that behind the scenes," Williams said. "Jim has experience working with Cuban refugees in Florida—he knows a lot of people across the gulf."

"She may not want our help, any help," McCord said. "I get the feeling she's been looking for this fight for a while."

"Funny," Williams said. "She would've gotten what she wanted even if you'd never met. Midkiff would have gotten what he wanted if we'd never spotted Konstantin Bolshakov taking a trip. Who knows what's going to happen to Parand Ghasemi in Iran with this stain on her record. Maybe Harward is right. Maybe we should be sitting things out."

McCord looked at his wife who was looking at him. He didn't blame her: her husband, the girls' father, had gone away on "business," just returned, and was back in the saddle.

"We'll talk about this tomorrow, Chase," McCord said. "But everyone who was actually in on this, not on the sidelines, would agree that what we pulled off was pretty amazing. And—*and*—despite Harward and Midkiff, I for one am very happy Iran took this one in the shorts and doesn't have a pair of nuclear warheads."

Williams thanked his intelligence director, who joined his family and the celebration and the preparing of food. Standing alone by a hedge, Williams drank his beer.

He did not, in his heart, believe any of the what-ifs he had rattled off. When he was in boot camp—back during the Civil War, it felt like—a conundrum had been posed by a drill instructor: "If you went back in time with the full resources of the modern military, would you have stopped the Japanese from attacking Pearl Harbor?" The initial consensus was "yes." Then the DI factored in the delay in the U.S. entering the war, allowing Hitler to take Britain, said delay also allowing him to throw more resources against Russia—and the Japanese concentrating on their domination of Asia and expanding westward. The result would likely have been a very different end to World War II, which would likely have allowed Germany to develop the atom bomb first.

Most of the new recruits changed their minds. But not Williams.

"No one turns a weapon against America if I am alive to prevent it," he said.

The DI was impressed with the clarity of purpose, the simplicity of the logic.

Williams still believed that. Come what may, he would never put self before country, career before patriotism.

I'd do the same damn thing all over again, he thought with a sense of pride as he finished the beer, dropped it in a trash can, and went to help Bankole and Gold with their groceries.

EPILOGUE

The Interests Section of the Islamic Republic of Iran was based in Pakistan's Embassy on Twenty-Third Street, a three-story, darkly fenced eagle's beak of a structure that was made in sections of gray, rust, and hay-colored stone.

It was dark when the black BMW SUV pulled up to the gate. It arrived alone and was admitted without fanfare or incident. Once it was inside, two men emerged. The first was First Lieutenant Bahadur İpekçi, the younger of the men by nearly twenty years. İpekçi was a sharpshooter with NEZAJA—the acronym for the ground forces of the Iranian army—and was now seconded to Iranian diplomatic operations in the United States. Nothing he did here had anything to do with statesmanship.

İpekçi had been driving, and he carried diplomatic papers to go with the diplomatic plates of the SUV. The documents had not been needed; he had made the trip from Reagan International to the embassy without being stopped or questioned.

His passenger, whom he had not met before tonight, was a

lean, tall, leathery man. He wore civilian clothes with obvious discomfort, as though they were the uniform of some rival forces— not the NEDAJA, his own branch of the service.

The Navy of the Islamic Republic of Iran.

With easy, efficient movements, the passenger grabbed his own suitcases from the tailgate while İpekçi, inherently wary, watched the street. The younger man did not know if the shooting at Quantico had been traced to him and surveillance assigned to his comings-and-goings; he did not think so, since he had not intended to kill the Bureau agent and had left the scene with careful haste. The action was in furtherance of a narrative, the specifics of which had not been shared with him. He was told only what he had to do, not why. And he was content with that. His job was to serve, not question.

As with this current task.

The men walked to the door where a night guard buzzed them in. By a gesture, İpekçi encouraged their distinguished guest to enter first. Ordinarily, the first lieutenant was not assigned chauffeur duties, what he called "hand-holding detail." But he was told that it was important this man be delivered to the embassy, and that he be extended all courtesies and resources that the facility could provide. İpekçi knew little more than that, though what he knew was profoundly exciting. His superiors in Tehran had told him that this undertaking was vital to Iranian prestige, not only at home but in the eyes of the government's Russian allies. And they assured him that it would not involve "supporting an agenda," as with Quantico. This time, as they had put it, "the shots will be real."

Whenever they were ready, the sharpshooter would be ready. Dr. Hafiz Akif and his family were already here. And whatever was required by his grimly silent countryman, he would receive. The first lieutenant could do no less for Captain Ahmad Salehi, late of the cargo vessel *Nardis,* which had been sunk by piratical Americans.

Americans who would be made to pay dearly for their criminal act.